A Brooke and Daniel Psychological Thriller

DESECRATION

J.F.PENN

Desecration
Copyright © J.F.Penn (2013). All rights reserved.

www.JFPenn.com

ISBN: 978-1-912105-64-9

Requests to publish work from this book should be sent to:
joanna@CurlUpPress.com

Cover and Interior Design: JD Smith Design
Interior Cabinet of Curiosities Artwork:
Copyright Suzanne Norris. Used with permission.

Printed by Amazon KDP Print

www.CurlUpPress.com

"The violation of the body would be the revelation of its truth"

Andreas Vesalius, 16th century physician, founder of modern human anatomy

PROLOGUE

THE BODY OF THE young woman lies on her back, blonde hair neatly arrayed in a sunburst around her head. She looks like an angel and I bend to adjust a lock of her hair, carefully disguising the deep wound in her skull. At least I can leave her face looking as beautiful as it did in life. Her lips are still painted with wine red lipstick, slightly smudged from where she drank with me. But that mouth whispered words of disturbing truth not so long ago, and I couldn't let her unleash that reality into the world. There is too much at stake and even she was not enough to make me give that up.

I pull on a pair of sterile gloves and breathe a sigh of relief as I slip into my second skin. They make me feel safe, a barrier against the world and yet somehow heightening the sensation in my hands. I always carry a pair, and tonight they serve a noble purpose. I brush her lips with gentle fingertips, some part of me wanting to feel a last breath. But I know she is dead, for I feel the lack of her. What made her alive is now gone and I wonder if she is already on another plane of reality, wondering how she got there, questioning why this life flew by so fast. This is but a body, just another corpse, and I know how to deal with corpses.

In a medical institution, it isn't hard to find a scalpel and I pull open the drawers in the training lab until I find an appropriate one. Returning to the body I use the 22 blade to cut a line through the crimson satin dress that clings to the curves near her hips. The material bunches slightly so I have to hold it down for the scalpel to slice through, but I manage to cut away a square of material, like operating drapes revealing the area for treatment. The blade is so sharp that I can sense the layer of material separate from the firmness of her skin and I feel a rush of pleasure at the sensation.

Beginning the incision, I slice across the soft lower belly. Her flesh is still warm, skin smooth and untainted, and I envy the beauty she carried so unconsciously. The scalpel slices down, a precision instrument in my hand and a line of blood rises to the surface. Even though her heart has stopped, it is as if this body still clings to life.

I feel something, a breath of air on my cheek and I freeze, scalpel in place on her skin. I know it must be nothing, but a shiver passes over me regardless. Perhaps it is the soul of the newly deceased taking one last look around this cabinet of curiosities, trying to understand her place amongst the many dead. For her body lies surrounded by tall glass display cases, packed full of the anatomical preparations for which the Hunterian Museum is famous. Body parts line up here in a macabre apothecary's shop, strange and bizarre with colors of pus, bone and decay. It is hard to tell what lies inside the conical jars of varying sizes until you lean closer to look inside or read the brief text that refers to each specimen. Stoppered and sealed with black tape, beads of condensation have formed on the lids as if what is inside still breathes. I can almost hear the dead cry out, drowned again each night in liquid preservation, and it makes me want to emulate the master anatomist in my own work. I stop for a moment to gaze at my inspiration.

Some of the organs are flower like, petals opening and fronds almost waving in the liquid, like sea creatures of delicate, strange beauty. Ruffles like tissue paper conceal a parcel of flesh that was once part of a living human. In one container sits a gigantic foot, cut off at the ankle, swollen with elephantiasis to four times life-size. Black toenails erupt from the end of grotesque toes, skin swollen to bursting, puckered and discolored. Every time I look into these cabinets I see something new, even though I have been coming here for many years, a pilgrimage to that which gives meaning to my own work. I glimpse the trunk of a baby crocodile, decapitated with its legs and tail brutally sawn off. Next to it, the trunk of a human fetus, barely as big as my hand, limbs and head removed, the tiny chest opened up to reveal the internal organs.

There are lizards, cut open, limbs posed as if they are running away, scuttling across this landscape of trapped souls. The body of a crayfish, tail curled under, protecting thousands of tiny eggs, and next to it, fat grubs and caterpillars, the larvae of hybrid insects. Quintuple fetuses are displayed in one case, tiny bodies with mouths open in horror, like corporeal dolls the color of ghosts. For the early anatomists were allowed to use the bodies of those that died within the mother, considering them specimen before human. Nowadays I have to work in secret, wary of judgment from those who don't understand the mysteries I can solve with flesh. This body is so precious that I cannot waste the opportunity to take what might further my research.

The sounds of the party filter upwards, laughter made louder by alcohol. Returning to my work, I cut into the young woman's flesh, digging down through the layers to reveal her inner organs. I use a self-retaining retractor to hold open the flap of skin and tissue to give me better access, blood slipping over my hands as I work faster now.

My gloved fingers probe her gently, making sure that nothing is damaged. The fetus is barely nine weeks old. Dead, like the mother, or soon will be. But its existence won't be wasted. Indeed, the knowledge it may reveal could be a greater achievement than most people could even dream of. I must get it back to the lab quickly.

Noises come from the hallway at the bottom of the stairs to the museum. I freeze, listening intently as my heart pounds in my chest. I can't be caught here, not like this. The work is too important and this specimen in particular must be studied. With the final cuts, I remove the uterus, placing it in her handbag that will have to do in place of an organ case

My work completed, I move to the doorway, hidden in the shadows. It sounds as if the people on the stairs are flirting and kissing, the party lubricated by enough alcohol to release the usual inhibitions. The noises grow fainter and I slip down the stairs as the unknown couple head off into a darker corner to fulfill their desires with each other. I pity them, for they can only find what they seek with living flesh. They know not of the darker pleasures of the anatomist.

CHAPTER 1

FROM OUTSIDE, THE LAVENDER Hospice looked like a school, with bright murals on the walls, a playground with swings, wood chips to stop the children hurting themselves. But those who entered this building wouldn't leave again and their voices were silenced too soon. Jamie Brooke pushed open the gate, hearing the usual squeak. She flinched slightly, adding the count to the list in her head, totaling the number of times she had walked through it. When she had first brought Polly here, finally unable to care for her at home, the doctor had said it wouldn't be long, maybe a matter of weeks. But the gate had squeaked ninety-seven times now, twice a day, so it was day forty-nine. Jamie sent up a prayer, thanking a God she didn't really believe in but still pleaded with each day. *Let her live another day, please. Take the time from me.*

The red wooden elephant by the door was looking a bit disheveled these days and Jamie made a mental note to talk to the Administrator about it. She knew the kids adored the jolly elephant, even though few of them ever made it outside to play on him. Practical help was about all she had left to offer.

Jamie checked her watch. She had moved to a tiny rented flat just down the road from the hospice, to be here for Polly as often as she could. Her job as a Detective Sergeant with the Metropolitan Police made the hours she visited complicated, but the nurses here were patient, understanding that as a single mother with a crazy job, she was trying the best she could.

Feeling tears prickle behind her eyes, Jamie took a deep breath, fixing a smile onto her face as she pushed the door open and entered the hospice.

"Morning," Rachel O'Halloran, the senior night nurse called cheerfully, as Jamie walked through the hallway.

"Hey Rachel. How's the night been?"

Rachel's face was a study in compassion and Jamie knew how much she loved the kids in her care, some here so briefly. There were people on this earth who were here to ease suffering and Rachel was one of the best, Jamie thought, and the kids instinctively loved the nurse in return.

"We had to increase Polly's morphine as she is getting a lot of pain from her spine now," Rachel said, "and her breathing is much worse. She might be drowsy when you go in." She paused, her eyes serious. "We need to talk, hun. You can't leave it much longer."

Jamie stood silently, closing her eyes for more than a second as she fought to keep her feelings under control. Despite her compassion, Rachel was an angel of death, her gentle arms helping the children to find their way onwards. But for parents, she represented only intense pain, for there was no avoiding the future she embodied. Jamie opened her eyes, hazel-green hardening with resolve.

"I'll come by on the way out."

Rachel nodded, and Jamie walked down the hall towards her daughter's room. The children's paintings on the wall attempted to add a veneer of hope to the place, but Jamie knew that the hands that had colored them were cold in the ground and the sorrow of years had soaked into the building. Parents and staff all tried to keep the spirits of the children up, organizing as much as possible to keep them occupied. But it seemed in the end that many of the little ones were more ready than their parents to slip out of the physical body. Exhausted with pain, debilitated with medication, their souls were eager for the next chance of life.

Jamie stood to the side of Polly's door, looking through the window at her daughter, whose body was distorted by motor neuron disease. Polly had Type II spinal muscular atrophy, and she was already past the life expectancy of children with the disorder. The deficiency of a protein needed for the survival of motor neurons meant that, over time, muscles weakened, the spine curved in a scoliosis and eventually the respiratory muscles could no longer inflate the lungs. Polly was already on breathing support and despite several operations, her physical body was now twisted and wasted. But Jamie could still remember the perfection of her beautiful baby when she had been born nearly fourteen years ago, and the joy that she had shared with her ex-husband Matt. He was long gone now, out of their lives with another wife and two perfectly healthy children he could play with to forget his past mistakes. Sometimes the anger Jamie felt at Matt, at herself, even at the universe for Polly's pain, made her heart race and her head thump with repressed rage. Her daughter didn't deserve this.

Jamie knew that the cause of Polly's disease was a genetic flaw on chromosome 5, a mutation somehow created from the alliance of her own body with Matt's. Perhaps it was some kind of sick metaphor for their marriage, which had collapsed when Polly started suffering as a toddler. But however difficult the journey, Polly had been worth every second. Jamie had always told her daughter that they were an unbreakable team, but now the bonds were beginning to fray and there was nothing she could do to stop it.

Jamie glanced in a mirror that hung in the hallway, visualizing the embedded genetic flaws on her own skin. If only she could dig out the part of her that worked and give it to Polly. Her long black hair was coiled up in a tight bun and she never wore make up for work. But with the dark circles getting worse under her eyes, Jamie thought she might have to consider changing her own rules. She looked pale and young, although she was the mature side of thirty-five these days. She touched her hair, tucking in a flyaway strand, claiming the little control she had left, clinging to this tiny victory. Threads of silver ran through the hair at her temples now, but the stress of the Metropolitan Police was nothing compared to living under the threat of Polly's death. Her daughter's every breath was precious at this point and Jamie fought for time away from the force to spend at her side. She turned the handle and went into the room.

"Morning, my darling," Jamie said as she approached the bed where Polly's twisted and wasted body lay, a tracheostomy tube in her neck helping her to breathe. She kissed the girl's forehead and put the wireless keyboard into Polly's hands, turning on the tablet computer, her daughter's link to the world. Her respiratory function had become so poor that the speaking valve was now useless but that couldn't stop her inimitable daughter. Jamie stroked Polly's hair as she watched her thin fingers tap slowly on the keyboard. Mercifully, the muscle wastage had started near the core of the body and left her extremities still able to move, so they had this method as well as lip reading to communicate. Jamie knew how important the computer was to Polly, the connection to her friends and a world of knowledge online, but the speed of her typing was painfully slow compared to even days ago.

6 videos last night. 3 more to finish multivariable calculus, Polly typed.

She had been progressing fast through the pure and applied math syllabus of the Khan Academy, an online video school designed to help children learn at their own pace, since many were capable of surpassing their classroom teachers. It was part of the incredible transformation of education, from an era of treating all kids the same, to targeting their specific talents and interests. It was also a godsend for children like Polly, who wanted to devour information non-stop. Even while her frail body lay dying, her brain was desperate for knowledge, although the drugs and her increasing weakness were now slowing her down. She was kept alive by the strength of her will, but that was dwindling like the leaves on the trees in the approach to winter.

Jamie knew that her daughter was fiercely intelligent and creative, as if in some way nature had made up for her physical flaws by giving her soaring intelligence. A picture of Stephen Hawking hung on the wall of Polly's room. The scientist was her idol, and she devoured his books - even at her young age she seemed to grasp concepts that her mother found difficult. Jamie had tried to read 'A Brief History of Time', but just couldn't fathom the science. Polly had explained the concepts in pictures and for a moment, Jamie had glimpsed the far galaxies in her daughter's mind. She had felt like the child then, instead of the mother. To be honest, she felt like the child now, as if nothing could ever be right with the world unless Polly could run and laugh again. But that couldn't be. This was not a journey Polly could return from and Jamie knew she couldn't go with her. Not this time.

Jamie met Polly's vibrant brown eyes, bright with a lively intelligence.

"I'm so proud of you, Pol, but you know I don't even understand what that means. Your Mum isn't exactly a math whiz."

Jamie pushed away the fleeting thought that it was pointless to learn when the brain would be dead soon. Polly's fingers continued to tap.

I'm doing the cosmology syllabus next. I'm beating Imran.

Jamie smiled. Imran was in a room down the hall, his body ravaged with terminal cancer but, like Polly, he was determined to cram as much into his intellectual life on earth as he could before he left it. On good days, when the drugs didn't rob them of consciousness, the teenagers could compete on the levels of Khan Academy. Both were competitive and determined to win. Jamie and Imran's parents were constantly astounded at their achievements, and Jamie credited her daughter's drive to succeed with preventing her own spiral into depression at the impending loss.

Did you dance last night?

Polly's eyes were brimming with the more detailed questions that Jamie knew she wanted to ask. She didn't need to type them because the conversation was one they had played out for years. Polly's greatest frustration with her body was not being able to dance and five years ago, she had asked Jamie to do it for her. "Dance Mum, please. Dance for me," she had pleaded. "And then come back and tell me about it. I want to know about the dresses and all the different people and how it feels to move so gracefully."

Jamie had relented at her insistence and taken up tango, a dance with its roots in the sorrow of slaves and immigrants, those oppressed by society. Tango was performed with a serious facial expression, emotion held within the dance. To her surprise, Jamie had found in tango her own form of release, and now the nights she danced enabled her a brief escape.

"Yes, I went to the *milonga* last night, Pol. I wore the silver dress and my hair down with the comb you made for me. I danced with Enrique first and he spun me into a close embrace ..."

So began the telling, the ritual they went through every day after Jamie could manage a night at tango. The erratic hours of her job made it difficult to go regularly, but she did find a sublimation of grief through the movement of her body. The late nights were worth the moments of clarity when focusing in the moment let her forget, albeit briefly.

Sometimes Jamie lied and told Polly stories of a tango night she didn't actually attend, an imagined evening where she had spun on the dance floor in the arms of a strong male lead, when in reality she had been at home, eyes red with weeping. Some nights, Jamie dreamt of walking along a beach, the ocean sucked back and the sand exposed, leaving sea creatures high and dry. There was a moment of calm when the waters receded, a suspended time of complete silence and rest. But she knew the tsunami wave would crash towards her soon, destroying everything in its path. Right now, Jamie held back the grief, but when it broke, she knew she would drown in its choking embrace. Part of her almost welcomed it.

Did you dance with Sebastian? Polly tapped with impatience.

Jamie laughed at her daughter's need for gossip. It was a marvelous moment of normality, although Jamie wished she was quizzing Polly about boys and not the other way around.

"You know I can't ask a man to dance, Pol. It's against the etiquette of tango. Sebastian was there but he was dancing primarily with Margherita. She's very good, you know."

Bitch.

"Polly Brooke," Jamie scolded, "enough of that language!" But Jamie couldn't help smiling, because the twenty-five year old Margherita was indeed a talented, beautiful bitch who dominated the London tango scene. Polly had seen her regular dancing partner Sebastian on YouTube and had become convinced that he should sweep Jamie off into a romantic sunset.

Polly's face suddenly contorted in a grimace of pain and she started making choking noises, a grotesque parody of breath. Increasingly now, the secretions in her lungs became too much and she struggled for air. Jamie had heard it described as similar to drowning, the body fighting desperately for oxygen. The keyboard fell to the floor with a clatter as Polly's fingers clutched at the air in grasping urgency. Jamie's heart rate spiked and she banged the panic button on the wall, knowing that the alert would be triggered in the nurse's area, silent so as not to alert the other children. She gripped Polly's hand.

"It's OK, my darling. I'm here. Try to relax. Shhh, there now, Pol. It's OK." Jamie couldn't hold back the tears, watching helplessly as Polly convulsed in pain, trying to cough up the stickiness that was engulfing her. Rachel swept into the room with another nurse and Jamie stepped back, letting them inject Polly with a sedative. Tears streaming down her face, Jamie felt impotent and useless as she could do nothing to take away her daughter's pain.

Rachel began to suction the fluid from Polly's lungs, the noise a hideous gurgling, but after a few seconds, Polly's tense body relaxed on the bed. Jamie stepped forward to take her hand, unclenching the fingers that had tightened in pain. She stroked her daughter's skin, touch her only communication now. The body on the bed was her daughter, but to Jamie, Polly was not an invalid in pain, a wracked, twisted, physical self. She was a soaring mind, a beautiful spirit trapped here by mistake. Some days Jamie wished death for them both, to escape together into an untethered future. She picked up the cuddly Golden Retriever puppy from the floor where it had fallen. Polly had always wanted a pet but the soft toy was the best Jamie could do. Polly had named it Lisa and kept it near her ever since, grubby now from a lot of love. Jamie tucked the soft toy under her daughter's arm.

Rachel stood close by, and gently brushed strands of hair from Polly's face.

"I know you don't want to have this conversation, hun," she said, "but sometimes it's better to let our children go. We can continue to keep Polly alive but her body is almost finished. You can see that, Jamie." Her voice was soft and calm, a practiced tone that Jamie knew she used with parents and children alike. "It's not something parents want to admit, but Polly's pain will only be over if you let her die. In any other society, she would have died of natural causes by now. We're just keeping this vessel alive, prolonging her pain."

Although appalling on one level, Jamie knew it was entirely appropriate to have this conversation in front of Polly, sedated or not. She didn't want to let her daughter's hand go in order to step outside the room, but also she knew that Polly had expressed her own strident wishes about the matter. They had talked about death and she knew that Polly wasn't afraid of it, only of the pain of passing. Jamie knew that Rachel talked about the end openly with the children and she understood the logic of that. There was an honesty at the hospice that cut through the crap of what was appropriate to discuss in polite society where the death of children was kept behind a veil of silence and denial. Here it was brutal in its regularity.

"I don't want to say goodbye," Jamie whispered. "I'm not ready yet."

"But what if Polly is?" Rachel said quietly, her voice speaking a truth that lingered in the antiseptic air.

Jamie's phone vibrated in her pocket, breaking the moment.

"It's work, I'm sorry." She pulled it out, seeing a missed call and a text. She scanned it quickly and felt her pulse quicken. Despite the desperation of Polly's illness, work was her sanity. "There's been a murder," she said. "I've been assigned to the case so I have to go Rachel, but I'll be back tonight. Just give me another day, please."

Rachel walked around the bed and touched Jamie's arm gently. "It's not me you're doing this for, hun. It's for your little one."

Tears pricked Jamie's eyes again, but she brushed them away, pulling the veneer of police business around her shoulders. Her job gave her a psychological anchor as well as paying the bills. Jamie was good at detective work, and her ability to solve puzzles and right wrongs gave her a little piece of lucidity in the face of inevitable loss. Every criminal brought to justice was another point added to her karma balance that she begged the universe to give to Polly.

CHAPTER 2

THE JET BLACK BMW motorbike pulled up in front of the Royal College of Surgeons in the square of Lincoln's Inn Fields, an area renowned for the legal profession and dominated by Georgian terraced houses. Jamie tugged off her helmet and dismounted the bike, putting her safety gear and protective leathers into one of the panniers. She had traded in her old car when Polly had entered the hospice. She couldn't stand to look at it anymore without feeling that her daughter had gone already. The bike was cheaper to run and the independence increasingly suited her. She wasn't meant to use it for getting to crime scenes but today she needed the mental space even though it rumpled her clothes. She straightened the black crush-proof trousers and tucked in her white shirt, pulling the matching suit jacket out with her handbag from the other pannier. Dusting the jacket down, she put it on and her transformation was complete. Polly sometimes called her the 'black work wraith', but Jamie preferred to wear the equivalent of a uniform to separate her professional life.

Glancing around and seeing none of her colleagues, Jamie pulled out a pack of Marlboro Menthol. Lighting one, she looked up at the imposing classical entrance to the Royal College. She smoked quick and fast, her breath frosty in the air, cheeks red with the winter cold. The cigarette was a shot of delicious poison, her own private rebellion against what she would have preached to Polly. What did it matter anyway, Jamie thought. Life is poison, drip drip drip every day until we die of whatever addictions hold us. Everything she lived for right now hung over her head like the sword of Damocles, so what difference would another cancer stick make? Besides, she needed just a little fix before facing the body that lay inside. The cigarette was a chemical separation between her home life and the professional, a space where she could squash her emotions into the mental box she kept separate from her police work.

Jamie took another drag, enjoying the mint fresh aftertaste through the harshness of tobacco smoke. In the old-school tango clubs of Buenos Aires, smoke filled the air, an important part of the culture where life was often short and lived intensely. In these brief moments Jamie recaptured that sensation in the little beats of time between her dual lives in this crazy city. She relished the start of a new case and already she was glancing around, her mind posing questions about the area. Why was the murder committed in this elegant part of town?

A gust of wind blew leaves along the road, brittle reminders of autumn tumbling over each other and rustling in the gutter. The sharp breeze bent the branches of trees in the park, a few skeletal leaves hanging on against the grey. Jamie looked up at the early winter sun, the only color in a sky that was as washed out as the commuters who walked, shoulders hunched, into the Aldwych. Winter was almost upon them and soon the British would begin their annual vigil, longing for spring as the nights arrived ever earlier. Jamie's thought ahead to Christmas, a time that Polly loved and she had always over-indulged. Would she be alone this year? Jamie pushed the thought aside, taking a final drag and pulling a small tin from inside her bag. She stubbed the cigarette out on the lid and carefully placed the end into it. The tin served as a way to monitor her habit but also to remove any evidence. She noticed there were already three inside, too many for this time in the morning.

Walking into the main lobby of the Royal College of Surgeons, Jamie gave her details for the crime scene log and put on protective coveralls and booties. A uniformed Officer directed her past the yellow tape of the perimeter to the first floor. The entrance hall was imposing, wide stairs with rich red carpet sweeping around in a curve, with marble balustrades to guide the way upwards. The hall was overlooked by extravagant paintings of the men who had once ruled this surgical empire. Artifacts from the museum were displayed in niches, drawing the eyes back through its illustrious history.

Upstairs, Jamie entered the Hunterian Museum, a place she'd never visited but vaguely knew of. It was one of those hidden treasures of London that few came to see but which changed those who did. She was partially glad of her ignorance, because she wanted to see it with untainted eyes before she polluted her instinctive impressions with fact.

Near the door, a uniformed officer sat with an elderly man, the Curator. He was agitated, wringing his hands and then rubbing his neck, repeatedly loosening his tie. Jamie recognized the body language of self-comforting and wondered if perhaps he had found the body. She would circle back to him in a bit. The officer looked up and Jamie nodded her head in a professional greeting, avoiding a smile.

She looked around, taking in the activity before her. Scene Of Crime Officers (SOCOs) were processing the area, and Jamie's eyes were drawn to a central space surrounded by walls of glass shelving that contained thousands of body parts in preservation jars. Jamie had seen many bodies in various states, but usually they were recognizably human. This was a collection of the macabre, and a strangely appropriate place for another dead body.

Jamie felt a familiar surge of excitement at a new case, a new puzzle to solve and a way to distract her from thoughts of the hospice. She registered the usual guilt as well, because for her to feel this way, a human being had to die. But Jamie was a realist and there would always be murder, violence and death. It was endemic to the human condition. She had a short window of opportunity in her life to make a difference and potentially lower the body count and it made her remarkable for just an instant. This job was not some office function where busy work whiled away the hours, counting for nothing. This work could save lives, bring justice and occasionally equilibrium to the small corner of the world that was Jamie's London. It was a chance to be extraordinary, the reason she had escaped her parents' home on the Milton Keynes housing estate as soon as she could. She had known growing up there that she had to get out of that rut or risk being trapped forever in mediocrity.

Jamie walked into the central area where a female body was laid out on the floor wearing a scarlet evening dress that had been slashed open. Her beautiful face was calm but there was a deep wound in her lower abdomen, looking more like a surgical operation than the butchery it must have been. The woman's blonde hair looked like an unnatural wig, the tresses freshly brushed and seemingly too alive to be attached to a dead body. Flashes of light from the crime scene photographer illuminated the corpse, her skin pale and posed like a model exhibit. Jamie stood still as she took in the scene. This was the moment when she knew nothing and her mind was filled with questions. Who was this woman and why did she die here last night. She noticed the red lipstick on the woman's mouth and imagined her speaking. What would she say?

"Jamie, good to see you."

Jamie turned to see Detective Sergeant Leander Marcus,

his slight paunch extending the dark weave of his suit trousers, visible through the thin protective coveralls.

"Hey Lee, were you first on scene?"

Leander nodded, his face crumpled with lack of sleep.

"Keen to get off it ASAP. I've been up all night and this only came in a few hours ago. Cameron get you called in?"

Leander arched an eyebrow and Jamie gave a complicit half-smile. Detective Superintendent Dale Cameron was respected for his accomplishments but he also seemed to have Teflon shoulders, deflecting any scandal onto other ranking officers, so his cases came with a health warning. With his salt and pepper hair and a body kept trim from marathon running, Cameron had the looks of a Fortune 500 CEO and his star was on the rise within the Metropolitan Police.

He had been appointed Senior Investigating Officer for the crime, assigning Jamie to the case along with a small team of Detective Constables as an inquiry team. Jamie had clashed with Cameron before, receiving a verbal warning for acting outside of protocol. She knew that she needed to rein in her independent streak, it didn't sit well with the rules and regulations of the Force. But she also knew that her exemplary investigation results meant she was given a little more leeway. Her methods might be unorthodox, but at least Cameron trusted her enough to get the job done and assign her to this case. She needed distraction, and losing herself in work was the best way, keeping her mind occupied while her heart was slowly breaking.

"So what have we got so far?" Jamie asked.

"The deceased is Jenna Neville," Leander said. "Her handbag is missing but we got a list from security of people who entered in the last 24 hours and she was easily recognizable after we got the names. You must have heard of Neville Pharmaceuticals?"

Jamie's eyes widened in recognition at the name.

"Of course, it's one of the biggest British pharmaceutical companies."

"Exactly. Her father is Sir Christopher Neville, the CEO, who mainly concerns himself with politics and media campaigning. Her mother is one of the top scientists for the privately owned company."

"Any indication of why she was here?" Jamie asked.

"There was a gala event downstairs last night for alumni surgeons of the college. Jenna Neville attended the event, along with her parents, who are benefactors."

Damn, Jamie thought. A medical style murder in the Royal College of Surgeons after a party filled with actual surgeons. No obvious suspects then. "How many people?"

"Around 90 guests, plus staff. The Museum was supposed to have been locked though, and it wasn't used for the function."

"Is a team on the statements already?"

Leander nodded. "There's several officers starting on it now we have the guest list."

"I don't envy them," Jamie said. " That's going to take a while." She looked up at the glass walls surrounding them, stretching two stories high and lined with specimen preservation jars. "Cameras?"

Leander shook his head. "There aren't any in the Museum itself and the ones downstairs show all those guests milling around. We need to go through the footage and see if any of them weren't on the guest list, but to be honest, there are other entrances. This isn't a highly secure building as it's not considered a security risk. There are no drugs here, or money, only old bones and bodies."

Jamie indicated a walled display of surgeon's tools.

"And scalpels, knives, hacksaws and other equipment that could be used as murder weapons."

Leander shrugged. "Of course, but the College says that these are historical objects and there are easier ways to procure knives around here. But they're checking the inventory now."

They stood in silence for a moment as a white suited figure finished examining the body. Jamie knew forensic pathologist Mike Skinner from multiple crime scenes but he barely strayed outside the boundaries of professional talk related to the case. He stood and stretched his back, then turned to them, inclining his head in a slight greeting.

"There's massive blunt force trauma to the skull and her neck's broken." Jamie could see that the head was positioned at an unnatural angle, and the hair had been pulled back from the wound. Skinner pointed behind them to an open space at the bottom of a flight of stairs from the upper level of the museum, now surrounded by crime scene markers. "There are blood and bone fragments over there so it looks she fell and hit the post at the bottom of the stairs. I suspect that the way she landed would have forced her head into hyper-extension with sufficient force to cause a fracture at the C2 vertebrae." Skinner demonstrated with his own neck, dropping his chin close to his chest. "It's a classic hangman's fracture and cause of death is likely to be asphyxia secondary to cervical injury. It only takes a few minutes. I'll confirm in the post-mortem but those would be my preliminary thoughts. Her body was then dragged to this central area and postmortem lividity shows she was on her back here when the body was cut open."

Jamie glanced down at the bloody wound, held open by a retractor. "Can you tell what was done?"

Skinner nodded. "Looks like her uterus was removed. Skillfully done too. It's a perfect Pfannenstiel incision, a Caesarean section, and it looks like the instruments used were from the Museum's collection."

Jamie tilted her head on one side. "That implies no premeditation, at least for the excision." She paused, looking around the museum at the specimen jars surrounding them, an echo of the mutilated body. "Was she dead when her uterus was cut out?"

"It looks that way but I'll know for sure after the autopsy. The lack of significant blood loss around the wound suggests that the heart stopped pumping during the operation."

Jamie felt a sense of relief that Jenna hadn't felt the invasion of her body, but why had it been done?

"Any idea of time of death?"

"Between nine and midnight, but I might get something more exact after the autopsy. I would say that it was certainly during the gala event. Right, I've done all I can here."

Skinner nodded at two other men, also in protective clothing and they came forward to remove the body. They bagged the woman's hands and laid down a plastic sheet. As the corpse was lifted, Jamie heard something fall from the folds of Jenna's dress with a dull thunk. She signaled for the photographer to capture it as she bent to look more closely, pulling out her sterile gloves and an evidence bag. It was a figurine carved of ivory, around four inches long, a woman laid on her back, torso opened in a detailed miniature dissection. The woman's serene ivory face portrayed a calm demeanor even as her body lay open and mutilated, her organs and loops of intestines painted a deep red.

"You can take the body," Jamie said to Skinner, who was clearly eager to get back to his lab. "I'll deal with this."

She waited until the body had been zipped in its bag and strapped to the gurney. Once it had been wheeled out, she beckoned to the officer by the door to bring the Curator. He shuffled over slowly, his face a mask of grief. Even surrounded by mementoes of death every day, it must have been a horrifying shock to find the newly dead body early this morning. After some brief introductions, Jamie indicated the figurine.

"Could you explain what this is, sir?" she asked, her voice coaxing.

The Curator's posture became more focused as he directed his attention to the figurine, bending down to look but careful not to touch it.

"It's an anatomical Venus," he said. "They were made from the seventeenth century onwards as a way to teach anatomy, but increasingly they became more of an attraction for the cabinets of curiosities belonging to various wealthy collectors. They wanted things that were strange or terrible, horrific or unusual, those that would provoke a reaction in the viewer."

"Is it valuable?" Jamie asked.

The Curator nodded. "Absolutely. We have some examples here but it's not one of ours. It must belong to a private collection, or a museum perhaps. Someone will be missing it, for sure."

There was a bustle of noise at the doorway to the Museum and Jamie turned to see Detective Constable Alan Missinghall enter, hunching over in an attempt to be less obtrusive. He failed miserably, his six foot five muscular frame dwarfing the other officers on scene. He was new in the department and so far Jamie was impressed with his work. Missinghall had only just turned thirty and many underestimated him, seeing in his physicality a propensity for violence. But he was gentle, his expressive face betraying an acute compassion for victims of crime and he had a way of standing that made others feel protected. As usual, he wore an understated dark blue suit, slightly too short in the leg for his height, but he still walked like a man with authority.

"What have we got, Sarge?" Missinghall said, bending to look at the figurine.

Jamie recapped what she had found out so far and he took notes on his pad, putting asterisks next to aspects for follow-up. Jamie appreciated his keen attitude, hoping that it would last, for he hadn't yet tasted the bitter side of detective work.

"This room is seriously weird," Missinghall said, glancing around at the glass walls. He walked over and stared at the rows of specimen jars.

Jamie took a picture of the figurine on her smartphone, bagged the item for processing and then followed him over. The jars looked marvelously benign until you leaned closer, until what was inside became clear. The specimens were organs grouped together across comparative species. A whole shelf contained jars full of tongues, fleshy camel, spongy lion, then a human tongue with soft palate and enlarged tonsils, wrinkled and puckered like an alien mouth. These jars of disease are evidence of our mortality, Jamie thought with a shiver, fragments of flesh and bone that once walked the earth, now imprisoned in jars of preservative, drowning anew each day.

The Curator shuffled over to the cabinets, noting their interest and clearly eager to distract his own attention from the misery of the crime scene.

"John Hunter was an eighteenth century surgeon," he said. "He introduced direct observation of the body and scientific method into anatomy, rejecting the flawed textbooks his generation used. Although his methods were unorthodox and he gained many enemies, he nevertheless changed the practice of surgery and made medical discoveries that saved countless lives."

"Is this all his work?" Jamie asked, indicating the glass shelving with a sweep of her arm.

"Most of it and more in storage," the Curator replied, "but much was lost in a fire. He worked with his brother initially, William Hunter, who specialized in medical education and gynecology. But John was the real anatomical genius, and he prepped the specimens perfectly as you can see. It became his obsession and he spent his life seeking out the strange and terrible from humanity and the animal kingdom in order to learn from them."

There was so much death here, Jamie thought, imagining John Hunter and the bodies he had cut to pieces to make this collection. It was certainly a triumph of science and reason at a time when the body was misunderstood, before anesthesia, before antiseptic, when surgery was more akin to torture and generally ended in death. But it was also a disturbing museum of the deformed and misshapen monsters that Hunter had found so fascinating. Jamie looked into one of the cabinets, staring at the face of a child with no eyes, covered in smallpox. Just a face, floating in liquid. This place was indeed a bizarre and perfect location for a murder.

"John Hunter eventually had his own anatomy school and private medical practice as well as working at St George's Hospital. He would hardly sleep, so driven was he in his studies." Jamie could hear the admiration in the Curator's voice, his respect for a lifelong obsession. "Hunter was elected as a Fellow of the Royal Society in recognition for his pioneering work and he was considered the authority on venereal disease, possibly even infecting himself to study its destructive course. He was obsessed with direct observation, hence the specimens you see here."

Missinghall leaned towards one of the cabinets and Jamie saw the grimace on his face as he realized he was staring at a set of diseased sexual organs. He shifted uncomfortably and turned back to the Curator.

"So where did the bodies come from?" he asked, and Jamie felt her own curiosity piqued too, for there were thousands of specimens even in this one room.

"That was … difficult," the Curator said, nodding. "But they had no choice, you see. Since the time of Henry VIII surgeons had only been allowed a small number of bodies each year, usually criminals hanged on the gallows. But there were too few to use for effective teaching and the surgical schools required each student to dissect several bodies in the course of their studies. John Hunter and his brother were part of a renaissance in anatomical teaching, but they needed fresh bodies every day in the winter dissection season. Summer, of course, meant the bodies putrefied too quickly." The Curator was speaking fast now, almost apologetic for what had happened all those years ago. "So they had to work with so-called Resurrection Men, grave robbers who would take fresh corpses from new graves, from the hospitals or poor houses and sell them to the anatomists."

Missinghall's expressive face showed his distaste, and although Jamie had heard of such practices, she hadn't really understood until now that many of the bodies were stolen, taken from graves without the consent of loved ones or sold because of poverty.

"Seriously?" Missinghall was incredulous. "Wasn't that illegal then? Because it sure is now."

The Curator shook his head. "The corpse was not considered property and the Resurrection Men were careful to only take the naked body, leaving the shroud and coffin so as not to be prosecuted for stealing. They were paid more for bodies that died of exotic diseases or deformities, and Hunter also wanted to recover the bodies of patients on whom he had performed surgery to see how they had healed." He pointed into the glass bell jars at the fetuses preserved there. "These little ones were priced by the inch. There are even some claims that the Hunters bought corpses murdered to order, particularly women at various stages of pregnancy for William Hunter's detailed study of the gravid womb." He paused. "Ridiculous rumors, of course."

Jamie didn't want to hear any more of Hunter's ghoulish past and Missinghall was looking increasingly queasy, even though he was accustomed to the newly dead. What mattered right now was establishing what had happened last night, not over two hundred years previously.

"Thank you for your time, sir," Jamie said. "We may come back to you with further questions."

The Curator nodded and walked away, his shoulders tense and rigid.

Missinghall shook his head. "Let's process this freakish place and get out of here," he said. "We can look into Hunter some more back at base, but I suspect this place will give me nightmares for weeks."

Jamie nodded, walking slowly around the glass-walled cases to the bottom of the stairs. She bent and examined the blood stains there, careful to avoid the crime scene markers.

"Why was Jenna even up here during the gala dinner?" Jamie thought aloud. "The body was clearly dragged from the bottom of the stairs, so it would be logical that she fell first and hit her head before being moved."

"Or she was pushed deliberately," Missinghall noted.

"Not a very effective way to kill someone," Jamie said, walking up the stairs to the next level. "It's not guaranteed that the person will die, only be injured in some way. And these steps aren't even that steep."

"Maybe it was an accident?" Missinghall said, as they both looked down at the scene below through more glass display cases.

"Cutting out her womb wasn't an accident."

"Maybe the killer has something against women?" Missinghall said. "Or perhaps this place just inspired impromptu surgical practice?"

Jamie ignored his black humor, understanding his need to keep a light tone with what they dealt with every day. She turned to look at the other cases on the second floor, which was focused on the history of medicine. In one was a life-size wax model of a hideously deformed victim of war, with half a face and its neck torn away to reveal the jawbone. One hand was burnt to raw pink skin with fingers missing, and there were slashes in the chest, open to bloody rib bones. In the next case, a whole series of surgical saws were displayed, all from a seventeenth century surgeon's kit. Jamie read the sign on an amputation saw, describing a time before anesthetic and antiseptic, when people's limbs were hacked off while they were tied down, dosed only with laudanum or alcohol. She turned away, before the imagined horror dominated her thoughts any further.

"We'll have to wait for the autopsy results on whether she was pregnant and we'll need the statements of the attending surgeons from last night." Jamie sighed. "So let's go talk to the parents in the meantime."

CHAPTER 3

THE STREETS OF CHELSEA were always busy but Jamie wove through the traffic with ease on her bike, while Missinghall followed in the squad car, eventually catching her up outside the Neville's residence where she jumped in beside him. The exclusive property had security cameras and the gates swung open as the police car drove up. Jenna's parents had been notified of her death earlier that morning, so they were expected.

"You're quiet today, Jamie," Missinghall said, finishing off a banana. The man never seemed to stop eating. "Do you want me to take the lead on this?"

Jamie stared out at the ornate garden as they drove slowly up the drive. The grounds were like a miniature Versailles, beautiful even in the chill of early winter, precisely ordered with not a blade of grass or stem out of place. Jamie wondered if her life would ever be this ordered. Right now, she felt it disintegrating around her, but she wouldn't share that with Missinghall, preferring to keep her distance with work colleagues.

"Sure," she said. "Why don't you talk to them first and I'll hang back a little. The father may respond better to you anyway."

"Isn't he some kind of minor aristocrat?" Missinghall

asked.

Jamie nodded. "According to the case file, the family is distantly related to Francis Galton, the eugenicist, and he was in turn related to the Darwins, so they have quite the scientific background. Their pedigree plays a prominent role in the marketing for Neville Pharmaceuticals. Lady Esther Neville is the brilliant scientist and Lord Christopher is well connected amongst the aristocracy, playing high stakes business with the manners of a perfect English gentleman."

"I'm not sure how well he'll like me then," Missinghall said, emphasizing his rough East London accent.

"But at least you're a man," replied Jamie, smiling a little. "He's apparently quite the chauvinist, with the media citing his preference for much younger women when out on the town."

"Marriage issues?" Missinghall said.

"They've been married since they were at Oxford University together," Jamie said, glancing through the notes on her smart phone that had been assembled by the murder inquiry office manager. "After thirty years of marriage, perhaps that kind of behavior is normal."

"Remind me not to ask you for relationship advice," Missinghall said. "I'm very happy with my missus."

Jamie remained silent at his comment, ignoring the unspoken questions about her personal life. Her own failed marriage and her parents' misery were the only markers she had against which to measure marital bliss.

Missinghall parked in front of the main doors, which were opened by an immaculately dressed butler before they stepped out of the car. Missinghall turned to Jamie, raising an eyebrow at the unexpected service.

"Good morning, Officers," the butler said as they presented their warrant cards. "Lord and Lady Neville are waiting in the library. Please come through."

The butler held the door wide and Jamie stepped first

into the hallway. It was sparsely furnished with a few taste-
ful pieces, but the walls were dominated by pictures, many
black and white or faded sepia. Jamie leaned close as they
were led through and she caught sight of famous faces. These
were ancestors of the Nevilles in classic poses, designed to
emphasize the visitor's inherent inferiority in this house of
distinction. There were also pictures of Christopher Neville
with senior political figures, CEOs and powerful media
moguls. Jamie even caught sight of one with her superior
officer, Dale Cameron, accepting some award, in the days
before he had risen to the rank of Superintendent. Christopher Neville was indeed well connected, she thought,
following the butler further inside.

The library was straight out of a Merchant Ivory film,
with tall bookcases of ebony and exotic hardwood filled
with leather bound first edition books, some behind locked
glass so that they couldn't even be read. It was another way
to impress and Jamie felt its effect, the delineations of social
class evident. She thought of her own rented rooms, clut-
tered with books for sure, but nothing on this scale.

Lord Christopher Neville was standing by the ornate
marble fireplace, his hand resting on the back of his wife's
chair. He wore a three piece suit in English tweed, the mossy
color palette blending into the library backdrop, like the
cover of a fox-hunting magazine. Lady Esther Neville sat
like an angular statue in a cream trouser suit, staring out
of the window into the distance, her blonde hair scraped
back into a tight chignon. She didn't even turn her head as
they entered. Jamie had the peculiar sense that the pair had
arranged themselves for some effect. She noticed the tension
in Lady Neville's body, her senses attuned as a dancer to how
people hold themselves. It was as if the woman was arching
away from her husband's hand, as if his very presence
repelled her. Jamie knew that the death of a child took many
marriages to breaking point, but this all seemed staged,

as if this is how a bereaved family was meant to look. She wondered what lay beneath the careful veneer.

"Detectives, what can we do for you?" Lord Neville said, his voice cordial with an undertone of impatience. He was bordering on corpulent, barely hiding the evidence of good living with impeccable tailoring and his voice was the epitome of aristocracy, honed by years of conversation in the upper echelons of power. His light grey eyes were clear and piercing, and Jamie noticed that they lingered a little too long on her own slight figure.

"We're so sorry for your loss, Lord and Lady Neville," Missinghall said, with a formal tone. "But we need to ask some questions about Jenna."

Lord Neville nodded. "Of course, we'll do everything we can to help you. Jenna was our precious angel."

Lady Neville's hand flew to her mouth at his words, and a stricken look passed over her face before her mask returned as her husband's hand moved to rest on her shoulder. Esther Neville was peaky, sallow-skinned and pale, as if she spent her days away from the sun. Jamie supposed that she did exactly that, shut deep in her lab generating fortunes for the company while her husband was out enjoying its profits. It looked to Jamie as if she would have got up and run from the room, but he imperceptibly held her down. Jamie felt a pang of pity for the woman touching the edges of her compartmentalized grief about Polly. But she couldn't let her preconceptions of motherhood cloud the investigation and, at this point, everyone was a suspect.

"We understand that you were both at the gala dinner with Jenna last night?" Missinghall said.

Lord Neville nodded. "The event was to raise money for the Royal College of Surgeons and we already fund a number of scholarships there. We're interested in supporting the education of a new generation as well as saving the lives of millions through our genetic and drug research."

Jamie thought he was about to launch into some kind of marketing pitch about the company so she jumped in.

"What time did you both leave?" she asked, pulling out her notebook.

"We've been through this already in the statement," Lord Neville said, a note of annoyance in his voice. "But Esther felt unwell and left around 9.30 and I am sure I left around 11."

Jamie thought she saw a spark in Esther's eyes at that, but her face remained downcast.

"And how was Jenna when you left?"

Lord Neville frowned. "I didn't see her before I went. She had left the table earlier in the evening to dance with one of her many beaus." Jamie noted a tinge of anger in his voice and an emphasis on the word many. She would have to investigate Jenna's love life carefully. Lord Neville paused. "We had an argument actually, I'm sure others will tell you of it, so I may as well. She'd had too much wine, and she said she had something to tell us, something that would change things. But she has said such things before, and nothing has come of it. I don't know why my daughter couldn't just leave the company in peace. She took its money easily enough." He looked away and his voice softened. "I guess it will be left in peace now."

Jamie wanted to explore the conflict around Neville Pharmaceuticals further, but she wanted to find out more from other sources first. People lied to themselves most of all. Those lies could hide the truth easily, and this was a family well used to displaying a public persona.

While Missinghall began to ask questions about Jenna's home life, her studies and the law firm where she worked, Jamie looked around and began to notice how unusual the room was. Lit only by table lamps, it was hard to see into the corners, but it was as if a veneer of respectability lay over more disturbing aspects. Above the fireplace was a large painting, at first glance just a woman holding her breast to feed an infant, posed as a Madonna and Child, seated with folds of light blue fabric around her. On second glance, Jamie noticed that her belly was in fact cut open to reveal her viscera and the baby in her lap was likewise a partially dissected cadaver. Jamie couldn't help but stare as it seemed to violate all sense of what would be acceptable to display in a public room like this. What made it all the more macabre was a framed photograph near the painting of a young Lady Neville with a baby, presumably Jenna, in her arms, the pose oddly reminiscent of the painting.

"I see you've noticed our interest in anatomy," Lord Neville's voice cut through Jamie's contemplation, and she turned.

"I'm sorry for staring," Jamie said. "But the painting is so unusual."

Especially given the location and style of the murder, she thought.

"I started collecting *memento-mori* many years ago," Lord Neville said, walking over to Jamie and looking up at the painting. "Tiny sculptures of skeletons and the dead in coffins that people would use to remind themselves of the shortness of life, the inevitability of death. To see a skeleton is to behold your own death and we all need a reminder that the end is inevitable."

A soft cry broke from Lady Neville's lips.

"I'm so sorry." She stood, wiping her eyes. "You'll have to excuse me. My husband will answer any further questions you have."

Jamie watched Lady Neville leave and heard her suppress a sob as she walked briskly up the stairs. The woman was clearly distraught, and for good reason, but she would have to find out more about Lady Neville. The interview would have to wait. She turned back to the room as Missinghall continued to ask about Jenna's life. But Jamie was impatient now and she wanted to get past the preliminaries. For a moment, she let Missinghall continue with his line of questioning and then allowed herself to interrupt.

"Did you agree with Jenna's career choice, Lord Neville?" Jamie asked. She was aware from the case notes that Jenna had started to specialize in the increasingly complex legal issues around tissue and DNA ownership, animal experimentation and other areas that could directly impact the practices of Neville Pharmaceuticals. There was also some photographic evidence that Jenna had participated in activist marches against the company and others labeled Big Pharma.

Lord Neville frowned and ran his hand through his thick dark hair.

"No, but my daughter was headstrong. She didn't want to come into the family business and in fact, she seemed determined to break it apart. I know she disagreed with some of the ethics of the company, but the money paid for her education, her prospects." Jamie could hear the disappointment and anger in his voice. "For some reason, she chose to leave us and live with that awful girl in a terrible part of town, getting into all sorts of trouble. I warned her, you know …"

His voice trailed off.

"And Lady Neville, did she support Jenna's choices?" Jamie asked.

Lord Neville paused, grasping for the right words. Jamie watched as he wrestled with what to say, finally settling on platitudes.

"Esther works too hard, spends long hours at the lab," he said softly. "She's wedded to the company, but she loves Jenna and she only wanted the best for her."

"Do you have any enemies?" Missinghall asked, changing tack. "Have there been any threats against you or the company, your family?"

Lord Neville walked to the other side of the fireplace and

waved his hand dismissively.

"Of course, we get so many threats that we have a full-time staff member who goes through it all and decides which ones to forward onto the police. Not that you lot ever do anything. My legal team has restraining orders on a number of individuals, but in this country, the right to protest runs deep. There are ringleaders, of course, and I'll get everything forwarded onto you for the investigation. I personally get several death threats a week related to the business, but it's *my* life, Detectives, and not something I expected to impact my daughter, especially given her activism. Do you think her murder was related to the protests against the company?"

"The violation of the body didn't suggest a crime of passion or an unskilled criminal," Jamie said. "In fact, quite the opposite. We're looking for someone with surgical knowledge. What about any disgruntled employees, people who have worked in your labs who may hold a grudge?"

"Again, I'll have the files sent on but the nature of our business attracts a fair share of crazies and psychos. To us, the human body is a treasure trove, an addiction and a fascination. The way my daughter's body was displayed was not unlike the models I have in my collection, and so I can see it as a warning of course. But of what? I have already left my body to science and it will be cut up the day I die, but for someone to do this to Jenna … It's unthinkable and I will see that person punished."

"Of course, Lord Neville," Missinghall said, a curious deference in his voice. Jamie could see that he felt the class difference keenly. "We'll be working hard to pursue the leads around the case."

"Did Jenna still have a room here?" Jamie asked. "Or did she leave any personal items with you?"

Lord Neville shook his head. "No, she was quite deter-mined to prove her independence. Anything she didn't want to take, she gave to charity. An animal rights charity, can you believe it?"

Jamie pulled out her smart phone to show him the photo of the ivory anatomical Venus found by Jenna's body.

"Do you recognize this, sir?"

Lord Neville looked at the photo and his eyes narrowed with interest. He hesitated just a fraction too long before handing it back.

"No, but I have similar pieces."

"It was with Jenna's body, wrapped in her clothes. We think she might have had it with her that night."

Lord Neville's expression was guarded and Jamie saw a flicker of doubt there. Was it guilt or just the devastation of a parent whose child had suffered too much?

"I don't know why she would have that with her."

Jamie nodded. "Of course." She hesitated, looking at the painting of the dissected woman behind him. The similarity to the museum exhibits in the Hunterian was too much of a coincidence to pass over. "May we see your collection? It might help us understand more clearly the artistic value of this piece."

"Of course, I'll have Matthews take you through. Is there anything else, or I will see to my wife."

Jamie shook her head. "Thank you for your time. We may be back with further questions."

Neville called for Matthews, the butler, who showed them through the library and out into another hallway, then up a staircase to the next floor. He led them into a salon that had been set up as a small museum with glass cabinets and even tiny handwritten labels. It was full of old anatomical teaching devices and artwork around the subjects of death and the human body.

"I'll leave you here to browse," Matthews said. "Can I bring you some coffee or tea?"

Jamie shook her head, walking further into the room.

"I'd love a cuppa, thanks," Missinghall said, then Jamie

saw his face fall as he realized that he hadn't escaped the macabre by leaving the Hunterian. She looked into the nearest case as Missinghall walked around the room, his body arching instinctively away from what he saw.

Jamie found herself next to an anatomical model of a female torso, her face turned into the room. Her perfect eyelashes lay on wax cheeks, one blue eye gazing into the distance. She had perfectly kissable lips and skin like alabaster but one side of her face was deconstructed down to bone and tissue. The jaw was opened up to display tongue and teeth, the veins in the neck exposed, and her internal organs opened to the air. The model was more disturbing because the limbs had been cut off, legs sawn through so the bones protruded through the middle of steak-like fleshy rings. Between the stumps, a vagina complete with pubic hair was expertly modeled. Like some kind of sex doll for necrophiliacs, Jamie thought, wondering where the line between teaching and pornography lay. Anatomical Venus indeed. She found herself wanting to hide the woman from view. This room was a testament to the development of science, but at the expense of human dignity.

"What do you think of all this?" Missinghall asked, his voice tinged with disgust. "I just don't get why people would want to look at this stuff?"

Jamie stared at the case with the dissected woman. Jenna had clearly inhabited a world where this was considered normal, where the human body was part of study and work. Jamie was sure that this had played a part in her death.

CHAPTER 4

LEAVING MISSINGHALL TO RETURN and process what they had so far, Jamie rode slowly through the streets of Rotherhithe towards the City Farm, where Jenna Neville had shared a flat. It was a strange suburb, a bleak, cornered world with houses crowded together, densely populated but seemingly empty. The area had missed out on the recent revival of the East End of London. Whereas the north side of the Thames had caught the imagination of the public and was now culture and party-central, this little corner of South London was concrete and unwelcoming.

Jamie parked the bike and walked to the end of Vaughn Street, looking out across the river towards Canary Wharf, the heart of London's modern financial district, and famed for obscenities of wealth. Some people lived in this area for the ease of commuting by ferry across the water but others, perhaps like Jenna, were here to protest against the high-rises and cocktail bars, six-figure bonuses and hedonism that thrived on the bank opposite. For a second, Jamie thought of Polly's impossible future, what she could have achieved in this city of potential. Feeling tears well, she sighed and pushed the thoughts away. She couldn't let her emotions leak into this investigation.

Turning back, Jamie walked down to number 15, knocking on the door of the little terraced house, unremarkable in a sea of similar properties. The door opened and Jamie showed her warrant card.

"Miss McConnell?"

Elsa McConnell was petite with a tousled head of ginger curls that she wore tied up with a lavender checked headband. Her face was clean of makeup, a few freckles were scattered across her nose and cheeks, and her blue eyes were red and raw.

"Yes, Detective. The police said you would be coming over … Please come in, and call me Elsa. Excuse me, I'm just so …"

She broke off to blow her nose as tears started to flow again. Jamie contrasted her genuine emotion with the strange stunted response of Jenna's parents.

"I know this is hard for you, Elsa, but I wanted to ask you some questions and have a look at Jenna's room, if that's OK."

Elsa nodded, stepping back into the hallway and turning towards the small kitchen. As Jamie followed her in, she caught sight of the back of her neck, crosshatched in a complicated geometric tattoo that wound beneath her clothes.

The flat was brightly lit, with all of the main lights and side-lamps turned on, almost blinding with intensity.

"I can't stand the shadows right now," Elsa whispered almost apologetically.

Jamie nodded, her eyes scanning the place for indications of Jenna's life. There were People for the Ethical Treatment of Animals posters on the walls and eclectic Indian throws over the furniture. The young women were clearly not into mass-produced goods, for the apartment was furnished with artisan products, all recycled and hand made.

"So, how did you and Jenna meet?" Jamie asked, while Elsa put the kettle on and pulled out organic peppermint tea from a cupboard.

"I've worked at the Surrey Docks City Farm for four years now, and about 18 months ago, Jenna started working there as a volunteer some weekends. She's a lawyer - I mean, she was a lawyer." Elsa wiped her eyes, sniffing. "She was so passionate about animal rights, as well as human rights. She wanted to learn more about the way animals could live within a city, and how the farm could benefit the community."

"And when did you move into together?"

"Pretty soon after we met. Before that she'd been living at her parent's London home." Elsa's voice became a sneer and Jamie sensed the undercurrent of resentment. "You must know of the Nevilles' place in Chelsea. But Jenna had become increasingly angry about the family business and just couldn't live under the same roof as her parents any longer."

Elsa passed Jamie a mug of steaming herbal tea. Jamie took it, then placed it back down on the counter top as she pulled out her notebook.

"Did she tell you any specific details of her work?"

"I know she was looking into the treatment of experimental subjects and tissue usage at the Neville labs." Elsa paused, looking a little guilty. "To be honest, I didn't pay too much attention to the detail. I'm not as - technical - as Jenna, so much of what she told me went over my head."

Jamie nodded. "Did she have a partner?"

A brief flash of anger passed over Elsa's face before she recomposed it into that of the grieving friend. Jamie noted that with interest.

"Rowan Day-Conti," Elsa said. "I guess he's her boyfriend right now. He was actually a friend of mine from way back, we were at Uni together, but he and Jenna have been seeing each other for almost a year now. They're a funny couple though, since he's so mod and she is - was - pretty vanilla." Jamie raised an eyebrow, her look clearly confused as Elsa continued. "You'll know what I mean when you meet Rowan. He indulges in body modification and believes in the use of the body for expression and pleasure. He says it's the ultimate canvas for art. Jenna, on the other hand, was pretty squeamish, despite the detailed investigations she had going into animal experimentation. I know he wanted her to start experimenting more but she wasn't keen. In fact, they had a huge argument only a few nights ago, lots of screaming and banging doors."

Jamie noted that down. "I'll be visiting Mr Day-Conti later today. Is it OK if I see Jenna's room?"

"Of course," Elsa nodded. "I haven't been in there … I was waiting for her mother actually. I thought she might come for Jenna's stuff."

"Were they close, Jenna and her mother?"

Elsa shook her head.

"Not at all. But I thought she'd come since the bitch would want to make sure there was nothing left of the Jenna she disapproved of. You know they do animal experiments at the Nevilles' lab, right?"

"I'd heard something about it," Jamie replied and added a visit to the lab to her list.

Elsa pointed to the stairwell. "Her room's the one on the right at the top of the stairs. I'll let you go up alone if that's OK. Here, take your tea, it's soothing."

Jamie took the pungent brew, and carried it carefully up the stairs. There was a bathroom directly at the top and then two rooms, one to the right and one to the left in a compact, modern design. Jamie ducked into the bathroom and poured most of the tea away, hating the hippy stuff. Give me black coffee any day, she thought, especially on days like these.

Going back out to the hallway, she opened the plain wooden door into Jenna's room, immediately noting the stark poverty of the place, despite the girl's wealthy background. Jenna evidently hadn't brought much with her, and clearly hadn't purchased much since moving in. There was a double futon with a plain white duvet and pillow, neatly made, and a white lampshade on the floor next to the bed. The dominant piece of furniture was an old wooden desk, but not the type of elegant antique you'd expect to find in the bedroom of an heiress. It looked like it had been discarded from a school and left, unwanted, at the back of a charity shop. On it, Jenna's diary and some papers were scattered haphazardly, in contrast to the neatness of the room.

Jamie put on her sterile gloves and opened the diary. It was a slender Filofax, nothing flash, something you could buy in any high street store. She flicked through the pages, but nothing immediately stood out. In fact, it contained very little for a woman who Jamie would have expected to be far more socially active. Perhaps she kept another diary at work or details were on her smart phone, which Missinghall would be processing along with the other evidence. Jamie checked the time and her stomach rumbled on cue. He should be getting back to her with something shortly.

She continued checking the papers, taking some pictures with her smart phone of the pages directly before and after the date of death. The only thing that looked strangely out of place was the word 'Lyceum' occurring this Saturday, in just a few days' time, at 11pm. Jamie wrote it down for follow-up, for there were several Lyceum theaters in London, and the word meant school in Latin, but 11pm was late for either of those possibilities.

Moving the diary, Jamie looked at the papers underneath, finding a sheaf of large artistic photos, beautiful but highly disturbing. A woman's naked torso was displayed in alabaster white, her breasts perfectly shaped, but under the right breast the body had been dissected away to show the internal organs. It was unclear whether the body was an artwork or in fact a real dissection. Jamie shuffled through the pictures and it became clear that Jenna was the model for the work.

There was a photo of her lying naked on the futon here in this room, her arms provocatively held above her head. She was beautiful, her body perfectly formed and her smile was that of a lover, her eyes inviting. The digital date in the corner of the shot was only a few months ago, so perhaps the photo had been taken by her boyfriend, Rowan Day-Conti. Jamie snapped a photo of the image and wondered how Jenna had felt about artwork that had been modeled on her body, then turned into a partially anatomized torso instead of the live, warm flesh of a beloved. Was this the source of the couple's recent argument?

Turning back to the room, Jamie went over to the freestanding clothes rack which served as a wardrobe, covered with an opaque plastic sheet to keep the dust off. She unzipped the front and pulled it back to reveal a small selection of clothes. Here was evidence of the heiress who couldn't quite leave it all behind, for there were several designer dresses and jackets in gorgeous fabrics. Jamie felt a tiny pang of longing for dresses like these, that she could dance in like a goddess, but she could never afford them on a police salary.

There was a shopping bag at the bottom of the makeshift wardrobe. Jamie opened it and pulled out a shimmering blue satin sheath dress. It was gorgeous, barely there and yet would hang like a gossamer dream on a body like Jenna's. The price tag was still on it. £2400. Clearly Jenna was still taking an allowance from her parents, Jamie thought, while at the same time becoming an activist against their company. For where else would this kind of money come from?

Next to the bed was a shoebox, simple, plain white. Jamie knelt down to open it. Inside were folic acid supplements, most often taken by women planning on being pregnant or in the early stages of pregnancy. The lab results were still outstanding but this might explain why Jenna's uterus had been removed, Jamie thought. So who was the father? Day-Conti, or someone else? Jamie looked around the room again. Why was the place so empty? Did Jenna really reject everything in favor of this simple life, or was there somewhere else where she kept her personal items? This didn't look like the room of a girl who had lived here for eighteen months, a professional lawyer, an activist, the heiress to a substantial fortune.

Jamie left the room, stopping on the stairs to look down into the living area. Elsa was curled up in a big chair, staring out of the window, her eyes fixed on something outside, her face a picture of Pre-Raphaelite beauty. She looked up as Jamie came down, and there was a hint of flirtation in her eyes, a suggestion of an invitation.

"Did you know Jenna was pregnant?" Jamie asked Elsa, watching for surprise. There was none.

"I wondered, to be honest, because she'd stopped drinking last month. Said she was over the drunken nights, but then she had actually been physically sick as well. Morning sickness, I guess. But she wouldn't talk about it. I did ask her, Detective, but we lived quite separate lives most of the time."

Jamie nodded slowly. "Was she seeing anyone else apart from Day-Conti?"

Elsa looked up, her eyes piercing, showing a level of hurt that was unexpected in a mere flatmate.

"Since we're being honest here, I think she was banging her boss at work, you know, that law firm. Perhaps you should ask him about it."

Jamie came down the stairs completely and knelt by Elsa's chair, intimately close, wanting to elicit her more personal thoughts.

"You loved Jenna, and that hurt you. Am I right?"

Tears welled up in Elsa's eyes, spilling over to run down her cheeks. She nodded.

"When she first moved in here, there was chemistry between us. I know she was bisexual, I've watched her with women at the clubs, and yes, I guess I was dazzled by her perfection. But she was also principled - about the things that matter." She indicated the PETA poster behind her. "We campaigned together, we worked on the farm together, and then she chose Rowan and I would have to listen to them fucking, when it should have been me with her." Her eyes narrowed. "She deserved more than that bastard. All he was interested in was her body, corrupting that perfection into some kind of perverted art. That's all he cares about." She looked down into Jamie's eyes. "You're going to him next, aren't you? Because he was always violent. It turns him on."

Jamie saw the shadows in her eyes. "Did you have a relationship with Day-Conti too?"

Elsa paused, then shrugged.

"Sure, at Uni, years ago but it was a web of intrigue back then and we all fucked each other. It didn't mean much, but he was darker psychologically than the others, he took everything to an extreme. That's when we all started playing with body mod and I got this tattoo." Her hand drifted to the back of her neck. "But Rowan took it much further because he has such a high tolerance for pain and expects others to enjoy it too. You'll know what I mean when you meet him."

Jamie stood, and handed Elsa her card.

"Thank you for your time, and please will you let me know if you think of anything else? That's my mobile number. Call me anytime, really, I want to find who did this to Jenna."

Elsa took the card and brushed Jamie's fingers gently.

"And you know where to find me, Detective, anytime."

CHAPTER 5

As Jamie pulled up on her bike, Missinghall stepped out of the unmarked car to greet her. With the information she now had from Jenna's flat, Jamie wanted the two of them to approach her boyfriend. He would always have been under suspicion in a case like this but more so given what Elsa had told her. The press would be onto the story soon, given how high profile the case was, but Day-Conti hadn't been informed of Jenna's death yet and Jamie wanted to observe his raw reaction to the news.

Missinghall was munching on a foot-long Subway, wiping the side of his mouth carefully to keep the crumbs off his suit. Jamie's stomach rumbled but she pushed the slight nausea aside. She felt a need to punish her own body for clinging to life while Polly lay immobile in her bed.

"We got the results back from the autopsy. It was rushed through because of the Nevilles' high profile," Missinghall said, pausing to take another bite as Jamie waited with barely restrained impatience. He offered her a piece of the sub and she shook her head, wondering even as she did so why she continued to resist even the slightest offer of help. "Jenna was definitely pregnant, around eight or nine weeks. Cause of death was asphyxia secondary to cervical injury and she was dead when her uterus was excised. There was some bruising on her hands, consistent with defensive wounds, so it's likely that she was deliberately pushed down the stairs."

Jamie nodded. "Anything interesting on her smart phone?" In so many cases now, phones provided intimate clues and almost exact time of death since people were so active on social networks or texting all the time.

Missinghall finished his last bite of the sub. "Work emails, the usual social networking with friends but nothing on her research into the Nevilles. Some angry text exchanges with Day-Conti, though."

He handed her a piece of paper with the printed texts, some highlighted. Jamie glanced through them, noting that it seemed the arguments were about Day-Conti's work but they didn't suggest a sudden escalation in violence and there were no actual threats. She frowned, sensing that pieces of the puzzle were still missing. But this was what she loved about her work, the moment where moving parts were beginning to be revealed and she needed to work out exactly how they fitted together. Her mind shuffled them around, but the edges didn't yet fit. It was a welcome distraction from the realities of the hospice, but Jamie's fist clenched as she thought of Polly lying there without her. There was a fine line between her desire to be at her daughter's side all the time, and her attempt to keep a hold on her job and her sanity.

Jamie and Missinghall walked together towards the Hoxton studio where Day-Conti lived and worked. The building was a huge brick warehouse, seemingly abandoned, but in this area of London artists were reclaiming the area and remodeling it into a trendy, creative haven. There was a large warehouse door marked Entrance that had a proper apartment door fitted into it. Jamie eyed the graffiti on the wall close by, unsure as to whether it was vandalism or art. Around here, it could be both.

She pressed the buzzer. There was no response after a minute so she pressed again, holding the buzzer down until the intercom crackled.

"Yes," a voice said, indolent, as if he had been woken from sleep.

"Rowan Day-Conti?"

"Speaking."

"I'm Detective Sergeant Jamie Brooke from the Metropolitan Police. I need to speak to you about Jenna Neville."

"Jenna?" the voice said, suddenly concerned and alert. "Is she alright?"

"Can you let us in please, sir, so we can discuss the matter."

The buzzer sounded and the door clicked open, revealing a large warehouse space. Jamie walked into the vast building, her first impression of a high ceiling, making the space light and airy. Her second was the smell, a heavy chemical preservative over the pungent stink of decay. Jamie noticed Missinghall's nose wrinkle, and she knew that he also recognized it. There was something dead in here. The huge space was bisected by great metal walls, creating a myriad of smaller rooms in the large warehouse, so it was hard to see where the smell might be coming from, but Jamie felt herself tense at the possibility of what they might find.

There was a clattering of feet down the metal stairs at the side of the warehouse and they turned to watch a man approaching.

"Is Jenna OK?" the figure called as he hurried over. Tall and gangly, he was dressed in shades of faded black that seemed to merge into his skin. As he came closer, Jamie realized that this was because he was covered in tattoos and in addition, he had small horns protruding from the front of his closely shaven head. Even his eyeballs looked different, as if they had ink on them too.

"Rowan Day-Conti?" Jamie asked, looking doubtfully from him to the picture in her hand, which showed a preppy, clean cut young man with blonde hair and a muscular body.

It was a long way from this clearly modified version.

"Yes," Rowan looked down at the picture. "That's the one on file, right. It's the way my family wanted me to look, the way they try to remember me, but I haven't been that boy for a long time."

As he spoke, Jamie saw that his tongue was forked, split into two, strangely grotesque but mesmerizing to watch. Rowan's eyebrows had been replaced by the intricately drawn wings of a dragon and there was a thick spike through his nose. Missinghall was staring and Jamie was trying not to, but Rowan was clearly used to it.

"Now, tell me about Jenna," he said, "because she's not answering my texts."

As Rowan turned slightly, Jamie realized that his left ear had been carved into an asymmetrical shape surrounded by rune lines making the ear more of a spiritual offering than a facility for listening. She had seen body modification in magazines and on TV but never so close up. Those who pursued it considered the body as an art form in itself, a tool to be shaped into something new, a canvas for self-expression and a way to differentiate from the pack.

"I'm sorry, Rowan," Jamie said, "but her body was found early this morning. It looks as if she was murdered."

Rowan froze, his face falling and he sank to the floor, kneeling on the concrete in his ripped jeans. He hugged his thin arms around himself and took deep breaths, exhaling loudly to calm himself.

"No, not Jenna," he whispered, panic in his eyes. "What happened? How did she die? Oh my God. When did it happen?"

Jamie crouched next to him, trying and failing to keep her eyes off his inked skin. From this angle, she could see that around the lower half of his cheek the tattoo revealed teeth inside a skeleton's jaw, a sweep of bone towards the eye socket as if the skin had been carved away,

"We're investigating exactly what happened," she said, "but we do need to ask you some questions."

"Of course." His eyes were haunted, uncaring of their judgment. "Anything to help the investigation."

Jamie stood up and looked around the warehouse, pointing to the metal walls.

"What do you do here, Rowan?" she asked.

Rowan's eyes changed, flickering to mistrust as if he suddenly realized that he could be under suspicion.

"I'm an artist. This is my studio, my livelihood."

"Can you show me some of your art?" Jamie asked, keen to investigate the source of the smell. It was death overlaid with sterility and it certainly wasn't innocent.

Rowan stood up, crossing his arms, his posture defensive.

"Don't you need some kind of warrant?"

Missinghall moved closer to Jamie, his bulk an effective backup.

"Not if you want to show us around as visitors," he said, his voice calm. "We're just here for a preliminary chat, after all."

Rowan paused, then shook his head in resignation. "I've got nothing to hide, so look all you like. This is all legal, although you might find it a bit disturbing."

Jamie raised an eyebrow, thinking of what they had already seen today. "I've been in the Met a long time so you'll have to try really hard to disturb me."

"Don't say I didn't warn you," Rowan said, leading them around one of the huge metal walls. A human cadaver sat at a desk, flesh ripped open to reveal its inner organs, as if it had been exploded from the inside out. "This is one of my works in progress."

Jamie didn't react and she was impressed that Missinghall didn't either. They just stood there in front of the body looking inside the preserved corpse, a compelling obscenity.

"This is your art?" she said.

Rowan walked to the cadaver and stood by it, forcing them to look at him. Jamie found it odd to see this modified living specimen next to a body that had been mutilated after death. One art form presumably chosen as a statement to the world, the other displayed intimately without choice.

"Have you heard of the Von Hagens Bodies exhibition?" Rowan asked. Jamie shook her head. Missinghall looked grim-faced, and remained silent. "It was made famous by the controversy over the provenance of the bodies, because some believed they were procured from Chinese prisons and used without consent. Whatever the truth, his technique of plastination has revolutionized anatomy preservation, and has also spilled over into art for private collections, as you see here." He pointed to the cadaver. "Plastination removes water and fat from the body and replaces it with certain plastics that can be touched, that don't smell or decay. It effectively preserves the properties of the original sample but in a state that will last over time. There are several Bodies exhibitions, including one in New York, that display the cadavers in modern poses so you can understand how the bodies work."

"Why?" Missinghall asked, finally breaking his silence. "What's the point?"

Rowan looked at him with disdain, as if explaining such meaning was beneath him.

"It's the intersection of art and science, confronting mortality head on. It's like seeing your future, looking inside yourself and realizing the truth. You are just flesh and you will die. The truth can set you free, Detective."

"You like playing God, Rowan?" Jamie asked, watching his eyes narrow as she spoke. There was a spark there, a defiance.

"I enjoy the confrontation of challenging established, so-called truth, yes. Most people remain in their safe little worlds, but I like to live in a way that makes them uncomfortable. Take the way I look, for example. People judge me, expect me to behave in a certain way because I believe in the right of each person to modify their own body. But most people are incapable of seeing behind the facade of skin to the true self."

"But is it your right to modify the bodies of others, even after death?" Jamie asked, pointing at the cadaver.

Rowan shook his head. "Of course, you don't get it. I didn't expect you to. Cops are on the side of the comfortable masses." Jamie felt herself bridling against that, but she forced herself to listen. "But you have to check me out before you take any action. I have all the permits and my flesh provider guarantees that these bodies are donated specifically for artistic purpose." He looked down at the body, running his fingers gently over the defined muscles in the neck. "I don't see a dead person here. I see beauty and a tool for learning, for the illustration of truth. You see, I customize my body while I am alive but life is too short, so I modify the bodies of the dead so that they might live forever. Of course we are not our bodies, Detectives, we are more than that. But I also want to demonstrate that our bodies can live on in this fashion."

Jamie considered his words, her thoughts flashing to Polly. She realized that she believed a similar truth, but from a different angle. Her daughter wasn't defined by her broken body any more than these were actual people that Day-Conti worked on. Once consciousness left with death, the body was a mere shell, so why did this instinctively feel wrong?

She walked closer to the cadaver, bending slightly to look into the partially-exposed folds of its brain. From one angle the face was intact and from the other, the cranium was open, displaying the preserved brain tissue. The body looked as if it was in the process of being dissected where it sat, the shoulder muscles on one side partially exposed. Some of the right wrist had been opened so the tendons and veins could be seen, like a belated suicide attempt.

Rowan moved back as Jamie deliberately invaded his personal space. She had read in the file that he was the son of a family similar to the Nevilles, who were appalled at his recent life choices and the alternative world he now chose to inhabit. Eton, Oxford, and now Hoxton, Rowan had become an artist dissecting bodies while indulging in body modification of his own design. It was extreme as rebellion went, but Jamie couldn't blame him from trying to escape his past, since she tried so often to forget her own.

"What else have you got here?" Jamie asked as she straightened.

"Follow me," Rowan said, leading them through a labyrinth of metal walls, until they rounded a corner into another workspace. Jamie blinked, trying to identify what she was seeing.

"This is what we call the explosion technique," Rowan said.

It was a decapitated head, plastinated in the same way as the other cadaver, so that it was a tan-color, preserved and dried. The brain sat intact with eyeballs staring ahead, tongue poking out from a deconstructed mouth. The rest of the head was peeled away in layers, skull carved in half with teeth intact grinning outwards. The face, skin and lips were peeled further out, fanned like a flasher in a horror movie, exposing what was meant to be hidden and intimate.

Jamie stood looking at the head, examining her emotional response to it. Logically it should be stomach churning, disturbing to the point of nausea like the worst murder scenes. But it was actually so far removed from anything you would normally see that it did indeed become objectified art instead of flesh. It was clean, sterile, ultimately fake-looking. Jamie had seen the decapitated heads of murder victims, and they were never as clinical as this.

"I am driven to view the body as a receptacle," Rowan said, waiting for their response. "As a mere container for who we truly are. Our skin, bone and physical flesh is but nothing in this life, only a carrier for our soul."

Jamie turned to him. "And what did Jenna think of all this?" she asked.

Rowan sat down heavily on a wooden chair, rubbing his hand along his jaw. He sighed.

"Jenna was a lawyer," he eventually said, his strident tone now gone. "We met at a body-mod event. She was research-ing the legal status of human body parts, consent for medical research and how that fitted with the use of bodies for art. There was an artist in the late 90s, Anthony Noel-Kelly, who was found guilty of stealing specimens from the Royal College of Surgeons. He and his accomplice were the first people in British history to be convicted of stealing body parts, even though the trade in bodies was centuries old. The body parts were classed as property because they were preparations, so there was actual work applied to the cadav-ers. Ironically, it would have been legal if the bodies hadn't been worked on. Jenna was exploring those legal issues as part of her specialization. When I learned of her interest, I showed her the artistic side of the anatomical world and one night, she stayed over. We've been seeing each other on and off for a while now, not exclusive or anything, but she was special. There was something different about her."

Rowan's voice trailed off.

"Not exclusive?" Jamie asked.

"No, we agreed to see other people, and that was fine with me, although lately I'd been thinking about her more seriously."

"Did she model for you?"

Rowan shook his head. "No, she would never do that." He went quiet. Jamie waited, aware of the photo from Jenna's flat in her pocket. After a full minute, he continued speaking. "But I couldn't help myself. I had taken some pictures of her naked. She looked so beautiful and I wanted to use them as inspiration for a new piece. A body came in, almost as perfect as hers and I posed it like she had lain for me on the bed."

"Before you carved it up, you mean," Jamie said, unable to stop herself.

"Fuck you," Rowan said, slamming his fist down onto his leg. Jamie didn't even flinch. "This is art, this is what collectors pay for. It's an evocative piece, imbued with emotion. I had a particular buyer lined up who was willing to pay a lot for it, but Jenna was furious when she found out what I'd done."

"What happened?" Jamie prompted.

"We had a huge fight, a real screaming match. She said she would find out where the woman's body had come from and make sure she was buried with dignity. She was going to stop the sale. Jenna refused to be the inspiration for what she saw as the abuse of another woman's dead body. That was two days ago, and that's the last time I saw her, although there have been angry texts from both sides, I'll admit that."

Missinghall looked up from his notes.

"Your name was down for the Gala Dinner at the Royal College of Surgeons last night."

Day-Conti nodded. "I think she wanted me to go as a 'fuck you' to her parents who were attending as well." He put his head in his hands. "I wish I'd gone now. Maybe she'd still be safe if I'd been there."

"Why didn't you go?" Jamie asked.

"To punish her, perhaps. She was disrespecting my work and I couldn't bear to be there if she was going to ignore me anyway, not when my appearance would cause such a stir amongst that stuck-up crowd. I'll admit it was a power-play." His hands clenched into fists. "But damn, she was good at winding me up."

Day-Conti must have realized what he looked like and relaxed his aggression, taking a deep breath.

"The piece she objected to," Jamie asked. "Were you were going to sell it anyway?"

"It's what I do, Detective," Rowan snapped. "The pinnacle of my art is to have it displayed in a collection, for other people's pleasure. I don't do this to have the final piece hidden away or buried, to rot and disappear into the earth like any other mundane piece of flesh. For this woman, the best way to be remembered was to be immortalized. This way her beauty won't ever fade."

"I'd like to see it if that's OK with you?" Jamie said as her phone vibrated in her pocket with a text message from the investigation team back at the station.

As Rowan led the way into another section of the warehouse, Jamie checked the text. *Day-Conti financials show that his gallery is on the verge of bankruptcy. Family have disowned him. He desperately needs cash.* Here was motive indeed, money on top of art.

Jamie shivered. It was colder down the back of the warehouse, and the lights were dim. They rounded a corner and saw a rectangular tent, made of opaque plastic, like a containment area of some kind.

"She's in there," he said, his voice hushed. "I'm still working on her."

Jamie pushed through the curtains and into the tiny space. On a lab table lay the plastinated body of a perfectly beautiful young woman, her breasts round and pert, nipples hard, with one side partially dissected, the same as the picture she had found at Jenna's flat. The woman's arms were held above her head, her legs provocatively crossed, as if tied, but willingly. Jamie could definitely see the echo of the nude picture of Jenna, but with one huge difference. The woman's head had been sawn off and the arms cut off at the elbows.

Rowan saw what she was looking at.

"I wanted her body to be the focus, not her face. This way she can be everywoman, a fantasy."

Jamie was struggling to contain her anger at such a desecration, yet she argued with herself that those feelings didn't make logical sense. This body was no longer alive, yet the callous treatment of the flesh was abhorrent to her. There was no sense of a person here, even less so because the face was missing. But it was the objectification of a woman mutilated and displayed without her consent. It was pornographic in some way, and yet how could anyone find this arousing?

"Has this collector bought from you before?" Jamie asked, keeping her voice even.

Rowan nodded.

"I don't know who they are though. They buy through a dealer, but I know this one likes vanilla skin, no mods at all. They do specify the partial dissection though, in order to see inside the bodies, always to their hearts."

Jamie shook her head, sure that the buyer would be untraceable, but her sicko alarm was blaring.

"I'll be needing all your permits, because I just can't believe this is in any way legal."

Rowan nodded. "I've been investigated before, Detective, based on a nosy neighbor's curiosity. So you've got all the paperwork for me at the local station. They know what I'm doing here and it's all legal, I promise you."

Jamie walked out of the tent, away from the disturbance of the body as Missinghall went into the tiny space after her. She heard his muttered expletives and knew how he felt. She had seen a lot of bodies, in various physical states because of violent death, but this casual arrangement of sex and death seemed much more of a violation.

She led the way back into the main gallery, then turned.

"So, apart from the fight over that piece, you and Jenna

had a good relationship?" Jamie asked, trying to refocus on other aspects of the case.

"She wasn't my usual type, you know, vanilla skin and all that, but she had a fucked up mind. I'm modified on the outside, but Jenna, she was pretty mod inside. That girl had some problems." Rowan shook his head. "You should talk to her family, right. They're a bunch of screw-ups. She hated them, did you know that?"

Jamie remained impassive. "So where were you last night?"

"I was here working alone until around 10pm and then I went to Torture Garden."

Jamie raised an eyebrow.

"Seriously?" Rowan said, his voice rising an octave with annoyance and frustration. "Check it out. It's all consensual and legal. Just because it's a fetish club, you reckon something evil's going on, right? At Torture Garden, there are lines you can't cross, it's not just a free for all. Seriously, I'd expect you to be more open-minded. We just want to express our individuality and that makes us far more normal than the rest of you. If you want to find some really fucked up individuals, look at the suits and ties and those who can only express themselves after drugs or alcohol. "

"Did you know Jenna was pregnant?" Jamie asked, not giving Rowan a moment to recover from his tirade.

He looked shocked. "Shit. No." He ran his hands over his scalp, rubbing the short hair upright. "Really? You think it was mine?"

Jamie could see that he really hadn't known about it. Her inner radar was going off over many things in this house of plastinated horror, but her gut told her that he hadn't known about the baby. He needed the money and he had motive around the sale of the female torso, and he definitely had the skills to carve up Jenna's body. But if he hadn't known about the pregnancy, there was no reason to extract her uterus.

She'd have to clear his alibi by checking out the cameras at Torture Garden, but she didn't think it necessary to take him in. She raised an eyebrow at Missinghall and he shook his head, clearly feeling the same way.

"Thank you for your time, Rowan," Jamie said. "Don't go far though, will you?"

He shook his head, still reeling from the news of the pregnancy. "Of course, I'll be here. Please Detective, let me know if I can help in any way. You might not approve of what I do, but I loved Jenna."

Jamie saw tears welling in his eyes as he turned away to show them out. They needed to speak to the other man in Jenna's life. Could an affair have led to her death?

CHAPTER 6

THE OFFICES OF LEIGHTON Bowen Winstone-Smyth were situated in the prestigious row of law firms on the north side of Lincoln's Inn Fields, just across the square from the Hunterian Museum. How convenient, Jamie thought, as she rang the bell on the imposing front door. Missinghall had returned to base to check out Day-Conti's alibi, so she had returned alone to question Jenna's employer and, possibly, her lover. The door was opened by an office junior, dressed in a grey suit that was just on the right side of being too small.

"I'm here to see Michael Bowen," Jamie said, flashing her badge and as she did so, a door opened further inside and a voice called out.

"Let the Detective in, please, Michelle."

A man stepped into the hallway as Jamie entered, her eyes adjusting to the changing light.

"Michael Bowen," he said, holding out his hand. "Come in, Detective. How can I help you?"

Jamie shook his hand firmly. Bowen was around six foot three, every inch of him perfectly turned out. His black skin demonstrated Afro-Caribbean roots but his cultured voice and the finely cut, designer suit betrayed his current allegiance to the City. Serious brown eyes showed curiosity at her presence but he was clearly used to dealing with the police and he displayed no trace of anxiety about being questioned.

"I'm here about Jenna Neville," Jamie said, looking around his private office at the ubiquitous bookshelves full of leather bound volumes. Even though most legal research was done online these days, places like this couldn't quite let go of the old traditions.

"Jenna?" Bowen replied, confused. "Is she alright? I'd assumed you were here about one of our open cases." He sat down, indicating a chair on the other side of the desk. Jamie sat and Bowen leant forward, placing his hands on the desk. Jamie saw the golden glint of his wedding ring, stark against his perfect dark skin and buffed nails.

"Jenna was found dead this morning, sir."

Bowen froze, one hand lifting towards his mouth and, as he turned away slightly, his dark eyes shifted from Jamie to one of the bookcases.

"My God, how?"

"I can tell you that she was murdered, but we're still in the initial stages of the investigation, which is why I'm here to talk to you."

"Of course, whatever I can do." His voice trailed off, and Jamie noticed his eyes flicking again to the bookcase. She followed his line of sight to where a few volumes looked scuffed and more worn than the others.

"May I ask about your relationship with Jenna, Mr Bowen?"

He nodded. "Of course, she was a brilliant young lawyer, perceptive, original. She was doing a private research project into the legality of using bodies and body parts in research, as well as art. She had quite the passion for it, as well as a keen legal mind."

Jamie nodded. "And what about your - more personal - relationship?"

Bowen looked at her sharply and Jamie could see that he wouldn't lie about this minor truth, suspecting he had bigger secrets to hide.

"Yes, we had an affair," he replied, meeting Jamie's eyes with no trace of embarrassment. "It wasn't long, and we finished it, by mutual agreement I would add, about three weeks ago. I was happy for it to continue in an ad hoc manner as it was mutually pleasurable, but Jenna moved on pretty fast." Bowen was twisting his wedding ring as he spoke. Jamie looked pointedly at it and he noticed her glance. "We all have our secrets, Detective, and I'm sure you have yours."

Bowen's brown eyes were piercing now, and Jamie caught a glimpse of the man he could clearly be in the courtroom, a formidable opponent. She could also see why Jenna would be attracted to such a man. There was a current of danger under the silk cravat, a tension of strength and sensuality under his refined speech. Perks of the job indeed, she thought.

"Did you know she was pregnant?" Jamie asked.

"No," he said slowly, and Jamie thought there was a hint of disappointment in his voice. "We always used protection so I know it wasn't mine. I may play the field, but I'm not so stupid as to have some bastard child when my marriage is so important to my professional life."

Jamie pitied his wife in that moment, but his steely ambition was also impressive in its single-mindedness.

"Do you know whose it might have been?" Jamie asked.

Bowen shrugged. "Maybe that so-called artist boyfriend of hers. Did you know she was investigating him secretly, trying to find out about his supply of bodies? She was obsessed by it, and she suspected something much bigger than what he was involved in." He hesitated. "Look, I think she was onto something because I received a threat in the mail yesterday."

"Why haven't you shown it to the police?"

"In the nature of our work, threats are regular occurrences and of course I know our legal rights. We have private security in the building and you know as well as I do that the police are unable to act on anonymous threats alone. But this letter was unusual."

"May I see it?" Jamie asked, unsurprised when Bowen walked to the bookshelf, pulling the worn books away to reveal a safe. With his back protecting the code, he opened the safe and removed a letter.

Jamie pulled on sterile gloves from her bag and took the envelope. The address label had been printed and stuck on and the postmark was from the Aldwych, just round the corner from the offices where they stood now. She tugged out a piece of paper from within the envelope. It was a picture from the Hunterian Museum, one of the teaching models, a torso with limbs sawn off strikingly similar to the artwork that Rowan Day-Conti had shown her. At the top was printed 'Memento Mori.'

"Remember you will die," whispered Jamie. Underneath was a short typed message. *Forget the Lyceum.*

"What's the Lyceum?" Jamie asked, aware that she had seen the very word in Jenna's diary for this coming weekend.

Bowen shook his head. "I don't know. The word means school in Latin but I've never heard of it used in this way before, more like the description of a place or a group of people." He paced across the office with agitation. "Look, Jenna was doing this whole thing on the side as a research project. She said it would bring us amazing press and some lucrative work if it paid off. She was well connected through her family, she was brilliant and I trusted her. She also continued to deliver all her other work to the highest standard, so I didn't meddle. But when this arrived yesterday, I was going to ask her about the Lyceum."

Jamie shook her head. "Unfortunately, that's not going to happen now. Could I see her desk?"

"Of course. This way."

Bowen led Jamie through a warren of offices that stretched surprisingly far back from the street. There was a focused atmosphere of tension and pressure, but perhaps Jenna had thrived on it. It certainly felt like the lifeblood of Michael Bowen's world.

"This was where she worked," Bowen said, indicating a slim desk by a window that looked out to a small interior courtyard. "I'll need to ask the tech team to get access to her computer but you're welcome to look at anything she has here in the meantime." He looked at his watch. "I need to get back to my own work, Detective, but please, dial 113 on the phone there if you need anything else from me."

Jamie nodded and he walked briskly away, his expensive shoes echoing on the parquet floor breaking the hush of the legal team working around them. She turned to the desk, which was tidy and neatly organized. She texted Missinghall to send over a tech to work with the legal firm's IT team to pull Jenna's data, but somehow Jamie thought that they wouldn't find much on her official drives. If the investigation was something that Jenna was threatened over, then it was likely she would have kept her research material somewhere safe. The question was where?

Jamie searched the desk drawers. She pulled one open to find a stack of printed material, photocopies of newspaper reports and articles. Sitting back in the ergonomically designed office chair to sort through them, she flicked the pages to check the headlines. The assortment related to multiple cases but Jamie couldn't see any common thread and nothing she could tie to Jenna's death. Then towards the end of the pack she found a sheaf of articles about grave robbery, how there was evidence of recent practice with bodies stolen from funeral homes before cremation as well as dug up from graves. Jamie pulled the piece out to read in more detail, fascinated to learn that body snatching wasn't only relegated to the past.

One article attributed the rise in grave robbery to the demand for metals that could be extracted from the bodies and sold. In an increasingly tough financial environment, people were finding easy pickings from robbing the dead. Another headline screamed cult hysteria as bones were removed for rituals and rites in communities honoring such practices. There were marks on two more articles about newly buried bodies stolen the night before their burial. Both individuals had suffered from genetic diseases that resulted in physical deformity. A yellow letter L ending in a question mark was written in highlighter at the top of these pages.

Turning the papers further, Jamie came to an article on necrophilia, only made illegal in the UK in 2003 and still legal in some states of America. Her eyes widened as she read of the erotic use of corpses and found herself shaking her head with resignation at the depths of depravity to which humanity sometimes sank. She knew that Jenna was undertaking a specific study on the legal rights relating to corpses and body parts. Were these practices also related to the mysterious Lyceum?

She took some pictures of the articles and continued searching the desk, but there was nothing personal and no more evidence of Jenna's investigation. She'd have to wait for the results of the tech team. Jamie rang through to Bowen and told him to expect them later that day. He thanked her, his voice courteous but she sensed that he had already moved on from the tragedy of Jenna's death, his mind elsewhere.

Leaving the building, Jamie stood by the park looking across Lincoln's Inn Fields back towards the Hunterian Museum, hunching her back against the freezing wind. Her mind was trying to capture the tendrils of suspicion that encircled this case, but in these pockets of calm, she could only think about Polly and what time she might make it back to see her. She lit a cigarette and inhaled the first, perfect drag.

"You really should give it up, Jamie."

Jamie turned to see Max Nester, one of the few men from work who could wring a smile from her serious demeanor. He ignored the fact that she was a woman and treated her like a blokey mate, albeit a prickly one, and she appreciated that. Max worked on the art theft and cultural crime that happened in the capital, a huge workload, since stealing specific artworks for collectors was a regular occurrence.

"Hey Max, are you on something local?"

"I was nearby and heard you'd been assigned to this murder case." He paused. "How's Polly?"

Jamie had told Max about Polly's illness a while back and he was one of the few who knew how sick she really was. She knew his concern was that of a real friend, but she needed to keep the separation between her worlds intact. Otherwise she would just break down and bawl her eyes out here on the street.

"Not good," she said, her voice constricted. "Best distract me, rather than talk about it."

"Sure thing. I did hear something about an ivory figurine being found and thought I'd drop by to see if I could help with identification."

Jamie smiled, taking another drag, the smoke curling up into the dying day. "I get it, you want in on the interesting artifact but not the dirty work of the murder."

Max nodded. "You know me so well, but I've heard it may have been stolen from an as yet unknown collection so I think there's some legitimate overlap."

"I'd appreciate any help on it, actually. I'm not sure how it fits into the murder, but I want to understand whether Jenna was carrying it that night and why, or whether it was left at the scene by the murderer. It could be important, but I don't know how we're going to pursue that angle."

Max took the cigarette from her hand and took a drag himself, an intimate gesture that Jamie wouldn't have allowed from anyone else. But Max was only interested in slim, younger men, so she knew his attentions were only ever out of friendship. He passed it back again in smoker's camaraderie, his face twisting into a grimace at the minty aftertaste.

"Can't you smoke something decent?" He pulled a slip of paper from his pocket. "If you've got nothing else, this guy might be able to help. Blake Daniel, at the British Museum. Here's his number, but I know he's there today if you want to drop by. He's a specialist in religious relics and figurines so I think this would be right down his alley." He paused, then grinned. "Bit of a looker, too."

Jamie smiled and took the paper. "Thanks, that's a great help." She noticed Max bite his lip. "So what aren't you telling me?"

Max sighed. "To be honest, Jamie, you'll probably think this is crazy. But he has certain - abilities - that make him unusual."

Jamie raised her eyebrows. "Sounds even more interesting. Do tell."

"He reads objects," Max said, watching for her reaction. "Some call it psychometry, or psychic reading. Blake calls it his curse and he truly is a reluctant psychic, not someone who broadcasts his skills."

Jamie considered what Max had said and weighed it against her bullshit detector. She trusted Max, even though his techniques could sometimes be a little unorthodox, and although skeptical, she had seen enough of the supernatural to not reject what he was saying outright.

"So how do you know him?" Jamie finished the cigarette and put the butt in her tin, slipping it back into her bag.

"I met him during a case at St Paul's Cathedral over a

missing relic," Max said, thrusting his hands in his pockets as he jogged up and down on the spot in the freezing wind. "Blake was called in as an expert witness, but he knew things that I knew he shouldn't. I took him for a drink afterwards and he became quite chatty after a few tequilas. Talking of drinks, you coming out tonight? Streeter's leaving."

Jamie turned to go and mounted her bike.

"You know I never drink with you guys, and besides Streeter's going off to do something in business right? Which means in about three months, he'll discover he's not happy. He'll miss the justice side, the making a difference …"

"The crappy pay, the long nights, the lack of weekends."

Jamie smiled. "But we love it, Max, you know we do." She pulled on her helmet. "I'll check out Blake Daniel. Thanks for the tip."

As she pulled away, she saw him raise a hand in a wave. For a moment, she regretted not going out for drinks over the years he had been asking, but at least he continued to try and persuade her. Everyone else had stopped and Missinghall hadn't even tried, knowing her reputation for staying aloof. But her nights belonged to Polly, and sometimes to tango. There was no room for anything else.

CHAPTER 7

BLAKE DANIEL BOUGHT A venti double shot latte with vanilla syrup and added more sugar before sipping the hot liquid and crossing the road back into the grounds of the British Museum. It had already been a difficult day, and he was severely behind on his workload. A pulsing hangover had kept him on the edge of nausea most of the afternoon, finally easing to a dull ache. The sugar was helping though, and when his stomach calmed, he would go to the greasy spoon down the road for a late bacon sandwich.

He rubbed his gloved hand over the rough stubble on his jaw and chin. It was thicker than he usually let it grow, almost at the point of softness now. Perhaps it was time to let it grow into a proper beard. He knew it made him look more like a serious academic and less like the lead singer of a boy band. His hair needed a cut too. He kept it at a number one buzz-cut: any longer and it tended towards the tight curls of the Nigerian heritage on his mother's side, incongruous with the piercing blue eyes that he had inherited from his Swedish father.

Last night was a blank, yet again, but the girl he woke up with hadn't seemed to mind much when he had politely asked her to leave. No regrets, he thought, holding onto a mantra that sounded more hollow each week. The London casual scene would continue to provide escape for as long as he needed it. He took a sip of the coffee and acknowledged that he did still need it. His nights were another life, far removed from his days shut in the bowels of the Museum, examining ancient objects and creating a past for them from painstaking research, augmented with his own special brand of insight. Right now, he was working on a series of ivory netsuke, miniature carved works of art that used to hang from the kimono sashes of traditional Japanese men. He found himself lost in each one, marveling at their intricacies and the echoes of past lives behind them. For Blake read the emotion in objects, and these were steeped in layers of its rich tapestry.

Blake walked through the museum, past the crowds of tourists. Although generally immune to the classical facade of the grand entrance, the glass-ceilinged Great Hall always lifted his spirits, although today even the weak sun hurt his fragile eyes. Finally sitting back down at his desk, Blake pushed some papers around while he drank his coffee, waiting for the kick of sugar and caffeine to give him enough of a boost to at least write a paragraph on the netsuke. The grant he was working under would only last a few more months, so he needed to produce something of worth to get it renewed.

He felt the sensation of being watched and looked up to see his boss Margaret leading someone towards his desk. Oh hell, Blake thought, what can she possibly want right now? Then he caught a glimpse of the woman behind. Her hair was jet-black, tied in a tight bun and she wore an unremarkable black trouser suit. But her face was alive with expression, her hazel eyes piercing with intelligence and she walked with an assurance he rarely saw in this academic environment. She was petite, her slim figure tightly compact, but Blake could see an inner strength and knew that this woman should not be underestimated.

"Blake, sorry to disturb you." Margaret ruffled with importance. "This is Detective Sergeant Jamie Brooke from the Metropolitan Police."

"Detective, good to meet you." Blake held out his gloved hand.

Jamie held his eyes, assessing him and Blake felt an inexplicable wave of guilt, perhaps something everyone feels in the presence of the police. What did I do last night, he thought.

She shook his hand, glancing down at the gloves. "Perhaps we could go somewhere to talk confidentially?"

Margaret looked at Blake with suspicion but accompanied them through to one of the private meeting rooms, shutting the door behind her as she left.

"Call me Blake, please," he said, sitting down at the wide desk, aware of the gossip that would now be exploding back in the main office about his possible misdemeanors.

"Of course." Jamie sat down opposite him. Blake was reminded of all those TV shows people watched, and wondered what was coming next. "I've been told you may be able to help with a special investigation."

Blake raised an eyebrow. "It depends what it is, of course, and who told you."

"Max Nester recommended you." That old queen, Blake thought as Jamie pulled a package, wrapped in cloth and plastic from her messenger bag. "This is evidence, but it's been processed and we can't pull anything from it. We're trying to determine how it relates to a particular crime scene."

"And how do you think I can help?" Blake asked.

"Your specialization here at the museum is ivory carving?"

Blake nodded. "I've been working on a series of netsuke, Japanese miniature sculptures used as fasteners for pouches and external pockets for carrying personal items. The man bag of seventeenth century Japan."

His witticism didn't raise even a hint of a smile from Jamie.

"Max told me that you've helped the police with investigations before and he mentioned your - special talents - I wondered if you might consider examining this piece."

Blake cursed Max and his own big mouth. Six months ago, he'd helped with a minor investigation into stolen property and then he'd gotten drunk. Tequila was an evil mistress, and he couldn't seem to escape her addiction. Blake wanted to deny everything, wanted to shy away from helping, but something in Jamie's eyes made him nod. "I can give it a go at least, but I can't promise anything."

Jamie was suddenly hesitant. "So how does this work?"

"If you could just unwrap the object and lay it on the table. Then I'll see what I can feel."

Blake wondered if he would be able to feel anything through the last vestiges of the hangover. Part of the reason that he drank was to deaden the visions, but as Jamie unwrapped a tiny figurine, only four inches tall, he became intrigued. It was a naked woman carved of ivory, but instead of the smooth skin of her beautiful body, the flesh was open to reveal the internal organs. The woman's eyes were open, her face impassive despite the mutilation of her body. Blake had studied Anatomical Venus figures before but this was a gorgeous specimen.

"Do I need to tell you anything about the situation?" Jamie said.

Blake shook his head. "Best not to. Just put it on the table."

Jamie placed the figurine down on the white tabletop as Blake pulled the glove from his right hand, revealing crisscrossed white scars on his cinnamon skin. He felt her eyes examining them, her questions unspoken. The thin canvas gloves he habitually wore prevented the casual visions that could intrude, but now he laid his bare fingertips upon the figurine.

Sometimes the visions were hazy and he expected to ease slowly into this one but immediately he saw the body of a young woman. Her lower abdomen was cut open, her organs on display like the figurine and her body was pooled in scarlet. He snatched his hand away and the vision faded as he stood, slamming the chair back and stepping away fast. He had been unprepared for such violence, expecting something like the art theft he'd worked on with the police before. He felt a wave of nausea return and cursed his hangover.

"This is from a murder victim," he said, his voice shaky. "Her body was cut open like this one."

He saw the surprise in Jamie's eyes, and understood that she had doubted his abilities. The look she gave him was one of respect tinged perhaps with a little fear, and her reaction was exactly why he didn't broadcast his peculiar sensitivities. In fact, he did everything he could to hide them.

She nodded slowly, the barest acknowledgment that he had seen the truth.

"Can you read anything else?"

Blake felt truly sick now but he braced for a longer look. His ability to see was always tied to an object, and it was more a collection of sensations than a strictly physical viewing. It wasn't as if he could psychically spin round in a room and see everything in detail, but he could pick up feelings and particularly heightened emotions that seemed to imprint a person's experience onto the object. He felt a little uncomfortable reading in front of Jamie, but he sat down and laid his hand on the object again, breathing deeply as he closed his eyes. He felt the rush of the images and the sensations that accompanied them.

"There's anger and hatred surrounding the figure, from both the girl and another. This wasn't premeditated murder, but there was logic in the death, and emotional connection between the people involved." He paused. "The dissection was deliberate."

Blake relaxed into the vision now, feeling sensation pulse through him. The experience itself wasn't unpleasant, but it was his own reaction to it that he feared. Occasionally he could be overwhelmed, unable to keep the visions from smothering him. It was the reason why he drowned his curse in tequila most nights, losing himself in physical oblivion.

"The figurine is from a collection," he continued, deeply focused. "And the woman's body lies in some kind of museum. Her imprint feels out of place as if she was interrupted in some kind of quest. She carried the figurine with her. It was evidence of something." Blake opened his eyes and shook his head to clear it. "I'm sorry, this doesn't seem like very useful information."

Jamie tilted her head to one side. "What's it like?" she asked, curiosity clearly overtaking her professionalism. "How does it feel?"

Blake slipped his glove back on, covering his scars. He was wary about explaining but somehow wanted her to understand. He could sense a deep pain in her and recognized a spirit on the edge of breaking.

"It's a sensation of another place, and sometimes another time. I have an impression of what has happened to the object and the emotions surrounding it. Of course, objects don't have feelings, they can't see, so it's only a projection based on the people who owned them or interacted with them. If they lie in one place for a long time, I get a much clearer idea of where they have been physically. For this figurine, I sense it is missing from a larger collection of macabre items, but then these miniatures were for teaching anatomy, so that makes sense." He paused, his eyes meeting Jamie's. "There's something else."

She nodded for him to continue.

"The girl," he said. "She was pregnant, wasn't she?"

Jamie nodded slowly, then stood and paced the tiny room. Blake felt his headache returning as the hangover beat his body with a vengeance. In contrast, Jamie was a bundle of energy and he could feel her vibrations across the space. He closed his eyes, trying to block it all out and return to his own equilibrium. The problem with reading was that it opened him up, and suddenly there was an overwhelming sensation of too much, color, sound, energy. The world was abuzz, and tuning it out was a huge effort once he had become sensitized. But he wanted to know more about Detective Jamie Brooke and, for some strange reason, he wanted her to trust him.

"I don't think you're entirely confident in my abilities, Detective."

He challenged her with a direct stare and she met his eyes, without flinching. Putting her hands to the back of her head, she pulled a comb from her bun. It was a simple thing, decorated with shells and looked hand made. Jamie laid it carefully on the table.

"What does this say about me?" she asked.

Blake pulled off his glove again and closed his eyes, letting his hand rest gently on the comb. He saw dancers in a tango club, the atmosphere heavy with smoke and the extreme eroticism of close embrace. He felt a maelstrom of emotion, grief and a silent strength honed over years that had now become a cage. He glimpsed Jamie, transformed, her long hair down in waves, wearing a tight silver dress that accentuated her curves and dramatic makeup. She was stunning and as she moved, he felt her sexuality, languid but restrained, held in check by fear and grief. He felt her love for a daughter that consumed her to the extent of everything else in her life. Blake was breathless at the vision, so different from the woman in front of him.

"You're a dancer," he said, opening his eyes. "Tango. You wear your hair down with your fringe held back by this comb. Silver dress. Smoky makeup. It's a good look on you, Detective."

Jamie visibly blanched and then her face flushed. He realized that this was a part of her life that she kept hidden and he had breached a forbidden barrier. Clearly she hadn't believed that he could truly read or she wouldn't have given him something so intimate.

"Is that all?" she asked, her voice almost breaking.

"It was made by your daughter," Blake watched Jamie's eyes as the shadows descended. "She's very sick."

Jamie whirled around, yanked open the door and strode out, slamming it behind her as she left. Blake looked at the figurine on the table, wondering if she would return. He sat silently and waited.

CHAPTER 8

TEN MINUTES PASSED. BLAKE was about to get up and leave, but then the door opened again and Jamie came back in, looking a little sheepish.

"Sorry I ran," she said, shaking her head. "I guess I found your ability a little disturbing. I don't let people see that side of my life and now that I know your gift is genuine, it's slightly odd to say the least."

Blake smiled. "I understand," he said. "Truly, I have no interest in prying."

"Would you consider helping me?" Jamie asked, her voice tentative. "I'm assigned to a special task force on this case. It's high profile because the victim is the daughter of a prominent aristocratic and business family. We've kept it quiet so far, but when the story breaks, we need to have answers. I think your sensitivity could help to point us in new directions. What do you think?"

Blake looked at Jamie, visions of her dancing still running through his mind. It wouldn't be so hard to spend time with her, and perhaps this would be some kind of redemption for the dark side of his gift. If he could use his unusual talents to help solve a crime, maybe it would go some way to righting the wrongs of his past.

"Anything you need, Detective," Blake said, and he saw

hope flicker in her eyes. "I'm happy to help if I can."

"I don't have anywhere else to go with this right now, so whatever you can glean from the figurine is going to help."

Blake looked at his watch. "Reading at the site of the murder would be the most powerful. We could do it now if you like."

Jamie shook her head.

"I'll need to get clearance for that tomorrow, since it's cordoned off as a crime scene. Is there anything else you could do right now? Any leads could help at this stage."

Blake felt the figurine taunting him with its macabre history, and wanted to try and explain the process of reading.

"There are layers to any object," he said. "Especially one as old as this. Ivory is similar to bone and a strong emotional medium. When I read, I see the most resonant places first but there may be something more in times before the actual crime scene that would help provide background information."

Jamie sat back down at the desk opposite him. "Please, try what you can."

"The problem with deeper reading is that I can go under for too long and it can become overwhelming. If you see me looking faint, would you just remove my hand from the figurine?"

Jamie looked concerned but Blake was determined to get something useful for her. He looked at the figurine again, holding his hand over it, feeling an almost physical resonance.

"It's macabre, isn't it?" he said. "I can see why they wanted such things as teaching devices, but I can't understand why someone would want to have a partially dissected body as an ornament. Let's see where it's been."

***

Jamie watched Blake's blue eyes change intensity, a summer sky suddenly filled with storm clouds, as he laid his hands gently on the figurine. It was as if he was no longer present, just a shell, although he still breathed. A sigh caught in Jamie's throat, for this was the emptiness she felt in Polly's body when the drugs kicked in and her consciousness slipped away. Something was gone, the vital part of the self. But if Blake's body was still anchored here, where was his spirit?

***

Blake parted the veils of swirling shadow in his mind and sensed his surroundings. He was in a large sterile operating room, cold and drafty with high windows to provide light and air, but he was aware that no one could see inside. The walls and floor were white, and precision surgical instruments were laid out on gun-metal grey trays, with scalpels reflecting light from the windows, sharp blades waiting to cut into soft flesh. The figurine was laid across the page of a medical textbook, used as a weight to keep the pages open. The book showed the uterus of a pregnant woman, similar to the dissected innards of the figurine itself and the text was in German.

Blake's attention shifted around the room. He could hear the sound of the wind whistling through the cracks in the windows, and outside there was staccato shouting and occasional gunshots. Overlaying this was a low moaning and he slowly became aware of figures in the room before him. A woman was strapped to a gurney, her mouth gagged to stifle the noises of pain. A man stood over her in a white coat, a doctor perhaps, but Blake could feel waves of agony coming from the woman, almost a physical assault to his heightened senses. The man was operating on her with no anesthetic and it looked as if he was opening her uterus, examining its function and comparing it to the textbook.

The man made another cut with the scalpel and looked into the deep wound, packing it with surgical sponges to contain the bleeding. Putting down the knife, he reached in with gloved hands and pulled out the woman's uterus. She arched against the straps holding her down, howled into her gag and then her head lolled back, unconscious with pain. The man cut away the organ and carried it to another bench. Ignoring the woman, he started to dissect it, pulling open the membrane to examine what was inside. Blake felt the world wrench as he witnessed the tiny fetus within, a life snuffed out before it had even begun. The man began to probe at the tiny figure with his scalpel, cutting matchstick limbs and opening the chest in a miniature autopsy. As he worked, the man wrote into an oversized journal that was next to the bench. It spotted with red as blood dripped from his fingers, but he continued scratching the lines, inscribing his findings in neat handwriting. Finally he seemed satisfied, the last full stop an emphatic black mark.

The man barked an order and two women came in, faces pinched and starved, eyes blank and unseeing. They wheeled the gurney with the mutilated woman out of the room and the door swung back behind them. Blake wanted to disconnect but he felt that the emotion imbued in the figurine from this time wasn't finished yet. He needed to know, so he waited. The doctor moved the figurine from the book, turning the pages to a drawing of twins, conjoined back to back. The doctor looked closely at the figures, tracing them with his fingertip as he examined exactly where the organs were attached, as if pondering how two bodies could be bonded this way. He hummed something, a jaunty tune that made Blake's breath catch.

The doctor turned and called to the next room. The door opened again and the women wheeled in two gurneys, each carrying a young boy, strapped down firmly. The boys were awake and alert, eyes darting around the room in fear, both gagged. The man motioned for the women to turn the boys over onto their fronts and cut away the clothes from their backs. They did so with an attitude of detachment, as if by swift obedience they could avoid being next on the experiment bench.

The man then stood between the boys and began slicing into the back of one of them. The boy's screams were high pitched and audible through the gag but the man kept cutting as he began to hum the tune again. The other child turned a deathly pale and froze, his stillness a primeval survival mechanism. Blake wanted to bear witness to the horror even as he knew he couldn't stop it, for these crimes were committed many years ago and it was too late to help the children. He started pulling away from the scene as the man reached into the first boy's open wound, his hands covered in gore.

***

Jamie watched as Blake's physical presence became stronger in the room. His skin tone paled, beads of sweat appeared on his brow and he took deep breaths to control his nausea. His eyes were wide as he struggled to return to full consciousness. Jamie reached out across the table and touched his scarred hand with gentle fingers. His hand grasped at hers and held it like a lifeline as his breathing finally slowed. After a moment, he let go and Jamie felt a moment of loss, as if the room had dimmed. Blake took a sip of water.

"I think the figurine belonged to Mengele," he said, meeting Jamie's eyes, an intensity of horror in his hoarse voice. "The Angel of Death."

Jamie frowned. "The Nazi doctor? You saw him?"

Blake nodded. "I saw what he did to a woman and then to a set of twins. It was horrific. He treated them as if they were lab-rats, to be mutilated and killed as he desired. There was something about to happen, something grotesque …"

Blake sat back in the chair and pulled his smart-phone out of his pocket. He Googled Josef Mengele and read from what he found.

"Here. Josef Mengele. German SS Officer and physician. Doctorates in anthropology from Munich and medicine from Frankfurt. In 1937, he was an assistant to a leading genetic researcher at the Institute for Hereditary Biology and Racial Hygiene. He had a particular interest in twins and it became his fixation at Auschwitz. He selected his subjects from the trains as they arrived, picking twins in particular but also collecting genetic anomalies like dwarves." Blake continued to scroll through the pages, jumping over sections, skipping through the horror until he found it. "My God, that's what I saw him begin." Blake paled, feeling his heart thumping with adrenalin as if he were still watching the crimes of over half a century ago.

Jamie took the phone from him and read from the screen. It detailed how Mengele had experimented on a pair of Roma twins, conjoining them back to back by joining their organs together. It was a particularly sick kind of evil.

"The bastard survived the war," she said, shaking her head. "He escaped to South America with the Odessa organization. He only died in 1979, despite being hunted for his war crimes. That's unbelievable. You'd think Mossad would have found him, like they got Eichmann."

Blake tried to sift through the visions for how this could help Jamie now.

"The figurine was with a medical textbook," he said, "and Mengele had a notebook. Perhaps they were all kept together as collector's items?"

Jamie frowned. "The Americans and Brits spirited a lot

of German scientists away after the War as well as keeping paperwork on the experiments they did. So much of what was done then has benefitted companies that still exist today, built on a bloody past." She thought for a moment. "There must be records about what happened to all the Nazi material, but it's going to take too long to track it down in time to help with the investigation. We've got to take a stab at what's most likely. The figurine was found with the body of an heiress - to a drug company - so perhaps there's some relationship to Neville Pharmaceuticals."

Blake nodded. "But was the figurine with the body some kind of threat to expose the company's connection with the Nazis? Or just a way of saying that the murder was punishment, or recompense, for the past?"

Jamie paced up and down the tiny room, then pulled out her phone and called Alan Missinghall.

"Al, can you run a check on whether any of the Gala dinner attendees were Jewish, or had any kind of Nazi links?" She paused. "Yes, I'll tell you more later, but that might help us." She hung up and turned back to Blake. "We know that Jenna Neville was working on exposing the company, campaigning for the rights of the tissue samples and bodies used in experiments. It could equally have been someone protecting the company from that exposure."

Blake sat quietly, rubbing his temples. "I want to take another look, but I can't do it today. The visions bring on migraines and I've already got a killer headache." He didn't mention the hangover. "But tomorrow, could we do it at the crime scene? That might bring more resonant memories."

Jamie nodded. "Sure. Meet me at the Hunterian Museum at 11.30 and I'll clear it. Are you sure you're OK?"

"All in a day's work." He smiled, but he could see in her eyes that she knew what the reading cost him.

Jamie picked up the figurine, carefully wrapping it in the cloth and placing it back in her bag. Blake watched her deft hands, bare of jewelry, as she put the comb back in her bun. For a moment, he had an overwhelming desire to unpin her hair and watch her dance. He pushed the sensation away as she thanked him and left.

Blake began to count the minutes until he could have his first drink of the night to drown the visions that morphed in front of his eyes. He needed to obliterate the image of Detective Jamie Brooke dancing with the Angel of Death as blood seeped from the wounds that the Doctor had inflicted on her body.

CHAPTER 9

JAMIE PULLED UP TO the hospice and sat for a moment on the cooling bike. She was late for her evening visit and she normally liked to be there for dinner time, but Blake had kept her longer than expected. His visions still disturbed her, the horror of Mengele but also his accurate perception of her dancing. She had doubted him and in doing so she had left herself open. She mentally kicked herself for being so careless with her privacy, for she had seen in his eyes a flash of pity that she resented. Despite that, she felt drawn to him, this haunted man who seemed so much older than he looked. Blake's blue eyes had the layered depth of a forest pool in an ancient wood that hid long-forgotten secrets, where the sun could not penetrate the thick canopy of twisted branches. She thought of the old scars on his hands, revealed when he removed the gloves, evidence of some kind of torture years ago. Yet he had the nonchalance of the truly beautiful, his face handsome and a body that he took for granted yet still turned heads in the street.

Getting off the bike, Jamie pushed all thoughts of Blake and the case aside and focused on her time with Polly. Being fully present was something that she tried to practice on a daily basis and it helped her separate the two halves of her life. She pushed open the gate. 98, she counted and sent up her prayer for another day. A flicker of concern nagged at the edge of her mind. Was she becoming obsessive-compulsive about her behavior? Did she really believe that her tiny actions could keep Polly away from the beckoning arms of death for much longer?

She walked through the hospice, greeting the Duty Nurse, who she recognized but didn't normally chat with. She was grateful that Rachel wasn't on duty tonight, because she didn't want to have any kind of serious conversation right now. Jamie knew she couldn't face that reality just yet and Rachel forced her towards a place she didn't want to go.

Pushing open the door to Polly's room, she found her daughter lying with eyes closed, her face relaxed in sleep or perhaps sedation. After the attack this morning, Jamie knew that the nurses would try to alleviate her suffering as much as possible and keep her comfortable. She bent to kiss Polly's hair gently and sat down next to the bed, watching her daughter's chest rise and fall under the covers. Jamie felt a rush of gratitude that she was still alive, that they had another moment together. She felt tears prick her eyes and she grasped Polly's hand softly, leaning forward to put her head on the bed covers as she concentrated on sending waves of strength to her daughter. In her practical world, in the daylight, Detective Jamie Brooke would have little patience for woo-woo energy work, but in the privacy of the night, she was just a mother doing anything she could for the girl she cherished.

After a moment, she felt a flutter in Polly's fingertips and a gentle pressure. Jamie sat up and Polly's eyes were open. The brown that had been so vibrant this morning was now dark and forbidding, a depth of mahogany that Jamie knew she couldn't penetrate.

"Hey Pol," she said softly. "How you feeling?" Polly blinked slowly and then mouthed, 'Bad'. Jamie noticed a tension around her mouth and her forehead was creased.

"Do you want me to up the pain relief?" she asked, reaching for the pump.

Polly barely shook her head, but it was still a negative and Jamie was grateful. The drugs brought unconsciousness and selfishly, she wanted this moment of lucidity together.

'You?' Polly mouthed.

Jamie tried to smile. "Oh you know, just another day in the big smoke. Chasing bad guys. Bringing justice to the city." She paused. "Actually Pol, you'd have found it interesting, lots of medical research and strange, exotic specimens. I know you love all those gory details." Her voice trailed off as Polly's eyes drifted closed. "Do you need to sleep, my darling?" she whispered. "It's OK, you know I love you. Sleep now."

Polly opened her eyes again, and Jamie was transfixed by the naked truth in their depths. Her daughter was pulling away and Jamie felt a stab of panic in her chest at the realization that time was running out. 'Dance for me tonight, Mum,' Polly mouthed. 'Tell me tomorrow.' Jamie took a deep breath and nodded. The last thing she wanted tonight was to dance but if she couldn't talk with Polly, then perhaps it would be the escape she needed.

***

Jamie stepped into the Zero Hour milonga, one of the best on the London tango scene. Her silver dress was faded in the daylight but in this darkened space it sparkled, a contrast to the long, black hair lying loose about her shoulders. She sat down briefly and changed into her four inch heels, completing the shift from day to night. Jamie transformed for tango, even using a different name if people asked, calling herself Christina. This was a part of herself that she wanted to keep separate, for the milonga was a shifting web of complication, not fitting her police persona. In her job, she was focused and driven but when she stepped onto the dance floor, Jamie embodied the spirit of Argentine tango. Some called it the vertical expression of a horizontal desire, vicarious pleasure, an obsession that allowed the dancer to leave behind the day's trouble and dwell in the moment.

Close embrace did not presume any further intimacy and Jamie preferred it that way. She could be held, swept through the music and then be released back into the world. It was physical experience without real engagement, and there was an etiquette to tango that centered around respect. It allowed Jamie to feel safe dancing with a string of men each time. Respect for the partner, for the dance and the culture permeated the room, albeit with an undercurrent of sexual tension that only served to heighten the pleasures of restraint.

The music began to wash the stress of the day away and, as Jamie watched the couples, she caught a glimpse of Sebastian through the crowd, handsome with his olive skin and dark eyes. He favored close embrace, his body square to his dancing partner as he swept her around the room. Jamie watched his sure steps, knowing that the dominance of the male partner was part of why she could lose herself in tango. Her roles as parent and police officer meant she had to assume authority, make decisions that affected lives and take responsibility. The beauty of tango was that she could give that up, relinquish control and just follow.

Jamie waited out the tanda, a set of songs, declining several partners because she wanted Sebastian tonight. It was selfish to wait for the best dancer in the room, but her body thrilled to be next to his and she craved his peppery scent. It was a chemical attraction but they had never even had a proper conversation or met outside the milonga. The asking, and then a thank you at the end of the dance was their only exchange of words, and that was all Jamie wanted. She felt that she would break right now if anyone asked any more of her than to move with the music and she needed to sublimate her pain.

There was an emotional darkness to tango, a broken spirit inside each of the dancers. She could see it in the older couples clutching onto one other, loss bleeding from their every step. Jamie looked away, not wanting to recognize her own future in their gait. Younger dancers had different problems, but the heaviness of the world seemed to anchor their feet, giving them gravitas, a center around which to spin. The words of the Argentinian poet Borges echoed in her mind, that tango converted outrage into music. She was outraged at how her daughter was being taken from her, angry at yet another murder and crazy mad at her own impotence to stop injustice. In tango, she could rise above those turbulent emotions and just feel. But to be swept away, she needed to dance with the best.

She kept her eyes on Sebastian and as he said his thanks to his last partner, Jamie stood and walked to the side of the dance floor near him. It was brazen to look at him in this way but she felt on the edge of mania and needed the steel cage of his embrace to root her to the earth again. He caught her eye, his look a question she had already answered. He walked to her, ignoring the others who wanted him, and in the cortina, the break between the tandas, he held out his arms.

As he drew her close, Jamie felt suddenly able to exhale, as if his physical strength gave her the support she so desperately needed. The music began and they moved, bodies becoming one, pressed close against each other as she followed his lead. As they swirled, Jamie let anger and grief move through her body, willing it through her feet and into the floor, letting it charge the air between them. She breathed in the space between steps as Sebastian spun her and then held her close, swaying as intensity deepened, the music a lament for dying dreams.

CHAPTER 10

THE INCIDENT ROOM AT New Scotland Yard was still in darkness when Jamie arrived the next day. Logging on, her fingers bashed at the keyboard, hammering out her frustration by typing up the notes from the case so far. Polly had barely opened her eyes this morning when she visited the Hospice in the dark early hours. Jamie had climbed onto the bed next to her and held her daughter, listening to her heartbeat, but there hadn't even been a spark of alertness. Polly had seemed blank and unsure, even of where she was.

Jamie had whispered to her of the tango night anyway, her voice spinning expansive tales of a world her daughter would never know. She had avoided speaking to Rachel again, unable to bear the quiet question in her eyes, coupled with an acceptance of inevitability that made Jamie crazy. The injustice of it and the anticipation of grief made her mad, and even tango last night had barely taken the edge off her anxiety. Escape into the complexities of solving this crime was her best way of distraction.

Spinning on her chair, Jamie paced the length of the large open plan office, the movement allowing her space to breathe. Finally, she stood with her forehead pressed against the reinforced glass, looking out over London. Lights from the early morning traffic flowed around the city and she could see the spires of Westminster Abbey only a few blocks away. For a moment, Jamie felt the scale of her insignificance in the world, a moment of clarity. If she disappeared, all of this would continue without her. London had thrived for over two thousand years, a hub of commerce and culture, its people surviving plagues, fire and flood. Jamie felt a pulse of passion, for she believed that it would continue to be the greatest city on Earth for many more years, whether or not she was here to see it. She acknowledged her inability to change what must inevitably come, but right now she could make a difference for the dead, and Jenna's case was still unsolved.

Walking back to her computer, Jamie began searching on one of the protected databases for any less public background on Neville Pharmaceuticals. Blake's visions couldn't be used as any kind of evidence, but if she could find something specific about the company it might give her leverage in questioning the Nevilles further. Today she was determined to speak to Esther about her relationship with Jenna and exactly why her daughter had protested against the lab.

The case room gradually filled up, the usual morning small talk ignored around her. Jamie knew that her solitary ways meant that she was considered cold and unapproachable but she still preferred it that way, avoiding difficult questions about her personal life.

"Morning." Missinghall placed his large coffee down on the desk in front of Jamie's, demanding her attention. "Anything I should know about?" He indicated her computer.

Jamie rubbed her eyes, lack of sleep beginning to catch up with her.

"Time of death has come back as between 10-11pm which puts most of the gala attendees in the building. But I'm just not happy with Day-Conti as a decent suspect, so I'm following up on the figurine and trying to find any leads as to why it was at the scene."

Missinghall raised an eyebrow as he took a sip of his coffee. "It's early days, though. We've still got to interview some of the others who were there that night and I need to plow through all the information from the taxi companies. That should help us alibi some of them out." He looked at her more closely. "You look awful. Is there something else going on?"

Jamie thought of Polly lying in the dark of the hospice and she hesitated for a moment, part of her wanting to share what was really on her mind. She knew that Missinghall was genuine in his concern.

She shook her head. "No, I'm fine. Just a late one last night. Who else have we got to interview? I'm keen to get on it this morning."

"This guy stood out from the pack." Missinghall passed a file over the desk. "Edward Mascuria. He was on the same table as the Nevilles and he works part time at the company while he completes his PhD. Get this, it's in teratology, the study of developmental abnormalities."

Like Mengele, Jamie thought, remembering what Blake had said about the Nazi doctor's obsessions.

"I'm not sure that I can cope with more medical specimens today … but I need the distraction, so I'll go talk to him."

She picked up the file and grabbed her coat from the back of the chair.

"Do you want me to come with?" Missinghall said, taking another bite of his morning muffin.

Jamie shook her head. "You couldn't keep up," she said, smiling and walking away.

***

It was raining hard outside, but Jamie relished the wet cold as she rode through rush hour, weaving between deadlocked cars and honking taxis. The weather enlivened her senses, reminding her that she still breathed despite the anxiety that pursued her. She relished the freedom of the bike and pulled up to the address in Clerkenwell in good time, hopefully before Edward Mascuria had left for the day.

Jamie rapped on the door and rang the bell. After a minute, the door opened a crack with the security chain on and a partially obscured face peeped out.

"Edward Mascuria?" Jamie asked.

"Yes," the man said, suspicion in his tone.

Jamie held her warrant card out for him to see. "I'm here to talk about Jenna Neville. Can I come in?"

The door closed again, then opened fully.

"Of course. Come in, Detective. Anything I can do to help the investigation. I work with the Nevilles, so of course I'm devastated."

Jamie noticed that his emphatic words didn't match the coolness of his dark grey eyes, which were more like a sharks, the irises bleeding into the pupils to give him a strangely unfocused look. His eyes were too close together and his face wasn't quite symmetrical. His skin was pale, even for an Englishman in winter, and Jamie felt her skin prickle, her senses alert with suspicion just to be in his presence. She found that this happened sometimes. A person of interest could become a suspect worth investigating when the physical meeting generated a gut feeling that everyone in the police understood. There was definitely something about this man that made Jamie uneasy.

She stepped into the hallway, decorated with light green William Morris print wallpaper. There was a scent of fresh pine in the air and a cashmere coat hung by the door. It seemed luxurious for someone who was apparently a student and worked part time.

"Please, come through." Mascuria turned and as he walked down the hallway, Jamie noticed he limped and his shoulders slumped to one side. His spine looked as if it was beginning to twist and hunch, but his shoulders were powerfully muscled and his arms pumped. He certainly wasn't weak, despite his physical disability, and he further compensated with his clothes. He wore a purple striped Marc Jacobs shirt over what looked like Armani jeans. Jamie didn't know much about fashion, but even she knew this was not a cheap outfit.

She followed him further into the flat, emerging from the corridor into a large living space with an indoor garden, enclosed in glass, with a light well open to the roof. It was sparsely furnished but as she glanced around, Jamie could see that this was more from choice than budget. In one corner was an ergonomically shaped desk with an oversized Mac. There was a huge flat-screen TV on one wall and opposite it, a large painting of a minotaur. The beast-man stood looking out to sea, his muscled back and heavy bull's head seen from behind, taut with longing for escape from his island prison. One strong hand pinned a white bird to the parapet, crushing the life out of this last symbol of hope. Mascuria noticed her gaze.

"Do you know GF Watts?" he asked. Jamie shook her head and Mascuria walked towards the kitchen. "To empathize with the monster in all of us is my life's work, Detective. Tea?"

"Yes, thanks. White no sugar," Jamie said, wondering where a graduate student like Mascuria would get money for a flat like this, or for a painting that looked original.

"You were seated on the same table as the Nevilles at the gala dinner?" Jamie asked, when Mascuria returned with her tea.

"Yes," Mascuria indicated a chair and, as Jamie sat down, he began to speak from the dominant position. She rose to her feet again, not allowing him the benefit of the high ground. She knew that the body language of power could make a difference to the perception of the suspect and Mascuria clearly knew it too. His eyes were sharp and deeply intelligent, used to manipulation. "I work for the Nevilles part time, helping with lab work, but I'm mainly working on my PhD. My studies are intimately connected with the Royal College of Surgeons."

"Your specialty?" Jamie asked.

"Teratology. From the Greek for monster, it's the study of abnormalities in physiological development, due to either genetics or environmental factors." He paused. "It's of personal importance to me as I have a spinal deformity."

Jamie heard a restrained aggression behind his words, daring her to look away, the natural human response to deformity and physical imperfection. But he didn't know about her daughter and Jamie just nodded, holding his eyes.

"Did you attend the dinner with anyone?"

Jamie noticed a micro hesitation, before Mascuria answered.

"I took Mimi, sorry, Miriam Stevens. She's just a first year student, and she couldn't afford the ticket. We're not seeing each other though. I'm not … her type."

Jamie considered his words, wondering at what was left unspoken.

"Can you describe what happened that night?"

Mascuria steepled his hands, as if about to begin a sermon.

"The dinner started late at 7.25 and the speakers went on too long, as usual. People wolfed down their starter, the main course was slower and then the mingling began. The dessert course was served on platters around the room to enable people to dance. Jenna was one of the first on the dance floor when the band started at around nine. Esther said she had a migraine and left the event soon after that, I think." Jamie noticed the familiarity with which he spoke of the Nevilles.

"Mimi wasn't feeling so well, I think she'd drunk quite a lot by that stage, so we sat at the table for a while. Christopher - Lord Neville - was engaged in conversation with the Dean about money. Not a surprise, the man is constantly hounded for funding."

Jamie caught a flicker of something in his eyes, but she wasn't sure what.

"And about what time did you leave?"

"We stepped out at around 10pm. I took Mimi for a walk around the square, I thought some fresh air might help her."

"And did it?" Jamie asked, well aware of what a walk around a square late at night after too much alcohol usually meant.

"Yes, we re-entered the party at around 11pm, and I saw Christopher there. But I didn't see Jenna again."

"That's a long walk," Jamie noted. "The square isn't that large."

Mascuria paused, his eyes unreadable. "We sat in the park for a while, talking. I gave her my jacket to wear as she was cold."

Jamie changed tack. "Do you know of anyone who would have wanted to hurt Jenna?"

Mascuria looked towards his glass-walled garden and his voice was wistful. "She was fiercely intelligent as well as determined. I believe she may have made enemies through the causes she was pursuing."

"Anything more specific?"

Mascuria turned. "To be honest, Detective, as part of her investigation she was going after the Royal College itself, focusing on the rights of the bodies that they have dissected over generations and trying to get recompense for the families, for victims of crimes against the body. She had probably made enemies of most of the people in that room, because she threatened their world."

Jamie sensed something more behind his words but she couldn't put her finger on what it was. She only knew that this man made her skin crawl, and looking at his thin white hands, she could only imagine what horrors he had dissected with them. Her years in the police had taught her that gut feel didn't necessarily mean the person was guilty of the crime being investigated, but it sure as hell meant something else was wrong.

CHAPTER 11

JAMIE HAD BARELY WALKED back in the office door before Missinghall called her over.

"You've got to see this footage. It's from Carey Street, a couple of streets back from the Royal College of Surgeons. Not somewhere we checked on the initial sweep of the cameras."

Jamie walked over to Missinghall's desk, pulling up a chair so she could watch the screen with him. It showed a dark road, cars parked close to the kerb and street lamps casting shadows into the gloom. The impressive Gothic architecture of the Law Courts towered above, creating an interplay of chiaroscuro that drew the eye.

"Watch this," Missinghall said and clicked Play.

Out of the darkness at the far end of the picture walked a man and a woman. The man was limping slightly, his shoulders misshapen.

"That's Mascuria," said Jamie, recognizing his gait. "But he said he was on the other side, walking in the park."

Missinghall nodded. "And the girl is Mimi Stevens. His plus-one."

Mimi stumbled a little and Mascuria put his arm around her waist, supporting her a little as he urged her faster down the road. Her head slumped on his shoulder, but she wasn't resisting. A door opened from a dark luxury car in the foreground of the shot.

"It's a Bentley Continental," Missinghall said quietly, as they watched Mascuria lead the girl to the car, pull the door further open and help her into the front passenger seat. After the door closed, he stood for a moment leaning against the outside of the car looking up and down the street. Missinghall zoomed the footage in. It looked as if Mascuria was attaching something to the car window before he stepped away. He slipped into the shadows of the law courts, melting into the darkness, but he could still be seen as a faint outline.

"He stands there for almost forty minutes," Missinghall said. "Let me fast forward."

The minutes sped past on the video until Mascuria moved again to return to the car as the door opened. He helped Mimi out, at the same time slipping whatever device he had planted into his pocket. The girl stumbled against him again, seemingly drowsy. Mascuria pulled her skirt down as he held her up.

"She doesn't remember anything at all?" Jamie asked.

He shook his head. "No, she says she has a blank for the evening after the starter course."

"Likely Rohypnol or some other date rape drug," Jamie said. "Get a couple of officers back to her place. There may still be physical evidence of assault … So who was in the car?"

Missinghall zoomed in the camera again.

"The number plate is obscured but the only Bentley Continental owned by anyone at the party belonged to Lord Christopher Neville."

Jamie slammed her hand down on the desk. "Bastard," she said. "But we don't have a visual on him. I'm going back to Mascuria's. I knew there was something up with him and I want to know what he put onto the outside of the car."

"There's something else," Missinghall said. "Look at the

time." He pointed at the screen. "Mascuria alibis out during the time of Jenna's death. This video clearly identifies him in that window of opportunity and if that's Lord Neville inside, then that's his alibi too."

"But we can still get the two of them on assault if there's enough evidence. It might give us some leverage to find out what else happened that night." Jamie bent closer to the screen, examining the figure of Mascuria clutching the drooping girl. "Can you print some stills I can take back out? If he acts as some kind of pimp for Christopher Neville we need to know, and if they were out there, we don't have an alibi for Esther Neville. Can you follow up on the taxis in the meantime?"

***

Twenty minutes later, Jamie pulled up outside Mascuria's flat again, her anger at his abusive behavior barely controlled. He opened the door, a clear expression of antipathy on his face this time, every trace of his helpful attitude gone.

"Detective, back so soon. What else can you possibly want?"

Jamie pulled out the photos of him on the street, one with Mimi and one waiting outside the car. As he looked at them, Jamie was gratified to see his already pale face blanch, before his eyes narrowed. Jamie saw the warning there, but she was angry with his lies and didn't intend to back down. He stepped away to allow her into the flat and walked ahead of her into the living room.

"You said earlier that you walked around the park," Jamie tried to keep disgust from her voice. "But it seems you took Mimi to Lord Neville's car and stood waiting for forty minutes. What happened in the car?" Mascuria was silent for a moment. Jamie knew that he was calculating how he could explain this in a way that would keep him out of trouble. "Just so you know, we're interviewing Mimi Stevens again, and there may still be evidence of assault." Jamie watched his face flush, with anger, perhaps jealousy. Had he wanted to be in the car with her? She went on the offensive. "Can you confirm that it was Lord Christopher Neville in the car?"

Mascuria turned away. "You don't have anything on me, Detective. I was just walking Mimi to the vehicle for a consensual private meeting."

Jamie knew there was only a small window of opportunity to take this further and she had to offer him something. She softened her voice.

"It's an alibi for the murder, Edward. The time of death was during the interval of that video, so you now have an alibi for the murder of Jenna Neville. I want to know who was in the car so I can also rule them out for murder."

Mascuria spun round, eyes suddenly hopeful. He was a bastard, for sure, but he hadn't committed this murder, and clearly Christopher Neville would be grateful for an alibi.

"Yes, it was Christopher," he said, with defiance. "But Mimi wanted to be with him."

Jamie waved her hand, as if brushing away his words. "I don't want to hear about it. But I do want the video you took."

"There's no video," he said too quickly, but his face was clearly guilty as hell and his eyes flicked over to the Mac. Jamie walked to his desk and pulled out her cellphone.

"Have you heard of obstruction, Edward? Shall I take your computer down to the station and get it processed? What else will I find on it?"

Mascuria came very close, invading Jamie's personal space and putting a possessive hand on top of the screen.

"You need a warrant for the computer, and you know it."

Jamie didn't back away, meeting his steely eyes with her own glare. She sensed that he felt her revulsion, but his physical deformity was nothing compared to his twisted morality.

"True," she said, weighing up her choices. She wanted that file. "But I can make a call and stand here and wait for it. I've got all day. Or you can just give me that one file right now, and I'll leave."

Mascuria stared at her, his shark's eyes calculating. Jamie felt a wave of violence emanate from him and she tensed her muscles, waiting for any indication that he would attempt to hurt her. She almost wanted him to try. After a few tense seconds, Mascuria breathed out slowly and she smelled decay on his breath.

"I'll give it to you," he said, stepping back. Jamie wondered what else he had on the laptop, because this clearly wasn't the only time he had done this, she was sure of it. Was he blackmailing Neville? Did that account for the wealth he displayed in his so-called student flat? Whatever else he had on that computer, she couldn't give him time to wipe this file.

She nodded and let him sit down at the desk. Mascuria turned the screen away from her and she stood with her back to the glass walled garden, watching him work. He plugged a USB stick into the side and quickly loaded it with a file. His eyes kept turning back to her, checking she was still far enough from him. After a minute, he pulled the USB stick out and thrust it at her.

"This had better be the right one," Jamie said.

"I think you'd better leave now, Detective. I don't have anything else for you."

Jamie saw the threat mounting in his eyes, but she held them with her own until he looked away. She walked to the door, her back muscles tense, waiting for an attack that didn't come.

Outside, Jamie mounted her bike and then looked back as she felt she was being watched. Through the wooden blinds, she could just make out Mascuria's face at the window, his features twisted with hate.

***

Back at the station, Jamie handed the USB stick to Missinghall, who plugged it into the side of a separate desktop, disconnected from their main system in case of computer viruses.

"It's clean," he said, after a moment. "Now let's have a look at what happened in that car."

The video shot was clear but only had one angle. It started with Mimi entering the car and sitting in the front passenger seat, looking dazed and confused. In the background, Lord Christopher Neville sat with his suit jacket off, his top shirt button undone. There was no sound, but Mimi looked surprised as the seat she was on reclined. She fought to stay upright for a second but Neville leaned over and pushed her down with one firm hand on her breast.

She was mainly out of shot then but Jamie watched the movements of Neville's hands, clearly pulling up her short dress. He clambered onto her, fumbled with his hands and then began a thrusting motion, the camera shot obscured by how close he was to it.

"I think it's clear what he's doing," Jamie snapped. "This is evidence of rape, since her statement says that she remembers none of this. It's clearly not consensual."

They watched as Neville knelt up and the scene changed as he maneuvered Mimi's legs, moving a slim stiletto heeled foot across his body. He reached forward, his body jerking a little with exertion, although he seemed to be doing whatever it was with some care. Presumably he didn't want to leave marks on her skin. Jamie leaned closer to the screen to see what he was doing, and then realized with a jolt of anger.

"Bastard. He's turning her over." Jamie started to rap her fingers on the table, a staccato beat that sped up as Neville reached his climax, his face reddening as he panted on top of the prone girl. Jamie hated to watch the rape, but she felt that witnessing the crime was part of her responsibility. The anger she felt for Mimi's abuse heaped upon her pent up rage and she felt her blood pressure rising. As much as the police could hack away at the darkness, inching their way forward and bringing light to the city, behind them the shadows reformed and evil flourished in the cracks. "Can you get this to the officers working with Mimi, and I want a statement from Lord Neville."

"Sure thing," Missinghall said. "But this alibis Mascuria and Christopher Neville for Jenna's murder. Can we eliminate them from that investigation?"

Jamie shook her head. "Not yet. I'm sure there's more to this. Let me sort out the warrant for Mascuria's computer and then I've got to meet a source back at the Hunterian. If we can get the paperwork sorted on this, we can arrest the pair of them by the end of the day. I'm sure that will result in new leads for the inquiry."

Back at her desk, Jamie was soon lost in the minutiae of paperwork for the warrant. It was a thankless, but important, part of any investigation and as much as she preferred the more active side of a case, it would give her great satisfaction to be able to bring Mascuria and Neville in.

Minutes after Jamie had logged the meeting with Mascuria and the request for a warrant up to the SIO, the door of the Incident Room opened and Detective Superintendent Dale Cameron walked in.

"DS Brooke," he called, his voice authoritative. "My office, please."

The room quietened slightly until he turned and left again, not waiting for her to follow. Jamie stood, wondering why her superior had made such a public scene. She went to his office and shut the door behind her.

"Sir. You got my update?"

Cameron stood behind his desk, looking down at Jamie, his patrician features composed. Jamie had been expecting praise at the new evidence, but his imperious tone suggested something quite different.

"Yes, and it disturbs me. I'm expecting you to focus on finding Jenna Neville's killer, not pursuing her grieving father for what was probably drunken consensual sex."

Jamie was stunned enough to stand in silence for a moment. There's no way that Cameron could have watched the video yet, so it could only mean one thing. She thought back to the photo of him in the Nevilles' hallway, the impossibility of moving on this quickly without his go ahead.

"But, Sir ..." she started.

"But nothing, Jamie." Cameron sat down behind his desk and Jamie felt like a child summoned to the headmaster. "Seriously, haven't you got enough on your plate with the murder investigation without heading down some sexual assault rabbit hole that has no chance of getting any further?"

"I can ..."

"I don't want to hear any more," Cameron interrupted, his hand held up to stop her. "I'll assign another team to investigate the sexual assault claims, but you need to focus on Jenna Neville's murder. The press are having a field day with our lack of progress. What about that Day-Conti, her boyfriend?"

"He's still a person of interest, but there's no evidence against him Sir, although we're still verifying his alibi at the nightclub. I do have some other interviews lined up today." Jamie decided to omit the detail that one of those was Esther Neville. If Cameron was compromised in some way, she needed time to collect all the evidence together.

"Continue with that then, but Jamie, I will not have you

anywhere near Christopher Neville unless you have some evidence directly linking him to Jenna's murder. I want the focus squarely on Day-Conti."

Jamie nodded her assent, but her eyes were cold. With such friends in high places, she could see how Cameron had earned his Teflon stripes, and she wondered what other investigations he had an interest in. But for now, there was nothing she could do.

CHAPTER 12

BLAKE LOOKED AT HIS watch for the fourth time as he paced outside the Royal College of Surgeons. Some part of him hoped that Jamie wouldn't turn up so he could go back to his research, but then he also felt she offered some kind of redemption, a way in which he could use his curse for good. The problem with being able to read the past was that you felt impotent and powerless, unable to change what had already happened. What good was an ability to see what had already failed, or died and rotted away? Perhaps this time, it would be different.

In preparation for today, he hadn't drunk anything last night, even though he had craved oblivion. Alcohol deadened the visions, shaded their vivid color and rubbed over their raw power until they faded like a mirage, and he wanted to be fully open and alert today. He hadn't read as deeply as this for a long time, and the possibilities both exhilarated and scared him.

He heard the roar of a motorcycle and a figure in black pulled up in front of him. He hadn't expected Jamie to ride a bike, but somehow it fitted her independence and need to be apart from others. As she removed her helmet, Blake remembered how she had looked in his vision of tango and tried to fit it to this leather clad wraith, her face devoid of makeup, hair scraped back as if in punishment. He realized that she had the face of a model, the kind who looked ugly in some shots and stunning in others, depending on the animation of her mouth, the look in her eyes or the way she held herself. At tango, she was a goddess, but right now Jamie's face was hard and Blake imagined that was the look that made criminals wary.

"Morning," she said, dismounting the bike. "Sorry I'm late. I had to see a man about a video."

Blake could sense her anger, the vibrations of intense emotion emanating from her.

"We don't have to do this now, you know," he said. "Maybe another time would be better."

Jamie shook her head. "If you're ready, I really do want to know whether you can shed any more light on the case." She smiled then, and he felt the shift in her, the way her attention could focus. He envied her ability to tune everything else out.

He nodded, pushing aside his own doubt. "Let's do this then. I can't promise anything but it's worth a try."

Jamie led the way into the museum, now cleaned of evidence but still closed to the public for a time out of respect for Jenna's family. Blake hesitated at the door, knowing that this place contained instruments of torture exhibited under the guise of the medical profession. There were saws that sliced bone from bodies, instruments to suck blood from flesh and knives to pare it away.

These were things he could not and did not want to touch, and he felt a wave of fear at being in such close proximity to them, a concern that he would be overwhelmed by visions of past horror. Blake took a deep breath, remembering his father's curses that had called on Hell to visit him with all its spectacles of evil to drive him mad. He felt tendrils of it in the museum and a pain began to pulse in his temples. But he felt that he deserved to face whatever was here, and only by embracing the visions could he find something to help Jamie and the murder investigation.

Removing his gloves, Blake stepped over the threshold into the Museum. Immediately he saw a wooden table laid out with a full dissection of the veins and arteries of the human body. Blake put his hand out to steady himself against the wall as a wave of bloody film swept across his eyes. He tasted a metallic tang and nausea made his head spin. He fell to his knees, hands clutched to his chest as he hyperventilated, shuddering, heart pounding. He had glimpsed the dissection beginning when the victim was still alive. In the vision, Blake saw the patient made anonymous by a hood, so the anatomist could focus on the pathology, eliminating the irrelevant human from the frame of the medically interesting, even as the body shuddered under the scalpel.

"Are you okay, Blake?" Jamie bent to him, her hand shaking his shoulder. "Blake ..."

This place was a museum of abomination. There was an ancient evil here, layered over centuries, and the deaths of many lay just under the surface of its gleaming exterior, clawing for release. Blake tried to regulate his vision, limiting the amount of sensation he was taking in at once and, as his breathing returned to something resembling normal, he tried to compartmentalize the complex web of emotion.

"I'm OK," he whispered, getting up slowly, making sure not to touch Jamie with his bare hands. He didn't want her energy swirling in this maelstrom as well, for she was alive and vibrant, her colors bold and bright. He needed to feel the edges of the palette of gray, where ghosts lingered, trapped by attachment to pieces of their unburied selves. "I need to establish a baseline for the energy of the place and then try to sift through that for Jenna. Her resonance should be greater because it's so recent." He grimaced, unable to hide his mental pain at the sensations pressing in on him. "Just give me a few minutes."

Jamie nodded, clearly worried about him but Blake knew she couldn't understand what he was going through. He was sure that part of her still thought he was a charlatan, but right now it was all he could do to hold onto the reins of his sanity. He had to face the horror head on and ride the wave into the past, and he could only do that by forcing himself to delve into the darkness.

Blake turned to a wall of glass jars exhibiting a collection of fetal deformity. Bracing himself, he placed his bare hand on the surface, deliberately exposing himself to sensation, feeling the agony of those who had suffered. In one jar was a tiny figure, with perfect arms attached to a human torso. Its head was like a lizard, taut skin pulled back over a deformed skull, slitted eyes, flat features and a gaping hole where its mouth should have been, while its legs were fused into a tail. Blake read the label, Sirenomelus, the word haunting but sweet on the tongue. He imagined the creature swimming around in the afterlife and wondered whether there was a soul out there mourning the loss of such a body.

In another bell-jar was a baby, its hair seeming to wave in the preservative liquid, its ears perfect little shells, soft as only a newborn's can be. But its face was a nightmare, with only a mouth and a gaping eye hole in its empty skull. The infant's body had been hacked open, with only crude stitching holding the corpse together for the preservation jar. Blake couldn't help but stare into the abyss of its eye, wondering at the horrors Nature could create and man could only imagine.

How could God allow these freaks to be born, he wondered. Blake knew that a woman's body would usually expel such damaged creatures, for Nature abhors malformation and human society keeps such things hidden. In times past, midwives would have been the bearers of such monsters and only some grew to adulthood, abused freaks. Now he could hear the screams of these drowned nightmares, their cries muffled by the thick preservative their bodies floated in.

In another jar, twins were joined by the face and chest and Blake's thoughts flashed to Mengele's lab. There was a macabre beauty in their perfect bodies with no faces, just a freakish pile of limbs without movement. Next to the jars lay delivery tools, a brutal pair of spiked forceps and a cranioclast, used for cutting or crushing the skull of the baby's head in order to wrench it from the mother. Blake shuddered and turned away from the violent images that flooded his mind, almost on the edge of what he could bear. But he knew he would soon reach the place when his brain was overwhelmed, fear spiked and then cool, calm would descend. He just needed to push his mind a little further.

He turned to a cabinet of diseased limbs and felt the resonance of disembodied flesh, some kind of muscle memory remaining in them, a persistent electrical impulse. Just as people with amputations felt an itch in a phantom limb, so the appendages themselves emanated a kind of psychical scratching as they were divested of the body that gave them life.

Blake walked on through the displays to a gallery of artwork. He stopped by a selection of repulsive images, sexualizing these human monsters into forbidden pleasure tinged with insanity. In one photograph a little girl, curls around her chubby shoulders, turned with an accusatory, feral glare. She crouched on deformed femurs, clutching at cloth with tight fists, as her over developed sex was exposed to the glare of the camera.

In another, a naked young woman stood, stomach bulging, her hair done up in a complicated style, topped by a bow. Between her splayed legs emerged a third leg, angled into the air from the knee, an impossible limb. It looked as if something had been thrust up into the girl but the leg was part of a parasitic twin that had grown inside her body. All three legs wore the same boots with long white socks. Blake couldn't help but look at it more closely, and read the label, 'Dipygus tripus, parasitic twin. Blanche Dumas/Dupont'. The name served to humanize the girl but he wondered what kind of life she had been able to have, or whether it had been one of constant abuse from the people making money from her deformity.

The photos were enough to push him over the edge, and his adrenalin spiked. Blake sat down heavily, pulse pounding as the visions took over his mind, whizzing through his consciousness in a cacophony of screams and flashes of grisly horror. He felt blood pulse at his ankles and wrists as if it would burst from his body, rising to a crescendo of overwhelm. His vision narrowed to a tunnel, his hearing dulled as if under a swimming pool and panic threatened to shut his body down. Then suddenly, it broke. Blake felt the cold aftershock and his heart rate began to slow as the panic subsided. This was the moment that he had waited for, and now he could regain control.

Blake looked up at Jamie standing a little way from him, her face concerned but also intrigued by his physical reaction. He could only imagine what horrors she had seen in her job, but she only witnessed the aftermath, while he saw visions of the atrocity in progress and actually felt the victim's pain.

"Do you want some water?" Jamie said, pulling a bottle from her bag. Blake nodded and sipped at it gratefully while his heart rate returned to normal.

"I'm ready now," he said after a moment and rose slowly, his legs feeling weak and sluggish. He pushed the baseline sensations of the Museum to a separate area of his consciousness and began to sift through the eddies of energy to find a strand of Jenna Neville. His eyes were drawn to the staircase and the heavy post at the bottom. Jamie noticed his gaze.

"That's where she fell," she said, walking towards it. Blake followed and then carefully laid his bare hands on the post.

He felt the extinction of life, her neck broken, the grasping suffocation of asphyxia. He shuddered as he experienced her panic and fear.

"She died soon after her neck snapped," he said. "But the baby didn't." His eyes met Jamie's and he saw a reflection of his own stricken face. "There's something about the child that explains why it was taken, why her body was violated. It feels different somehow but I can't get a clear vision." Blake grasped for a truth that was tantalizingly close and he knew that he had felt whispers of it in the cabinets. There were echoes and reflections of Jenna here and the past of this museum had come to life in the present. Jamie leaned closer, waiting for his words.

"Her baby was a miracle," Blake finally whispered. "Jenna was like one of these specimens. She shouldn't have been able to get pregnant. You need to find who created her."

CHAPTER 13

PARKING THE BIKE A few blocks away from Neville Pharmaceuticals Head Office, Jamie went into a little coffee shop. She was early for her meeting with Esther Neville and she wanted to review her notes on the case so far. Ordering a black coffee and dumping two sugars in it, Jamie considered how Blake's words had disturbed her. Although she still had some doubts about him, he had definitely been affected by the Museum and seemed convinced that Jenna and her baby were somehow special. Esther Neville would be the only person who could answer that but there was no evidence with which to start such a discussion and all of the records indicated Jenna Neville was her biological child. What did Blake even mean about the baby being a miracle? Was he just disturbed by the craziness of the Museum, filled with dead things that seemed about to wake at any moment?

Jamie examined the file on the Nevilles that Missinghall had pulled together. Lord Christopher Neville was a distant descendant of the Darwin-Wedgwood-Galton family and had been raised in aristocratic circles. After Eton, he had read Philosophy, Politics and Economics at Magdalen College, Oxford and was expected to go into Law. But at Oxford he had married Esther Galloway, a distant cousin from another branch of the same distinguished family. Esther studied

•

medicine at Oxford and then worked in the pharmaceutical industry, increasingly specializing in genetics after DNA had been sequenced in 1977.

Neville Pharmaceuticals was started in 1979 with an investment from the family fortune and was now one of the most highly respected private genetics companies in the world. Jenna Neville, their only daughter, was born in 1985. Jamie read a couple of the articles from various pharmaceutical magazines profiling Esther Neville as a brilliant scientist, in total command of the business and scientific side of the research. Christopher Neville seemed to play a more social role, schmoozing with potential investors and clients, leaving the serious business to his more than capable wife. There was evidence of a number of affairs between Christopher Neville and young society women, and Jamie presumed that Esther turned a blind eye to her husband's indiscretions. It was certainly one way to keep a marriage of power together.

Her phone buzzed with a text from Missinghall.

Taxi dockets show Esther Neville picked up alone 10.45pm.

Interesting, Jamie thought, since Mascuria had indicated that she had left the gala dinner around 9.30. What had she been doing in that missing time period?

Finishing her coffee, Jamie drove down the road to the imposing company headquarters of Neville Pharmaceuticals. It was situated on the western edge of London, close enough to the City for ease of access but far enough out for the company to have a high rise building encompassing both official office suites and functional labs. The blue glass exterior reflected the cool winter sun as Jamie parked the bike in a visitor spot and headed in.

After the usual security protocols, Jamie was led into a long boardroom on one of the upper floors, with a giant window looking out over the city. There were a couple of pictures on the walls, magnified images of cells that were monstrous in close-up. Jamie stood, gazing out at London, considering the pulsing mass of humanity that crowded together below her.

"Detective, how can I help you?"

Jamie turned to see Esther Neville at the doorway, a tailored white lab coat cut close to her body and stiletto heels making her thin body appear like a stork picking its way through the marshes. She looked completely different in her own domain, clearly a scientist first, rather than a society wife. Her expertly highlighted blonde hair was tied back with a black clip, and under her lab coat she wore clothes of mourning black. Yesterday, at home with her husband, she had seemed timid, submissive and even fearful, yet here, she walked with authority. Jamie reassessed her opinion of Esther Neville and her position at the company, for this was an empire that she definitely would not want threatened, especially by her own daughter.

"Thank you for seeing me, Lady Neville."

Esther inclined her head and sat at the head of the boardroom table, her eyes emotionless as she spoke.

"What exactly do you need from me? I'm keen to help find my daughter's killer but I'm sure you understand I'm a busy woman."

Jamie sat down to one side and spread her files out in front of her, keeping them closed. She noticed Esther glancing sideways at them, achieving her purpose of making the woman wonder exactly what she knew.

"Can you explain a little of what Neville Pharmaceuticals does? Just for some background."

Esther inclined her head, beginning a clearly well-practiced speech.

"Our main business is genetic engineering for the agricultural and farming industry. You must know of the increasing pressure that food production has experienced with dramatic population growth. We investigate efficient ways to feed more people cheaply, researching faster growth methods for protein sources. We also have a smaller part of the company that researches genetic mutation and how to eradicate birth defects in animals caused by environmental toxins. The exact details are protected, as the work is for the Ministry of Defense, but it's both a profitable business and an important one for the world. Do you think that the company is related to my daughter's death?"

Jamie shuffled her papers to detract from Esther's piercing scrutiny.

"What did you think of Jenna's legal investigations and protests against the company?"

A flicker of disturbance flashed across Esther's face.

"Oh, she was just going through a rebellious patch, encouraged by that man she was seeing." Esther was haughty with a tone of dismissal. "Jenna seemed willing to do anything to undermine me and her father. Although she reaped the rewards of what we do, she was determined to bring it all down and to make victims of the - very few - bodies we use for research."

"Bodies?" Jamie pushed.

Esther sighed. "The best way to learn anatomy is to dissect the human body, Detective. We all want surgeons to know what they're doing, don't we? But Jenna would never acknowledge that truth." Jamie waited, counting the beats of silence until Esther continued. "You have to break humanity before you can fix it. John Hunter knew that. He was driven by the need to understand life, and he wouldn't take accepted wisdom as truth. He would only believe the evidence of his eyes, and only by dissecting the bodies of animals and of people, could he truly understand their inner workings."

"So you objected to Jenna's legal work?"

"We argued about it, yes. But the use of the dead to benefit the living is entirely scientific. It has always been this way. It's superstitious nonsense to think that the body has to be intact for the resurrection, or that somehow we are dishonoring the dead by using them for scientific matters. There are those who would prefer not to think of this side of things, but they are also the ones who expect medical science to cure them, for their drugs to work and for treatments to be pain free. But drugs must be tested on human subjects and the surgeon must know exactly where and how to cut. What are they to practice on, if not real flesh? Of course, these days there are computer simulations but that doesn't give the proper sense of cutting into a body, the push of a blade through resistant skin. It doesn't part like butter, you know, you have to cut. Surgeons sweat as they work, it can be physically draining." Her voice was strangely wistful. "The human body is so well put together, it can be hard to pull it apart. "

Jamie looked down at her notebook to leave some silence between them, as she considered Esther's vivid words. After a moment, she looked up again.

"Can you talk me through your movements on the night of the Gala Dinner?"

Esther froze, her face stony, then slowly answered.

"I had a headache that night. I get migraines and one was threatening. I put up with that odious dinner for as long as I could, but I got up to leave as the dessert was being served. I felt giddy so I sat in the toilets for a while." She looked away from Jamie. "I don't know how long I was there. The pain was all I could think about, and eventually I caught a taxi home."

"And did you argue with Jenna that night?"

Esther laughed, a shrill sound that seemed out of place in the austere surroundings.

"Of course. I argued with my daughter whenever we spoke, Detective. That night wasn't any different."

Jamie decided to change tack and circle back on the alibi

later. There should be some footage from near the bathrooms of the Royal College of Surgeons, and she could check on the migraine medication.

"What about Jenna's active membership of the National Anti-Vivisection Society? The marches against this office, against you and Lord Neville personally."

Esther rolled her eyes and shook her head. "I know she meant well, but she was misguided. Come with me and I'll show you how humane we are. I want to give you the scientific side of the story so you'll understand."

She led the way out of the lab, into a corridor and then to a lift. Esther pressed the −3 button, and Jamie noticed that there were five floors underground as well as the twenty above ground. It was an extensive facility. Esther was silent in the lift, and Jamie said nothing either. Finally, the door opened to an atrium, which smelled of disinfectant, like a vet's surgery.

"This floor is where we keep some of the animals and also where we perform legal vivisection."

Jamie noticed her emphasis on the legal basis of the research. "Can you explain to me exactly what that is?" she asked.

"In the UK, any experiment involving vivisection, where we use a live animal for experimentation, must be granted a license from the Home Secretary. The license is only given when the benefits to society outweigh the adverse effects to the animal."

"What's your definition of adverse?"

"It depends on the procedure. The definition of vivisection is that the animal is alive when we experiment but of course we use anesthesia, so there is no pain. We also have an external ethics committee."

"Why was Jenna so against this practice?"

"She believed it was morally wrong to inflict pain or injury on another animal, for whatever reason, and so any kind of animal experimentation would be unacceptable." Esther shook her head. "But Jenna was short-sighted about this, she only saw the propaganda spread by the anti-vivisectionists, and she put everything in the same box."

"What do you mean by that?" Jamie asked.

"Well, I agree that it's pointless to test household products by spraying them into the eyes of rabbits, and there are some needless experiments where positive results on animals have no application to humans. But here, we carry out genetic research, and since we cannot experiment on humans, we must make do with animals, as did the great John Hunter. Although of course, he did experiments on live animals with no pain relief."

"Which we would now consider barbaric and inhumane," Jamie prompted.

"In our culture, yes," Esther replied, her eyes curiously blank, her mouth tense. "But think of how operations were back then. No anesthetic and no antiseptic, they didn't know about germs or infections. Surgeons would go from the dissection room to the operating theatre, reusing equipment that was encrusted with the blood of the previous patient and the gore of the recently dead. The patient would be tied up or held down, then the surgeon would progress as fast as possible. Many didn't survive. Hunter became known as one of the greatest surgeons in England because he was so much better than the rest, and he was better because of his experiments. Dissection and experimentation were a means to gaining insight. It wasn't a macabre obsession, it was more about expanding his own knowledge in order to help the living."

Jamie was startled at her words, her passion suggesting that only the law was stopping her from experimenting on humans.

"And what exactly do you do here?"

Esther led the way into the next lab, dominated by a

quiet hum of medical equipment and the smell of antiseptic. One side of the room had refrigeration units with clear glass doors. As they walked past, Jamie glimpsed racks of labeled test-tubes and larger jars containing monkey fetuses of varying sizes. She couldn't help but stare at the recently extinguished lives, so similar to human babies but distinguished by tails and longer toes. It was eerily reminiscent of the Hunterian Museum, but these specimens were much more recent, and presumably modified by design.

They walked deeper into the lab to find a group of scientists in lab coats and expressionless masks surrounding a monkey. It was anesthetized and strapped to a bed, eyes shut, and Jamie felt her heart thump in her chest as she recognized a kind of kinship with the creature.

"This macaque has been exposed to specific environmental toxins whilst pregnant," Esther said. "Now we're waiting for some key stage developments, at which point we will operate and extract the fetus for further testing."

"You kill it?"

Esther looked at Jamie, her eyebrows raised as if the question was entirely irrelevant. "It was never meant to be born, so how are we killing it by extracting it early?" Jamie said nothing, but she was beginning to see why Jenna had protested against her mother's company. Esther continued in a superior tone. "Jenna accused me of being like Mengele, an animal Angel of Death. She painted me as this architect of Nazi-style experimentation, but I'm only seeking medical truth and these monkeys don't even suffer any pain."

Jamie was shocked to hear Esther mention Mengele. It seemed too much of a coincidence after Blake's revelation. Could the book that he saw be here? She looked down at the face of the macaque, whose baby was about to be ripped from her body and she felt a wave of anger, as she supposed Jenna would have done. But had Jenna's objection been enough for her mother to have acted against her?

"I think I've seen enough," Jamie said. She spun on her heel and walked out of the lab, breathing deeply as she tried to regulate her emotions. A few moments later, Esther Neville walked out of the lab behind her.

"I didn't think you'd be so squeamish Detective, considering you must see real violence on the streets."

Jamie thought of what humans did to each other, supposedly prevented by the law, but that didn't stop the horrors that went on behind closed doors. After all, there was no license from the Home Office necessary to have a child. These animals didn't choose to be treated this way, but at least there was some legal protection in place to limit their suffering.

"Did Jenna ever come down here or visit the other parts of the lab?"

Esther nodded. "Of course, when she was younger I hoped that she might continue my work, but once she went to university and began to study ethics and law, we had to ban her. We even took out a restraining order to keep her from coming near the premises."

Jamie wondered how far the conflict had gone between the members of the Neville family. A restraining order on their own daughter seemed extreme, and surely Jenna couldn't have sat easily with them at the Gala dinner.

They walked towards the lift, and Jamie suddenly felt trapped underground in the lab, desperate to emerge into the light. Even though it was high tech and shiny, the lab felt like a dirty prison. Being kept down here in the dark and experimented on was a modern nightmare that wasn't so different to the horrors of Hunter's time.

"I'll show you out," Esther said, and Jamie thought she heard a tinge of triumph in the woman's tone.

As the lift took them back up to the lobby, Jamie decided that she had nothing to lose by testing Blake's theory.

"I need to ask a more personal question Lady Neville."

Jamie waited as Esther hesitated, then nodded. "Was Jenna your natural child?"

Esther's eyes narrowed, her lips pursed and she began twisting her wedding ring, remaining silent as the lift door opened. In the lobby, Esther ushered Jamie into a small meeting room at the side of Reception, obviously keen not to be overheard as she finally answered.

"It's an ironic twist of fate, Detective, and one which sometimes seems to occur when scientists investigate an area of medical research. Cancer researchers get cancer and neurosurgeons get brain aneurysms and I have a rare genetic mutation that means I couldn't have children. It was this that led to my constant drive to eradicate mutation in animals and humans." She paused and her eyes flickered to Jamie's. "Back then, the lab was purely experimental, investigating mutations at a time when genetics was really just beginning. I worked with a fertility specialist to remove my mutation and enable my egg and Christopher's sperm to make Jenna. So yes, she is my child, but she started life in the lab. She was a miracle, because so many of the fetuses we engineered were corrupted."

"Could Jenna have had children?" Jamie asked quietly, her suspicions heightened as she realized that Blake had gleaned a truth at the Hunterian.

Esther stared out the window, silent for a moment. When she spoke, her voice was wistful.

"She shouldn't have been able to."

Jamie opened her mouth to ask more but at that moment her phone buzzed urgently in her pocket. She took it out and checked the display. The Hospice. Her heart hammered.

"I have to take this, sorry."

Jamie stepped out into the corridor and answered the phone, a sense of dread rising within her.

"Jamie Brooke," she said and it was as if her voice wasn't her own.

"You have to come now," Rachel said. "Polly needs you."

A coldness swept over Jamie, raising goosebumps on her arms. She wasn't ready. She leaned against the wall, her hand clutching it for support.

"I'm on my way."

CHAPTER 14

SCREECHING TO A HALT outside the hospice, Jamie wrenched her bike helmet off and ran inside. The lump in her throat threatened to choke her with tears at any minute but she had to hold it together. She had to believe that this wasn't the end, not yet. Not her beautiful girl. She saw Rachel at the door of Polly's room and her face crumpled.

"Breathe, hun," Rachel said, her hand firm on Jamie's arm. "Polly's calm now, but she's drowning in the respiratory secretions and we can't suction it off fast enough anymore. She's hypoxemic, which means she's not getting enough oxygen."

"Is she in pain?" The tears came now, streaming down Jamie's face.

Rachel nodded. "She's been in pain since she was a little girl, you know that, but now her body has had enough. We've given her morphine and midazolam to dull the discomfort, but you know her wishes. We haven't fully sedated her yet, so she's just conscious, waiting for you. But, it's time, Jamie."

Rachel stood back and pushed the door open and Jamie walked slowly into the room while the nurse followed behind. It was so bright, the sun shining in from outside. For a moment, Jamie couldn't believe that anything bad could happen on a day like this, but then she looked at the bed. Polly was lying on her back, eyes closed. Her skin had a bluish tinge and her lips were almost lavender. Her rasping breaths were harsh in the room, and every inhalation was hard fought, the sound of torment even though it was dulled with analgesia. Jamie knew that the drugs could help Polly peacefully into another place, but everything in her screamed for her to stay. She bent over her daughter and kissed her forehead.

"Pol," she whispered. "I'm here, darling. It's OK. I love you." The tears came freely now and Jamie couldn't hold them in anymore. She took Polly's hand in her own, squeezing it. Polly opened her eyes slowly and Jamie saw eternity there. In that moment, she knew that this twisted physical body was only a trap, a temporary home for the tremendous spirit that was her beloved child. More than that, Polly would go further than she ever could in transcending this physicality. Wherever she was going next, Jamie couldn't follow and she knew she would never see her daughter again. Looking down into Polly's eyes, Jamie saw that she only asked permission to leave.

With a fierce need to save her child from pain, Jamie looked up at Rachel and nodded her consent. The nurse readied a bolus of medication to sedate Polly and let her die pain-free and then injected it into the cannula.

"It's OK, Pol, you go now my darling." Jamie wept openly, knowing that Polly didn't want to hurt her but desperately needing her to find release. Trying to keep her here was only selfish. Jamie kissed her daughter's face gently. "I love you Polly," she whispered. "I'll miss you but I understand. I love you."

Rachel turned off the ventilator and stood by, a witness to the transition she had seen so many times before. Jamie sobbed, her body wracked with silent heaving, for she didn't want Polly to go with the sound of pain in her ears. She clutched her daughter's hand, pressing it to her own cheek.

Jamie pleaded with God, with the Universe, anything to have her baby back. But Polly had been her gift for fourteen years, and now her time was over. The girl's rasping breaths stumbled and skipped, hoarse gasps becoming weaker.

"No," Jamie whispered. "Please, no."

She felt Rachel's hand on her shoulder and then rubbing her back, like a mother comforting a child. Like she used to do with Polly.

"I'll remove the tubes now," Rachel said, her voice choked. "Let me make her your baby again and you can hold her as she goes."

Jamie nodded, still clutching Polly's hand. It was so warm and soft, relaxing now as the pain dissolved from her face. Rachel removed the tube from Polly's neck, wiping her face carefully as her breaths became sporadic.

"There you go, hun," Rachel said quietly. "You can curl up on the bed with her now. I'll come back in a bit."

Jamie heard Rachel leave and shut the door quietly behind her. She climbed onto the bed and pulled Polly carefully into her arms, folding her daughter's head onto her chest and stroking her hair. She rocked Polly back and forth, something she hadn't been able to do properly since she had become bedridden. She felt the thin body, spine twisted and misshapen and Jamie cried silently, her tears soaking the pillow and Polly's bedclothes. She wanted Polly's agony to be over, but she also wanted to crush the girl's body to her and breathe her own life into her daughter's lungs.

Time seemed to slow down, held back by each faltering breath as the sunlight dimmed outside and night fell. Jamie listened to the evening routine of the Hospice, lives that continued even though she felt hers was over.

Finally, after a last breath, Polly's body was still, released from pain. Jamie had a sense that while her body had held Polly captive for so many years, now she was free. Her spirit had gone, and Jamie hoped that she hadn't looked back. For whatever her daughter became next, at least she wouldn't have to rely on this mess of a body to carry her there.

Jamie held Polly's body tightly against her own, knowing that these last moments were for her own precious memory. In the depths of her misery, she knew she was grateful for the years she had Polly in her life, for the joy her daughter had brought. She was grateful that the physical suffering was finished and thankful that she was able to be here to let her daughter go, that she didn't have to die alone. Although Polly's body was still warm, Jamie knew that her girl wasn't inside. She already felt the absence, the emptiness. Her daughter's pain was over now, and her own, she would bear as penance, although she felt she would never stop crying.

Polly's tablet lay next to the bed, and Jamie reached for it, wanting to see her words. Turning it on, she saw only one line of text. *Dance for me, Mum.* The tears welled again and Jamie sobbed as if she would never stop.

***

Much later, Rachel knocked at the door and came in slowly, holding a steaming cup of milky tea. Jamie disentangled herself from Polly's body and sat up.

"Here you go, hun." Rachel said as she put the tea down next to the bed. "I know you're hurting, but it was time."

Rachel's eyes were red-rimmed and Jamie could only imagine the tears that the nurse had shed for the children over the years. Jamie blew her nose, adding to the pile of wet tissues on the side table.

"Thanks Rachel." She took a sip of the tea. It was sweet, just what she needed. Rachel walked around the bed and together they arranged Polly's body, tucking the sheet around her, so she looked like she was sleeping.

Jamie took a deep breath. It seemed like it had all happened so suddenly even though the moment had been approaching for years. "So what happens next?" she asked, feeling a need to understand the process, to reach a point of completion. She had prepared hypothetically for this but suddenly her mind was blank on the next steps.

"The doctor will sign the death certificate and we'll get the funeral director to prepare her body."

Jamie nodded, remembering the difficult discussions with Polly over the choices. Her little girl had been independent minded, even about her own death.

"She wanted to be cremated, taken by fire and smoke into the freedom of the sky." Jamie's voice broke, as the tears came again. "She watched a history documentary about the Viking boat pyres … and afterwards she wanted her ashes to become part of the flowers. She loved the first daffodils of spring."

"Of course. And what about your family? Do you want me to call anyone?"

Jamie thought of Polly's father, Mark, her own parents and the fights they had engaged in over the years. She couldn't bear to talk to them and right now, she didn't even want the funeral to be for anyone else. Polly had been her life, and no one else had the right to be there as she said her final goodbyes.

But then she faltered. Of course Mark had to be there, if only for him to acknowledge their remarkable daughter. He seemed to live in denial of the miracle that they had created together, seeing primarily her disability. But Jamie knew he would mourn in his own way and she had loved him too, once. Polly's school friends would want to come as well, and a funeral was a chance to honor her memory with those who loved her.

"I can't face talking to anyone right now," Jamie said. "I need to leave all that for tomorrow. Let's just do the essentials. "

***

Much later, Jamie returned to the flat in darkness. She left the lights off, sitting on the sofa alone, for the brightness would only illuminate what she was missing. This moment had been on its way for nearly ten years but she still wasn't prepared for how lonely she felt. Polly had been her reason for everything and without her, there was nothing. Jamie's head pounded, the headache that had been growing all day exploding into her consciousness. She embraced the pain, wanting it to consume her.

The Funeral Director had come quickly to the Hospice and Jamie had wept again to hand Polly's body into their care. It was so wrong: a daughter should weep for her mother, not the other way around. Jamie rose and went to the bathroom, opening the cupboard where she kept her sleeping pills. For a long moment she looked at them, oblivion in a bottle. She twisted the cap off and tipped out two pills, then four more, then the whole bottle into her hand. Release called to her, a tangible desire to swallow these down and follow Polly's spirit onwards.

That thought made her stop, for if there was another side and Polly was there now, she would be disappointed at these self-destructive thoughts. Jamie poured the tablets back into the bottle, keeping only the prescribed two. Even in death, she didn't want to disappoint Polly, for one of the things that she had been most proud of was Jamie's job, the fact that she brought killers to justice. Jamie tried to put the two deaths into perspective. Polly had died surrounded by love, and was now mourned and missed. Jenna Neville had died violently, her parents rejecting her passionate cause, and her killer was still out there. Jamie knew that right now, across London, across the world, other crimes were being committed, other people injured and killed. If she were to stay alive, her role would be as one of those who stood against the dark tide, part of a dam that held back at least some of the monsters.

She clenched her fists, remembering the sensation of holding Polly's hand and the fierce determination in her daughter's eyes when she wanted to learn something new. She could have been the next Stephen Hawking, Jamie thought, smiling a little because every parent would say that their kid could achieve something unique and amazing. But hers could have, for sure, because Polly's mind had been special and sometimes Jamie wondered how she had brought such a being into the world.

Jamie thought of her own mother, years of not speaking creating a wall neither of them could cross. She rummaged in the back of a drawer and pulled out a card, the one that had finally broken their relationship years ago. It had a quote from the gospel of John 9:2-3.

His disciples asked him, "Rabbi, who has sinned, this man or his parents, that he was born blind?"

"Neither this man nor his parents sinned," said Jesus, "but this happened so that the work of God might be displayed in his life."

Jesus had healed the blind man and Jamie's mother had said to pray in faith that God might work a miracle in Polly's life. But Jamie could never reconcile the thought that God would have condemned a little girl to a life of torture in order to save her later. Her mother's constant acceptance of suffering as God's will was something that Jamie couldn't bear, as if the violent anguish she saw every day was condoned by the Almighty. She hadn't spoken to her parents for six years now, and cutting them completely out of her life had made the separation easier. It had just been her and Polly against the world, fighting for one more day. And now it was just her. Jamie pulled Polly's cuddly dog, Lisa, to her chest and the tears came again as she wept for an empty future.

CHAPTER 15

THE NIGHT WAS LONG and lonely. Even when Jamie managed to drop off to sleep, exhausted from weeping, she woke with a start from nightmares of Polly dying over and over again, forced to watch as she had to let her daughter go. In the end, although she knew that she should rest, Jamie could not bear lying there any longer.

Standing in the shower, she tried to think of what was supposed to happen next. Time seemed to have slowed down and her brain just wasn't functioning properly. The pills in the cabinet called to her again and she rested her palm against the wall, anchoring herself to the physical world as the wave of longing washed over her. It was all she could do to resist the pull of oblivion. Fight it for just another heartbeat, she told herself, for this too shall pass.

Eventually, she managed to drag herself out of the bathroom and started getting ready to go to the funeral directors. Jamie was dreading the practicalities and the finality, holding onto the last moments she had cuddled her daughter on the bed. That was what she wanted to remember. That, and living as passionately as Polly had wanted her to. Jamie's hand flew to her mouth and she held back a sob as the wrenching in her chest made her stop dead in the middle of the room. This was how people died of a broken heart, and even with all her years of police work, she hadn't been prepared for the violence of her own grief. She breathed into the silence until the tightness eased and she could move again.

It was still early but Jamie rang Detective Superintendent Dale Cameron anyway. He didn't answer so she left a brief message, grateful that she didn't have to talk to him because she couldn't bear his false sympathy right now. She followed up with an email to him and the HR department taking her allotted bereavement leave. She had told the Met about Polly's illness previously and given them notice of her potential need to be off work, so there would be no problem with it. Jamie felt a lingering guilt and responsibility over Jenna Neville's case, especially as Cameron had seemed to be directing the investigation away from the Nevilles. She still had her notes on Esther Neville to file, but her suspicions paled into insignificance now. They would have to find someone else to continue the investigation, because nothing else mattered anymore.

**

The entrance hall of the funeral directors was tastefully furnished with fresh flowers and cream decor, a light and airy atmosphere that seemed a respectable overlay for what must happen behind the scenes. Jamie didn't want to think about Polly's body being prepared for cremation: she wanted to remember her alive and vital, not as a shell of a corpse. In other cultures, in other times, she would have been the one washing the body and preparing her daughter for the grave. Perhaps that would have been a way to help the desolation, but Jamie couldn't bear the thought of grieving so openly in front of others. This pain was hers to bear privately.

She rang the bell, pacing the little room with barely controlled nervous energy. As Jamie waited, her phone buzzed with a text from Missinghall.

So sorry about your daughter. FYI. Day-Conti arrested for Jenna's murder.

Jamie frowned. Firstly at how her private life had been so clearly exposed but also, she couldn't understand how Day-Conti could be arrested, given the little evidence against him and the open lines of investigation still to be followed up. Jamie wondered whether her visit to Esther Neville had stirred the hornet's nest. Had Cameron used her absence to change the direction of the case? But then again, what did it even matter? She had more important things to think about right now. She pushed the investigation from her mind.

A door at the back of the entrance hall opened and the funeral director stepped out, rubbing his hands together in an awkward way.

"Ah, Ms Brooke," he said without meeting her eyes and Jamie felt her heart thudding in her chest.

"What's wrong?" she asked, sensing the man's discomfort.

He pursed his lips and twisted his hands, adjusting his tie. "I'm so sorry, we're investigating right now. This has never happened before."

"What's happened?" Jamie cut him off, impatient for him to get to the point. "What do you mean?"

"Oh, no one called you?" The man looked embarrassed and shocked. "I'm so sorry. It's your daughter's body. It's missing."

Jamie's head spun, confusion buzzing in her ears. "What do you mean it's missing? How can that even happen?" Her voice escalated to a shout. "How can you lose my daughter?"

The man wrung his hands together, clearly distressed and worried about his business.

"I'm so sorry, but there was a break-in last night and by the time security got here, her body had been taken." The man was flustered, his face reddening with every second. "It's never happened before and to be honest, we don't know why anyone would even want to steal a body."

Jamie felt a chill at his words and rising anxiety rippled through her body. It was too much of a coincidence. Jenna had been investigating the theft of bodies and was then killed, and now she was analyzing the same evidence. Was this some kind of retribution for her investigation?

Hysteria rising within her, Jamie felt a desperation to shake the man. It seemed too much to take in and she was only just clinging to the edge of sanity. The funeral director was still speaking but Jamie was no longer listening. She was thinking back to Esther Neville's clinical detachment about bodies, the horrors of Day-Conti's studio, the evidence against Mascuria and Christopher Neville. The last forty-eight hours had been steeped in dissection, mutilation and desecration. This theft had to be related.

Inside, Jamie was screaming. Someone had taken her daughter. Someone had known about Polly's condition, her death, and because of her, they had taken her body. She had to do something.

"Have you called the police?" Jamie asked, her voice outwardly calm.

"Of course, they're sending someone down to interview the staff soon."

Jamie knew this would be a priority for the Met. The theft of a body was unusual at the best of times, but when it was the daughter of a serving officer, she knew they would fast-track the case. The police had their problems, like any organization, but they certainly looked after their own.

She called Dale Cameron's office and was put straight through. She explained what had happened and her suspicions surrounding the Neville case.

"Jamie, this is terrible ... unbelievable. Of course, I'll contact the officers assigned and explain the situation. We'll find Polly's body, I promise you." He paused and Jamie heard caution in his silence, before he continued. "I can't believe it's related to the Neville case, though. And, of course, you know that you can't be involved in either now. You're too close."

"But, Sir …"

"I'm sorry for your loss, Jamie, but you're now officially on extended bereavement leave. I'll keep you up to date."

Jamie's heart was thumping and her fist clenched the phone tight as Cameron hung up, dismissing her with barely concealed relief. But there was no way she could stay out of this case, especially as she was sure that the theft was related to Jenna's murder.

Looking at her watch, Jamie suddenly felt a sense of lost time. It was Friday morning and the Lyceum had been marked on Jenna's calendar for tomorrow night. It was one of many unanswered questions in this case, but she remembered the news clippings from Jenna's office, the stolen bodies marked with L. Images of the specimens from the John Hunter museum flashed before Jamie's eyes, twisted spines and diseased body parts floating in formaldehyde, torn from the bodies of their owners. She had to find Polly before she was displayed in a labeled bell-jar, her flesh carved up and trapped in liquid limbo. She would let the Met start their own investigation, but there was no time to follow the correct protocol. She needed to bring her daughter home.

CHAPTER 16

THIS PART OF LONDON was always busiest in the dark. Artists worked nights and slept the days away, and the oldest profession in the world was always active. Debilitated from grief and lack of sleep, Jamie had taken a couple of ephedrine tablets, stimulants that would keep her awake for the investigation ahead. She wouldn't rest until she held Polly's body in her arms again. With the spike in energy helping her recover, at least physically, she parked the bike and slipped along the street towards the studio of Rowan Day-Conti.

Since he was still in police custody, Jamie knew that his flat would be empty. She was determined to find out more on his sources for the bodies he worked on and the mysterious buyer for the naked female sculpture. Tugging her leather biker's jacket tighter around her, Jamie pulled a pair of thin gloves from her pocket. Slipping them on, she flexed her fingers and then rubbed her hands together. The night was cold and Jamie felt light-headed, her body fevered, running hot and cold. The tears had finally dried up, to be replaced by anger and determination. The thought of someone using Polly's body in an artistic collection of mutation made her want to vomit. It was an abomination.

She was about to commit a crime by breaking in, but Jamie understood the risks she was taking. She could lose her job or even face charges if discovered, but right now, it felt like her life was over anyway. She would leave her colleagues to pursue Polly's case in the legal fashion, but she needed to follow the less respectable route, as time was critical. This had to be connected with her own investigation of the Jenna Neville case, and perhaps, in finding Polly, she could also bring Jenna's killer to justice.

Arriving at the flat, Jamie blocked the view of the lock with her body and, without looking around, picked it to gain access. There was no elaborate security at the studio. Why bother when no one would want to steal the dead bodies Day-Conti worked on, but then why steal Polly's body, she thought. Rage bubbled again and Jamie's face hardened with resolve.

Inside the flat she put on a head torch, the powerful beam stretching all the way to the high ceilings of the warehouse space. The hum of a generator pulsed gently in the background, keeping the remains cool. The smell of death seemed stronger now, disinfectant barely hiding decay. Jamie imagined the naked body of the decapitated young woman lying behind the panels, alone in the dark. She shuddered, imagining the flesh reanimated, body lurching blindly for a weapon to avenge her mutilation. Jamie shook away the thoughts. These bodies were dead flesh, preserved as an echo of reality, with not a shred of humanity left. What had defined those people was gone, back to the stars and the earth.

Jamie shone the torch back to the staircase that led to Day-Conti's living space. How the man could live in such proximity with the dead, she didn't know, for the smell must impregnate his clothes and his skin. Jamie padded across the floor and up the stairs, freezing as a creak echoed through the space. But no sound came after, no answering noise, so she continued upwards. At the top, she opened the door into the living area. Incense, some kind of heavy patchouli, hung in the room, disguising the smell of the dead but pungent with its own depth of scent. Jamie wrinkled her nose. Perhaps Day-Conti had damaged his sense of smell with all the preservatives. Jamie tried to imagine Jenna here, their intimacy amongst the dead. What had she been thinking? Had she been pursuing a similar goal in trying to discover the origin of the bodies and who wanted such specimens? Or had she really loved him?

Shining the torch around, Jamie could see the place was sparse and minimalist, with a basic desk in the corner and a second-hand filing cabinet against one wall. Jamie pulled it open, using her head torch to illuminate the thin folders within. One held clippings, with articles on the New York Bodies exhibition, interviews with practitioners of the plastination process and controversies over provenance of the bodies. Another file contained receipts, thrown haphazardly into paper envelopes marked with the month of spend. Jamie opened one and thumbed through the paper, looking for where Day-Conti bought his materials. The vendor of the plastics could be a lead, so she snapped a picture on her smart phone and replaced the receipt.

Jamie opened another file. In it were five separate sheets, each one an order form for an unspecified piece of art. There was only one name, Athanasia Ltd, and as the item would be picked up by courier from the warehouse, there was no delivery address. The company name rang a bell and Jamie Googled it on her smartphone. Athanasia, meaning the quality of being deathless or immortality. She took more pictures.

Pulling more files from the cabinet, Jamie discovered notes on different artistic projects, records and photos of stages of the plastination process for each artwork. She laid them out on the desk, scanning pages, and replacing each as she processed them. She flicked open one folder and stopped suddenly, appalled by what she saw. It was a child, no more than ten years old. A boy with deformities of the spine and twisted limbs was posed naked on a metal table that Jamie recognized as the one downstairs where the woman now lay. In the first picture the boy was lying, eyes closed, almost sleeping, as if he could wake up. The next picture showed the body turned onto its front, the spine dissected so as to demonstrate his deformity more clearly.

Jamie gulped for air, feeling the rise of vomit as her stomach clenched at the violation of the child. Seeing a door off the main room, she barged through it into a tiny bathroom. She fell to her knees, holding the toilet bowl as she heaved the meager contents of her stomach out, shaking with the effort as her head spun. She retched again, the sound reverberating around the flat and then she was dry heaving, her stomach spasming.

Finally Jamie lay down on the floor, placing her aching head on the cool tiles, waiting for the tremors to pass. The image of the dissected spine hovered in front of her eyes and she wished she could go back and un-see it. That little boy was tortured in life with disease and then mutilated in death. And to what end? Did the same people have Polly's body, because that close up of the spine could have been her daughter's. Jamie wished for a moment that Day-Conti was here and her hands clenched into fists at how she would teach him some respect for the dead.

Pushing herself up from the floor, Jamie took some deep breaths. She swilled her mouth out with water from the tap, and spat into the toilet, flushing the evidence away and pouring bleach down after it. She wiped the floor tiles with disinfectant and toilet paper and flushed that too.

Walking back into the main room on unsteady legs, Jamie snapped some photos of the image of the little body, trying to separate her emotions from what she was seeing. This was evidence, and this boy was dead. It wasn't torture when the body was no longer alive, was it? Jamie replaced the files into the filing cabinet, careful to put them back in the right order. She shone the torch around the room again, preparing to leave, and the light flickered on a photo in a frame next to the bed. Rowan and Jenna, lit by the summer sun, sitting by Camden Lock and eating ice-cream. Rowan's arm was around her shoulders and Jenna's smile was wide, natural and at ease. Jamie felt sure that he wasn't responsible for her murder. He might well be guilty of other crimes, but not this one, and she wondered again what strings Cameron had pulled to get him arrested while the Nevilles walked free.

Next to the photo was a diary, just a small one, easily overlooked. Jamie picked it up and opened it to the past week. Day-Conti had TG as a regular Friday night appointment and sometimes TG O. TG must be Torture Garden, the club that Day-Conti frequented, but who was O, and would they be there tonight? Jamie looked at her watch. Just before midnight. She replaced the diary next to the bed and slipped down the stairs into the night.

CHAPTER 17

JAMIE CRUISED PAST THE entrance to Torture Garden, slowing down on her bike to get a look at the crowd entering the club. Everyone was dressed up or carried bags, presumably with costumes, that were being searched by the bouncers. Parking a few streets away, Jamie used the mirror on the bike to apply heavy kohl eye makeup, and for good measure, did her lips in black as well. She let her hair swing loose. With pale, feverish skin and deep shadows under her eyes, she looked ghoulish, and black leather suited any occasion. Polly wouldn't like this look, she thought, and a lance of pain thrust through her with the realization that her daughter would never judge her outfit again.

Pushing the heaviness aside, Jamie tried to assume the persona of a sexy party-goer. She tried a smile in the mirror, knowing she had to get into the club because it was the only place she had left to go. Still no good, she thought. She pulled off her biker's jacket and took off her long-sleeve t-shirt, revealing her black bra underneath. She'd lost weight with the last few months of worry, but she still had enough cleavage to attract some attention. It would have to do. She pulled the jacket back on and strode towards the club.

Torture Garden was one of the world's largest fetish and body art clubs, a place where people could indulge in fantasy and experiment on the edge of extremity. Sex had been the last thing on Jamie's mind over the last few years of Polly's illness. There were moments in tango when she felt the thrill of attraction, pressed against a hard body and reveling in the intensity, but that ended when the dance finished. This place was a little outside her comfort zone, but then she was only here to hunt for those who might know Rowan Day-Conti. She had his more recent mugshot in her pocket, but she was aware that this wasn't the kind of place where people wanted to talk to the police. She was here as a seeker, and right now, she felt on the edge of her own sanity. Jamie looked around at the queue of people and thought that perhaps this was exactly where she belonged.

With not much more than a cursory look at her revealing outfit, the bouncers waved Jamie through. She walked into the club as dance music pumped through the atmosphere, making her heart beat in time. Jamie bought a bottled beer and stood on the edge of the dance floor, watching the crowd. There were plenty of people in skin-tight rubber, many with cutouts revealing nipples and buttocks. Couples gyrated in suspended cages, some simulating sex, others presumably doing it while dominatrixes prowled, whipping gimps in face masks. Women danced in little more than string, bound flesh poking from their bonds, but nothing was shocking about the BDSM scene anymore. Most of these people were bankers, lawyers and consultants in the city, taking pleasure in the slick darkness and then returning to work the next day with their secrets intact.

The perfection of the human body was on show, along with every variation on the spectrum of bizarre. Once the eye was used to so much flesh, nudity wasn't interesting anymore and the eye wandered. Jamie was more interested in the people who had crossed the line into true fetishism. A fat man wrapped in Mummy-style bandages stood at the edge of the dance floor, a parody of plastic surgery, dotted lines drawn over the bandages and blood seeping through the female pubic hair drawn over the groin area.

A figure close to Jamie in the full ruffles of Elizabethan dress turned towards her and she saw that the face was an alien mask, a vertical gaping mouth with razor teeth and no eyes, just purple bleeding flesh. Jamie couldn't help but shrink back as a woman in a latex SS officer's uniform pressed herself against the alien creature, her breasts pushed up, nipples revealed by artful holes. Jamie watched the figure's hand go under the woman's short skirt and begin to thrust and rub. She turned away, not wanting to watch the strange coupling as the music faded to a backbeat and then segued into an oriental track.

The crowd turned towards a central stage as the lights dimmed. A spotlight focused on a naked woman standing with her back to the audience, her hands wrapped around a shining silver pole. The bulbous head of an octopus inked in pitch dominated her back with its tentacles winding around her body. The music lifted and she began to dance. As she undulated, the octopus seemed to be moving her limbs, as if she were a puppet unable to escape its grasp. One tentacle wrapped up around her neck, entwining in her hair, another draped around her waist and dipped down between her buttocks. The work was intricate, each sucker on every tentacle finely drawn, the craftsmanship breathtaking. This was truly using the body as a showcase for art, a canvas for creation. Jamie thought how daring the woman must be, to use her body in this way, to make it a physical display and allow people to judge her.

As the woman turned in a slow dance, the full extent of the tattoo was revealed. More tentacles circled her small, tight breasts, one curving around a nipple and the other seemingly caressing the underside. The woman lifted her arms towards the audience, offering herself and it seemed the limbs of the octopus moved with her. One tentacle caressed her stomach and wound down between her legs, tattooed as if it penetrated her there.

The woman used the pole to swing her body up and then hang upside down, stretching her legs wide apart into splits. She tilted her hips towards the audience, showing that she was fully tattooed between them, her sex hairless but black with ink. Jamie could only imagine the pain that this woman had gone through to have her body marked this way, yet there was a surprising lightness in her face as she danced. She wore only pale makeup, keeping the attention on her body, but the slight lines around her eyes suggested that she was in her mid-thirties. Her hair was pixie-cropped, almost white and cut close to her skull. She kept her eyes closed, almost as if she were dancing for an unseen god instead of this hungry crowd. There was a brutal sexuality in the perfection of her body under the lights, but in her face there was only peace. Jamie felt a strange pang of jealousy. This woman was free of expectations, behaving as she wanted and empowered to use her body as she desired. The liberation must be extraordinary, and Jamie felt humbled by the gift that this woman offered, a glimpse into another way of living. Her own freedom seemed so far out of reach.

As the music rose to a crescendo, the woman draped herself away from the audience, leaving the spotlight on the head of the octopus on her back. Jamie presumed that this must be O, the name from Day-Conti's notebook and she was determined to meet her. As the music ramped up the beat and the floor thronged with dancers, Jamie edged around the club toward where the woman had left the stage and slipped into the side corridor away from the main club.

"Hey, this is private. You're not allowed here," a deep voice said, as one of the bouncers stepped from the shadows.

"I need to see O," Jamie said, taking a chance on the name. "It's a personal matter."

The bouncer shrugged, and took a step towards her.

"Sorry lady, it's off limits back here."

Jamie knew this wasn't the time to produce her police credentials, but she was so close.

"Please," she asked, with gentle deliberation. "I'm a fan, and I'm sober and clean. Seriously, I just need to talk to her."

"You're going to have to go back to the club or I'll help you leave." The bouncer sounded final this time, still polite, but dominant.

"Wait," a voice came from down the corridor. Jamie turned to see the woman peering out from one of the doors. "It's OK, Mike. I'll see her."

The bouncer shrugged and stepped back to let Jamie pass.

"Alright, but just call me if you need anything, O."

Jamie walked down the corridor a little way to where the woman stood, the beat of the club fading behind her. O's eyes were a light, cornflower blue, shining with an innocence that jarred with her naked performance of a few minutes before. An ivory robe was loose around her shoulders and one of the octopus tentacles could be seen creeping up her neck, caressing her throat.

"Why did you let me through?" Jamie asked.

O looked at her, and Jamie felt a power in her gaze, as if she could see beyond the surface. Her eyes were much older than the body she wore so well.

"I recognize pain."

Jamie paused, then nodded.

"Then thank you. I'm Jamie."

O stepped aside. "Come in. I'm just getting changed but you're welcome to talk for a while."

Jamie walked into the little space, at once a makeshift powder room for the performance artists and a storage closet. It smelled of old leather with a hint of must and a top note of sandalwood. A long mirror was propped against one wall and Jamie caught sight of her own reflection, scarcely recognizing the gaunt woman in black, harrowed features outlined in kohl. O stood behind her. With her ivory robe, almost white hair and pale features, Jamie felt that she was the demon here and O, an angel.

"Do you know Rowan Day-Conti?" she asked, breaking the momentary silence.

O's eyes met hers, as if chiding her for not asking the deeper questions.

"I heard he'd been arrested," she said, walking a few steps to where a bag hung on the wall. She slipped off the robe and reached for the bag.

Jamie was so close that she could have reached out to touch O's inked, naked skin. On her back, the head of the octopus seemed obscene, its eyes black orbs but still strangely compelling. Jamie wanted to touch it, to touch her. She swallowed. O looked back over her shoulder.

"It's homage," O said, meeting Jamie's gaze and turning, totally secure in her nudity. "The octopus is what you would call my totem animal, a being I feel kinship with."

Jamie nodded, understanding the sentiment and wanting to know more.

"Octopi are so alien to us," O continued, "so unlike our human physiology and yet they have tremendous intelligence. In my country, Norway, there is a legend of the great Kraken, a monster that will sink ships and drag men to the depths. In Japan, there's an artistic tradition depicting violent octopi raping women with thrusting tentacles. And in Hawaiian myth, the octopus is the final survivor from the wreck of the last destroyed universe. So, you see, the image has great power and resonance."

"It's amazing work," Jamie said, "but why ink your body so completely?"

"I can see you're internalizing your pain." O's blue eyes darkened. "Whereas I wear mine on my skin. It reminds me of what I am, of what I've lost." Jamie wanted to hear more, her own troubles briefly forgotten, but O turned away. "Enough of me, Jamie. Why are you here?"

O pulled her clothes from the bag, putting on underwear, a plain t-shirt and jeans. Jamie waited until she was fully dressed, using the time to try and construct a story that didn't reveal too much. Yet she also felt a strange need to be honest with this astonishing woman.

"I saw that Rowan was going to meet with you tonight, and now he's in custody. So I can't talk to him and I was hoping that you might be able to tell me anything you can about his work."

O looked curious. "What, in particular, about his work?"

"I need to know where he gets the bodies, and who buys his finished works."

"Why?' O asked, her face stony now, protecting her friend.

Jamie felt a rising frustration and the feverish headache that had been building couldn't be held back much longer. She couldn't get the image of the dissected little boy out of her mind and she had to be honest, at least about Polly.

"I'm not sure you'll believe me, but my daughter, Polly." Jamie's voice cracked and O's face fell a little, in sympathy. "She died yesterday and her body has been stolen. She bears a resemblance to some of the bodies used in Rowan Day-Conti's artwork and it's the only lead I have right now. I have to find my daughter."

O shook her head slowly, and breathed out, as if making a decision.

"Did you know Jenna Neville?" she asked. Jamie started at the name of the murdered girl.

"Not personally, but I know of her murder and her connection to Rowan. Why?"

O rummaged in her bag and brought out a key.

"I became friends with Jenna, closer friends than with Rowan really. She was investigating Rowan's supplier and his buyers too. She came to me only a few days ago and asked me to keep something for her. Come."

O led the way out of the tiny room, down the corridor away from the club. At the end was another storeroom with lockers in.

"We keep our personal items here when we perform." O explained. "Jenna came to me directly after last week's performance so I left the envelope here." As she unlocked the door, Jamie caught a glimpse of a marine biology textbook and some photos inside. O pulled out a plain blue envelope. "She said she'd received a threat to stop investigating and she wanted to leave this with me instead of carrying it with her. Just in case." O spoke haltingly. "I didn't ask enough about it. I thought she was being overly dramatic, she had that tendency sometimes. But we're used to that here, it's part of the character of the place."

Jamie knew that the envelope should be handled with sterile gloves and placed in an evidence bag. O should be interviewed at the station with proper protocol. All of those thoughts ran through her mind, but there was no time. She would get the envelope to the police in the morning but right now, she had to follow where this path might lead.

"Can you open it now?" Jamie asked.

"I guess Jenna's not coming back for it." Tears welled in O's eyes. "So we might as well."

She tore the top of the envelope and pulled out a wad of white tissue paper. Unfurling it in her hand, O revealed a key. Just plain, no special markings.

"Is there anything else in there?" she asked. "Any indication of what it opens?"

O handed over the envelope and Jamie looked inside, tearing it open for some clue, an address, something. There was nothing.

"I should give this to the police, shouldn't I?" O said. "It might help with her murder investigation. It might even help Rowan, because he can be a bastard, but there's no way he killed her."

"I know he didn't." Jamie said, wrestling with whether to tell O she was with the police. But it would change the dynamic of the situation, betray the woman's trust. Being honest with herself, Jamie wanted O to like her, to see her as an equal, someone who fitted in here. And tonight, Jamie didn't even feel like a cop. She was just another desperate seeker.

"Can I take the key?" she asked, holding her hand out. "I know someone who might be able to find out what it's for."

O hesitated. "What about the police?"

"I think we should leave them out of it for now. Please. They're too busy with the murder to worry about the theft of my daughter's body. I think this key might help."

"If your friend can't find what it's for, then it needs to go to the police," O insisted.

"Of course." Jamie nodded. "First thing tomorrow … How do I find you again?"

O smiled, the drama returning to her eyes. "I'm a performance artist, darling, you can find me everywhere. Online, in the clubs, on the stage."

Jamie felt she had caught a brief glimpse of who O was beneath the tattoos, but now the veil was drawn again as she returned to her stage persona. But her bold example made Jamie want to ink her own pain into her skin.

"Thanks for your help, O, and I loved the show."

O stepped forward and kissed Jamie gently on the cheek, her lips cool on fevered skin.

"Come back soon," O whispered.

Jamie walked back down the corridor and out of the club, passing the freak show on the dance floor. Her heart was scarred like these bodies, her spirit just as twisted. For a moment, Jamie felt a part of them, with an understanding that the body could be a canvas, an external expression of self. She pulled the motorbike jacket tighter around her as she walked away from the club, out into the London dawn. She needed to find out what the key opened without going through official channels, and there was only one person she could think of to help her.

CHAPTER 18

BLAKE SLUNK INTO BAR-BARIAN, the unobtrusive entrance down an alleyway towards Tottenham Court Road in Soho. They knew him well enough in here, understood his habitual drinking, and didn't question his gloved hands and haunted eyes. There were dark posters on the walls of Arnold Schwarzenegger as Conan and Jane Fonda as Barbarella, their swaggering poses a declaration of confident sexuality. Fake double-edged blades hung glinting in reflected light, homage to an era when the struggle to survive eclipsed cerebral concerns. People came here to edge closer to chaos, to tame the crazy and to forget.

Rock music pumped through the bar, heavy enough to thump the heart in time. Blake found that the beat anchored him to reality and he welcomed the throbbing pulse. Seb, the barman, nodded at him and started pouring before Blake had even sat down on one of the tall stools by the chrome counter. It was always the same. Two shots of tequila and a bottle of Becks.

"Bad day?" Seb said, his voice as caring as any barman interested in his alcoholic customers could be, a tone between solicitous and encouraging so that the pounds were all spent before complete oblivion was reached. Blake used to come to the bar only on bad days, but they seemed to be happening more regularly now. He couldn't stop the visions leaking into his waking consciousness, and his ability to hold them back was weakening.

Tonight he was haunted by the mutated monsters in the bell jars of the Hunterian, their preserved flesh trapping them as undead, floating obscenities. He couldn't stop thinking of the scientific brutality of Mengele cutting into live bodies, seeking his perverted truth in vivisection. Over these nightmares, he watched Jamie dancing the tango but as she spun around, her partner was revealed as the Angel of Death, his teeth stained with blood. They were dancing over the bodies of the damned, her spiked heels piercing flesh, her eyes fixed on a horizon that she would never reach.

Blake thought it curious that his mind was spinning dark fantasy from an amalgamation of the visions, but it also worried him. Jamie was clearly affecting him, and he wanted to both protect her and push her out of his life. Helping her was dangerous, for she was already under his skin. He felt the pull of her pain, as a wrecked ship is pulled down to crushing depths.

Slamming back the tequila shots, one after the other, Blake took a pull of the beer. It chased the fiery liquid down, and Blake visualized it burning his visions and dark thoughts away. He waited for the kick of spirits, sipping the beer, now concentrating on the myriad bottles behind the bar, exotic liquids from far flung countries. Sometimes two shots were enough to chase away the demons that lurked in the corners of his mind, but tonight he needed more. The tequila buzz was dulled by years of habituation. He signaled Seb for another round.

Two more shots and another slow beer.

After a few minutes, Blake finally started to feel his tension soften and a tequila haze began to drown out the noise of his inner world. This is what tequila did for him, more of a drug than mere alcohol, changing his perception of the world into some place brighter. It swept the shadows from the corners of his mind and revealed them to be lies, planted there by the curses of his father.

Without the drink, he was alone in the darkness, sure that his true nature was a twisted, rotting thing feeding off pain and memories of torture. He struggled daily against that perception, and the tequila freed him from the chains of lies that his father had told him as a child. Blake pulled off his gloves and ran the fingers of his right hand over the scars on his left, criss-crossed lines of ivory on his cinnamon skin. These patterns intimately marked him, and he knew every stripe.

He thought back to the long nights on his knees by the altar, his father calling desperately to God for deliverance. As a child, Blake had mistakenly thought to share his visions, puzzled by the mirage he glimpsed, a tableau of the past. His father had gathered the faithful and they had held him down, forced his shaking palms out. His father had whipped his hands, prayers driving him into a violent frenzy. Blake was considered possessed, a child used by the Devil for dark purposes. "And if your right eye offend you, pluck it out and cast it from you," his father would intone, his voice carrying the authority of Christ himself.

Blake's hands were the instrument of the Devil's work, so his hands were punished, caned and whipped until they dripped with blood. His mother had wept hysterically and tried to stop the violence, tried to protect her son, but Blake had believed his father was right. He had to be. The man was a prophet in the Old Testament tradition, a figure of gravitas, strength and unshakeable faith. He was a Jeremiah of the present times, weeping for his people even as he ushered them to God's judgment. When he spoke of possession, others listened. Even Blake.

And so he had taken the beatings, clutching at his damaged hands, silent tears spilling down his cheeks as he bore the pain. He almost relished the days afterwards while the scars were forming because he couldn't touch anything and he was freed from what he usually saw in the objects of the world. So many times he had thought the visions gone and he was blessed again, then his father would hold him close and praise God for his redemption. But days later, when the wounds were still raw and weeping, Blake would touch something and the visions would return. His father would push him down to his knees and call for the inner circle to pray again, confident in their ability to eventually vanquish the evil in the child.

Blake took another swig of his beer as the memories flooded through his mind. Perhaps the answers to his present despair lay in the past. He remembered the last time, the final escape from the cycle. He had knelt in penance at the altar, listening to the frenetic prayers of the elders, as they called down power from God in the beginnings of the exorcism ritual. As they were praying, Blake had laid his hands on the Bible that they read the lessons from in the center of the church. In a hazy vision, he had seen what these trusted men were doing, the perversions that were hidden by their veneer of holiness. They touched their daughters, they found pleasure in destructive addiction and even his own father wasn't as holy and blameless as he pretended to be. Blake saw the lies and understood that he was only punished as a scapegoat for their own sin, the beatings harder to cover their own guilt.

As the men had turned to lay their hands upon him once more, Blake had seen anticipated pleasure in the eyes of his father's most trusted minister. The man whipped down a cane and split open a recent wound, blood spotting his clothes. Blake saw excitement in his violence and as the pain lanced through him, he knew that this wasn't God's way, but only man's invention. This curse was just the reality of his life, not Satan's hand. Blake had pulled his hands back so the cane missed on its next swipe and stood to face his tormentors. His father's prayers had faltered at his son's audacity and then he began to shout. "Out, Satan. Leave my boy." But in that moment, Blake had seen eye to eye with his father. During the years of repeated abuse, he had grown into a young man and they had no power to keep him there anymore.

Blake had walked out of that church and never returned to his parent's life. His father was still preaching messages of judgment, destruction and apocalypse; his mother was still in thrall to her prophet. The visions wouldn't leave him, and so Blake had tried to live with them, adapt them to a useful life in his museum research. He had to believe that a normal life was still possible. Blake turned back to the bar and signaled Seb for more tequila.

The fifth shot.

This was the one Blake craved, because this was when the visions of reality finally left him and he slipped into memory loss. A little brain death never hurt anyone, he thought, slamming it back. Swallowing it down, he breathed out in relief, feeling the prick of tears behind his eyes, from the alcohol or his morbid thoughts, he didn't really know which anymore. He blinked the tears back, wondering where the rush of emotion had come from. He didn't want to care for Jamie, didn't want the complication of her in his life. He looked around the bar, searching for the kind of oblivion that could easily be found on a night in London.

The bar turned into a nightclub as it grew later, full of girls in tight tops, hair loose about their faces, taut stomachs curving down into fitted jeans. Blake turned on the stool to watch a girl dancing, appreciating the glimpse of soft flesh, wanting to lay his head there and forget. Young men circled around the edges, predators waiting for the sedation of alcohol to lower inhibitions. But Blake knew that there were women just as predatory, and there was a point when tequila turned him into willing prey. Women were drawn to him, the very fact that he generally avoided them was nectar that drew them in. Like cats, some women were best attracted by a kind of detachment, an inattention they had to conquer. Blake knew his bone structure helped, for sure, and despite his lack of care, his body was strong and muscular, clinging to life even as his mind struggled to escape it.

A woman danced closer and then leaned into him, her long blonde hair reflecting the spotlights. Her eyes were sultry, inviting.

"Dance with me," she whispered, placing her hand on Blake's chest. He felt a surge of desire, a need to bury himself within her and forget this day. He stood and pulled her towards him as a heavy bass rocked them. His hands slid down to cup her buttocks and tug her closer. He felt the tendrils of her life knocking against the walls of his vision but the tequila haze kept them far enough away and Blake reveled in the release.

The woman smelled of vanilla and coconut and he breathed in her scent. Then the woman's hands were inside his shirt, touching the muscles on his tight stomach and edging downwards. It was permission: all he had to do was bend to her mouth and tonight he could lose himself in her.

Lifting his head, he caught sight of their reflection in one of the barbarian blades, just another couple desperate to lose themselves for a few hours. London was full of this need, an attempt to stave off loneliness, even though in the morning there was so often regret. Under his close-cropped hair, Blake saw the shadows under his eyes, making his face even more angular. He looked haunted and there was no escaping, least of all from himself. Even the fifth tequila could not drown his life right now.

"I'm sorry," he whispered to the woman and opened his arms to let her go. She shook her head slowly but in her eyes was a crazy need and she backed into the dancing crowd. She wouldn't be alone tonight, but Blake felt that he should be.

CHAPTER 19

JAMIE PULLED UP IN front of the tall terraced houses of Bloomsbury, distinctive in this area of gentrified London. Street lamps lit the quiet streets with a glow that only seemed to accentuate the fog of chill air in the hour before dawn. The area was dotted by large garden squares, many of them locked for residents only, but Jamie could just make out the trees of Bloomsbury Square Gardens, where in the summer, students and tourists lazed by opulent flowerbeds.

She wondered how Blake could afford a place here, right around the corner from the British Museum. The area was saturated in history and academic brilliance, from the London School of Hygiene and Tropical Medicine, to the Royal Academy of Dramatic Art and the University of London. It had been made famous by the Bloomsbury Set, an influential group of British writers, artists and intellectuals including Virginia Woolf, EM Forster and John Maynard Keynes, luminaries who had lived or worked here during the early twentieth century. Jamie looked up at the blue plaques on the houses in front of her, marking places of historical significance across London, littering this district with great names from British history. Darwin and Dickens once lived here, as did JM Barrie, whose Peter Pan visited Wendy Darling amongst these rooftops. Jamie smiled as she remembered Polly finding that out on the internet after they had read the book together. Her daughter had always wanted to know more, never satisfied with what was on the surface. The memory stung her with a jolt of grief and she caught her breath, willing it to pass.

Now she was here, Jamie desperately wanted to ring Blake's bell and get him out of bed, to plead for his help. But she knew she looked like a crazy Goth, and at this time in the morning he was unlikely to be conducive to helping her on unofficial business. Jamie slumped on the bike, her shoulders dropping as a wave of tiredness hit her. The ride from the club and the thrill of finding a clue had invigorated her, but now she felt unsure. Should she just take the key straight to Cameron and the investigation team? But then what? Jamie suddenly felt very alone.

She heard footsteps and looking up, she saw a figure weaving up the street, his silhouette familiar. As he drew closer, Jamie realized that it was Blake, and he was singing something unintelligible in an actually half-decent voice. He was definitely drunk and, as he reached his door, Jamie made a decision. She got off the bike and holding her helmet, ran across the quiet street.

"Blake," she said, as she approached. He spun round to see who it was, his face confused for a moment as he looked at her. "Hi Blake, it's Jamie."

He squinted at her, then grinned and the smile transformed his face, like a little boy proudly showing off his skills.

"Jamie ... hot Detective. You're really here?" He shook his head in wonder, like she was the fulfillment of some kind of wish. "Wow, you're looking... hot tonight. Love the black. Very alternative you."

His cobalt blue eyes raked over her body and Jamie could see his blatant appreciation, the alcohol preventing any form of inhibition. He stammered into silence as Jamie met his eyes, bemused. She was definitely stepping over the line being here with him in this state, but she needed his unique talent. If she took the key to Cameron, it could disappear into evidence for days and she needed to find what Jenna had hidden before the Lyceum deadline tonight.

"Why are you here?" Blake asked. "It's a bit late for me to help on police business tonight and I ... may have had a few drinks." He finished in a loud whisper. "Sorry."

Jamie stepped closer to him.

"I need your help, Blake, but it's not for the police right now. It's for the case but I'm investigating it separately." Blake looked confused. Jamie shook her head. "It doesn't really matter, but it's urgent and I need you to do a reading."

"Shh. Keep your voice down," Blake hushed her. "I don't like to talk about that in the open. You'd better come up."

He fumbled in his inner pockets and pulled out his wallet and key fob. His hands were bare and the scars reflected light from the street lamps. Jamie thought of the body art at Torture Garden, self-inflicted shades of pain that revealed inner lives. But Blake's weren't artistic markings, they were violent cuts, evidence of another wounded soul. For a moment, she wanted to reach out and trace the lines.

Blake managed to get the key in the lock, pushed open the door and led the way into a darkened hallway. There were a number of doors leading to inner flats and a staircase heading upwards.

"This way," Blake whispered, pointing at the staircase. "I'm right at the top."

He took the lead, swaying a little on the way up and Jamie wondered if he would be any use at all for reading. Part of her doubted it would work, but right now she would take any help she could get. At the top was a tiny landing and one faded red door.

Blake turned another key in the lock and pushed open the door for Jamie to enter. The space was small but neatly laid out with a few pieces of wooden furniture, creating a homely feel. Jamie was immediately captivated.

"It's not much," Blake said, "but I can't resist living in a real artist's garret in Bloomsbury. It's my spiritual home." He pointed to the large window. "Check out the view."

Jamie walked three steps to cross the flat and gaze out the window, over the rooftops to the moon shining above the chimneys and spires of London. Jamie thought of Polly, flying off to Never-Never Land across these skies. She turned.

"I'm sorry to come to you privately like this, but I need help with something." She reached inside her jeans pocket and pulled out the key. "I need you to read this. I have to find what it unlocks, because I think there's information there that I need urgently and time is critical."

Blake rubbed his head and then sat heavily on the bed, his eyes drooping with tiredness.

"I'd love to help you, Jamie, but this is the way I numb the visions. This is how I kill them. The finest tequila will always crowd out any demons that threaten my peace. Please don't ask me to try and pierce the happy haze." He looked up at her and Jamie caught a glimpse of the little boy again, asked to do things he didn't want to and then punished for it anyway. But she pushed aside her guilt.

"But can you?" she asked, desperate to know what might be possible.

"I don't know. I don't want to know." He shook his head. "You don't realize what my life is like. The visions come to me unwanted, unasked for. I see too much, Jamie, and this is how I numb them." He gazed out the window, speaking softly. "But it's taking more and more tequila these days. I don't know what will kill me first, the madness or the booze."

Jamie felt a surge of pity, for whatever Blake heard and saw, it was real to him. Whether it was mental illness, a supernatural gift, or a part of the brain he could access that most could not, she didn't know. But she could see that he was hurting and alone, and she recognized her own torment in that state. Part of her wanted to pull him to her, to soothe their pain together but instead, she sat next to him on the bed, careful not to touch him.

"My daughter, Polly, died yesterday." Jamie's throat tightened with emotion. She heard Blake's intake of breath but she kept staring out the window, wanting to tell him the story. "She's been ill a long time with a genetic disease, but she was only 14. Too young to die, even though we'd been preparing for it for years. I wanted to say goodbye in the way she had chosen, a cremation where she could be released to the sky and then her ashes buried to bloom into flowers. She knew exactly what would happen after she died." Jamie stopped and turned to Blake, looking into his eyes. "But her body has been stolen and I have to get it back."

"No," Blake gasped. "Seriously, what are the police doing?"

"They'll do their best, but I can't be a part of the official investigation as I'm too close to it, and I can't just sit around and wait."

Blake shook his head. "Of course ... but that's just awful, Jamie. I'm so sorry."

Jamie heard the truth of his concern in Blake's voice. Yet how could this man care so much for her so quickly? She remembered he had seen Polly in his vision of her. He had felt her pain, and his empathy scared her. This man knew her inner world and yet they had only just met. Jamie felt laid bare, part of her wanting to run out the door right now and never see him again, because she didn't let people get this close. It was the way to ensure she was never hurt again, but she couldn't run. She had sought Blake out, and she needed his help.

She stood and walked to the window.

"I think Polly's body was stolen because of what I've

been investigating on the Jenna Neville case," Jamie said. "I thought perhaps you might be able to help and I can't wait until morning. This is urgent, Blake."

He considered for a moment. "Tell me about this key."

"It was Jenna's and she gave it to a friend. I only found it an hour ago and if I give it to the police, the processing will take too much time. But if you read it, we might be able to find the place it belongs to. It might lead me to Polly's body, Blake, and perhaps help me to solve Jenna's murder. They have to be related." Jamie paused, and then decided to tell Blake as much as she knew. There was nothing to lose anymore. "Jenna Neville had noted something called the Lyceum in her diary for tonight. She also had articles on body snatching at her office, marked with an L, and she was warned off investigating them. I think that what she discovered led to her death, and I think they have Polly's body too." Her voice cracked a little. "I can't stand the thought of them cutting up my daughter's body like a specimen for their cabinet of curiosities. I can't let that happen to Polly and so, I really need you, because I don't know what else to do right now."

"The specimens in the museum … the mutilation of dead bodies … Mengele and the dissections. Oh, Jamie," Blake said, his voice betraying horror at the possibilities. Even through the fog of tequila she could see he understood the parallels. "You think the same people have Polly's body? And if they do, they will …" He went silent for a moment, and Jamie saw his eyes darken. " Of course, I'll try to help." Blake dropped his head to his hands. "Shit. This is serious. I guess I can try but I've never read after this much tequila before. That's kind of the point."

Jamie nodded. "I understand, but anything you can give me is better than nothing. This is the only clue I have. Please try."

"I'm not promising anything but put it on the table."

He pointed to a low table at the side of the room under the window. It was dark wood, plain, with nothing on it. "Give me a minute."

Blake stood and walked into the adjoining tiny bathroom, shutting the door behind him. Jamie placed the key on the table with some reverence, hoping like hell he could get something from it. There was a part of her that was screaming disorder at this whole process, the skeptical part of her, the police officer who at least tried to play by the rules most of the time. That part of her wanted to run out of there, hand the key over and leave it to the investigation team.

But Jamie knew the system. She knew that, however hard the police worked, there were priorities, and investigation according to protocol took time. Time she didn't have, and after all, she was Polly's mother, her protector in life and death and her daughter was not resting in peace. The image of her body on a slab, like the little boy at Day-Conti's studio, dominated her mind.

Blake emerged, his hair wet from splashing his face.

"Do you want coffee?" Jamie asked. "Would that help?"

Blake shook his head. "Not at this point. Just sit quietly while I read and note down anything I say. I can't promise much, though."

Jamie nodded and sat on the bed, a piece of paper and pen on her lap as Blake knelt in front of the table. From behind he looked like a penitent, praying at a shrine to emptiness. He breathed in and out slowly, rolling his shoulders around in an attempt to relax. He picked up the key. Jamie waited, trying to breathe quietly, not moving for fear of breaking whatever trance state he went into.

Blake was silent for nearly two minutes before he spoke.

"Corinthian columns. Yellow."

Jamie frowned, writing it down.

"Looks like a church or a temple, but definitely yellow." Blake's voice was strained as if he were peering into the gloomy distance. "She's worried, afraid. She knows some-thing she shouldn't. More yellow." Blake paused. "Green apple." He went silent for a moment and then put down the key. He turned on his knees to look at Jamie, his face distraught. "Sorry, that's it. There's an overwhelming sense of yellow. I don't know whether that helps but there's no deeper level on an object like this. It's a new key with only her imprint, but it's all so faint."

Jamie felt disappointed at what he had told her. His words seemed like impossible clues.

"Look," Blake said, "Why don't you stay here and use my laptop to do some online research. I need a couple of hours' sleep but then I can try again. Or you could go home and come back later."

Jamie thought about her empty flat, Polly's belongings reminding her of everything she had lost. "I'd like to stay, if that's OK. You've given me a few things to check out … if you don't mind."

"Sure. There's coffee and a bit of food in the kitchen. Help yourself. I'll sleep like the dead so you won't wake me with any noise." He stopped, realizing what he'd said. "Sorry, that was a stupid thing to say."

Jamie shook her head, smiling at him gently. "It's alright, seriously, go to sleep. I can see you need it."

"You look like you could do with some too," Blake said softly, and Jamie felt the deep fatigue that had seeped into her body over the long night. She shook her head.

"There'll be time for that later when I've found my daughter."

Blake logged onto his laptop and Jamie sat at his plain IKEA desk with a side lamp on, her back to the bed as she heard the rustle of him taking off his jeans and slipping under the covers. There was a curious intimacy between them, and she felt a moment of wanting his comfort. If she went to him now, what would he do? Jamie knew that she would shatter with physical touch, grief would pour from her and the waves of desolation would crash against them both.

She pulled herself together and went to the bathroom. She washed her face, wiping off the black makeup until she was scrubbed clean. Emerging quietly, Jamie listened to the noises of the house. The pipes groaned and there were creaks, the sounds of an old area, a good house. Outside, she could hear the city waking up, buses going past and cars starting up.

At the laptop, Jamie opened Google and went to the Maps application. She went to London and zoomed in to a scale that showed where Jenna Neville had worked and where she had lived South of the river. She added in the Torture Garden Club in East London. It was a good few square miles, but not exhaustive. As she studied the screen, there was a meow at the window and a faint scratching. Jamie looked up to see a black cat with white paws and a cheek smudge pawing at the glass. On the windowsill she noticed a saucer with a little dry food. So Blake was a cat person, bonding with the independent. She smiled and got up to open the window a little way so the cat could wend its way in.

"Hello, puss," Jamie whispered, stroking as it nibbled at the food. It butted up against her hand. She smiled and picked it up, holding it close to her face, feeling its warmth. There was something therapeutic about stroking. The Lavender Hospice used animals as part of their therapy for the children, although perhaps the parents needed it more. She carried the cat back to the desk and sat down, stroking it firmly on her lap. It circled a little, kneading its paws and then settled against her. Jamie was glad for its companionship. She caressed the cat with one hand and with the other doodled on the pad where she had written Blake's words.

She tried to put herself in Jenna's shoes. She had needed somewhere to keep secrets from her flatmate, her parents, her work, basically away from anyone. Jenna certainly had a trust problem, Jamie thought, and she could relate to that. But what could be so secret that it was worth killing her for?

If it was some files, like Jenna had at work, they could be kept within a small locker. Jamie wrote down locker, then brainstormed options around that. The threat of terrorists meant that most train and bus stations no longer had lockers, and libraries and gyms cleared them out most nights. Jamie wrote down 'gym' since sometimes they rented lockers long term, but whatever Jenna was hiding might not be something so small. The key could unlock a safe or even something as big as another flat. Despite her activism, Jenna still had money, so that wouldn't have been a problem.

Jamie nuzzled down onto the cat's head.

"Too many options, puss," she whispered, stroking it and feeling its purr resonate through her.

Maybe she should just try using the words Blake had given her.

She typed "yellow + lockup" into Google.

The first results were technical errors for Ubuntu software, yellow lockups on splash pages. She scrolled down to Skull Candy yellow lockup belts and yellow transmission belts, becoming lost in the technical rabbit hole she had stumbled into. But further down, Jamie found Big Yellow Self Storage, a company with lockup space of all sizes dotted around the country and with a number of sites in London. Jamie felt a wave of excitement run through her. It fitted, now she just had to narrow the location down. After a few more mouse clicks, she found there were a few units around the places Jenna lived and worked and also near Torture Garden.

Using Google Maps street view, Jamie started to examine the pictures of the locations. The minutes ticked by as she virtually walked the streets of London, using the technology to view snapshots in time.

Then she saw it.

Opposite the New Cross storage facility was the Lewisham Arthouse, featuring a classical entranceway with a large door framed by Corinthian columns, fitting Blake's description. Jamie virtually walked down the street a little way and found a pub called the Flower of Kent. On the sign above the door was a picture of a tree and a green apple on the ground under it, representing the tree under which Newton had been sitting when the apple fell, giving him the idea for the law of gravity. It had to be the place.

Jamie checked the opening time for the storage facility. 8am. It was only 6.40am now, so she could be there when it opened. Looking behind her at the bed, she could see a mound of covers under which Blake slept silently. She still found his ability disturbing and it wasn't admissible in court, but anything she found at the site would be. She could keep the secret of how she found the place but she could still give the key and the address to the investigation team after she'd discovered what was inside.

She wrote a short note to Blake saying thank you and that she would call him, that he was a star. He'd probably read it and wonder what the hell he'd done the night before under the tequila influence. Jamie rose and gave the cat another cuddle, relishing its warm body for a moment longer. She put it down gently on the chair, stroking it so it settled into her warm patch. Then she let herself out of the flat, pulling the door quietly shut behind her.

CHAPTER 20

JAMIE PARKED THE BIKE down a side street off the main road of Lewisham Way. There was still some time before the storage office opened so she walked down and got a takeaway coffee from a service station. She poured two sugars into it and grabbed a Mars bar at the same time. The spike of sugar and caffeine would keep her going just a little bit longer.

She sat on the steps of the Arthouse looking at the Yellow storage units, and wondered what Jenna had hidden here. What was so secret that she kept her research away from her work and home life? And would there be clues to the location of the Lyceum?

At five to eight, Jamie watched a car pull up and a woman reach out the window to key in a code on the main gate. The gate swung open and a few minutes later Jamie saw her unlock and enter the office. At exactly one minute past eight, Jamie walked across the road and rang the bell.

"We're not quite open yet. Can you wait five minutes?" The voice was hassled, clearly annoyed to be buzzed so early.

"I'm from the police," Jamie said, deciding to approach with official credentials, omitting the fact she was off the investigation. "Detective Sergeant Jamie Brooke. I need to speak with you about one of the storage units."

"Oh," the voice sounded unsurprised. "Of course, come on in."

A buzzer sounded and the pedestrian gate clicked open. Jamie walked in and showed the manager her warrant card. The woman was in her mid-forties, Asian, her dark hair tied back into a ponytail. She had the efficient air of a born organizer, and she nodded at the credentials, clearly used to dealing with the police.

"How can I help you, Detective?" she asked. "There hasn't been a break-in, not that I know of. We had one last year, but you can't be here about that."

"I'm actually investigating a murder, and it looks like the victim had a locker here. I need to see inside."

The woman looked at once appalled and intrigued. The cop shows on TV made people want to be part of crime scenes these days.

"Of course, we have strict privacy regulations here but ..." Jamie could see the interest in the woman's eyes. "What was the victim's name?"

For a moment Jamie wondered if Jenna could have used a fake name, but there were so many rules around multiple forms of ID, it was unlikely.

"Jenna Neville."

The woman tapped on her computer. "Yes, I have her here. Number 714. It's a mid-size lockup, able to store a three-bedroom house worth of stuff."

Jamie pulled the key from her pocket. "Would this be the key for it?"

The woman glanced up. "Oh no, they're all number coded on a keypad, but I can let you in with the override. I'll take you right up."

As Jamie wondered what the key could actually be for, the manager led the way through the sterile complex, the bright yellow walls only serving to highlight the dead space.

Full of secrets, Jamie imagined. What else might be hiding in the corners of this place? What stories would be revealed by the objects within?

On the second floor, at the very back of the complex, the manager stopped in front of one of the myriad yellow doors. She tapped a code into the keypad and the door clicked.

"Go ahead, Detective," she said. "I'll leave you to it. Just come and check with me before you leave."

Jamie nodded, wondering at her lack of curiosity about what might be inside. Perhaps it wore off after years of working here. She listened to the woman's footsteps receding down the hallway, echoing around the empty space. She imagined Jenna coming here alone, keeping the location quiet and not trusting anyone with the information inside. Blake had said that she was afraid, worried, when she held the key, and Jamie felt the same way right now. She was afraid to go in, because the contents might not be enough to give her the answers she needed. What if this didn't lead her to Polly? What would she do then?

Jamie pulled on a pair of sterile gloves, took a deep breath and pulled the door open. The space was about six foot wide, almost the same deep, with a high ceiling so that boxes could be stacked up. The only thing on the floor was a heavy metal safe and Jamie felt for the key in her pocket. She stepped inside the unit and saw that the walls were plastered with images and maps. Here was Jenna's extensive research spread out and expanded, and Jamie could see that the notes she had seen in the legal office were just a tiny part of the whole.

There were newspaper cuttings about crimes involving bodies, notes on art shows using body parts, photos of teratology specimens, historical references to John Hunter and other anatomists, as well as gruesome pictures of anatomy and quotes from legal papers on the rights of the body. On one wall was pinned the logo of Neville Pharmaceuticals and radiating out from it were all kinds of documents and sticky notes, curling at the edges. There were pictures of vivisections and animal cruelty as well as a photocopy of a very old newspaper article about the violent death of a PhD student at Oxford, back when the Nevilles were students. There was a photo of Esther Neville, looking pale and gaunt, her arm thrust out to obscure the view of the camera. It wasn't the type of picture that a daughter would usually want to keep of her mother.

Clearly, Jenna had quite a story here. Jamie couldn't quite work out all the links but it was far bigger than she expected. She couldn't keep this from the police investigation, but she could get a head start on finding the Lyceum. Pulling the key from her pocket, Jamie squatted down and opened the safe. With her heart beating in anticipation, she pulled open the metal door.

Inside were a just couple of pieces of paper. Jamie knew that she was breaking all the rules of police investigation but she was well past caring at this point. She had to know what was going on. Carefully lifting the top paper from the pile, Jamie unfolded it. A photocopy of a title deed for a piece of land in West Wycombe. Jamie frowned, not seeing any immediate significance, for there was no mention of the Lyceum.

"Found something?" The voice made her jump and she looked up, startled, her posture immediately defensive and shielding the safe.

It was Blake, holding two cups of coffee. His body was slouched against the door, languid confidence in his stance and Jamie couldn't help noticing how good he looked, all tousled and sleep-rumpled.

"Damn it, Blake," she said, "How did you find me?"

"Browser history." He shrugged. "I woke up and found you gone but your note had me hooked. Plus, I want to help you."

Jamie's eyes softened as she stood to take the coffee from him. Her fingers touched his gloved hand briefly and even through the cloth she could feel a spark between them. She realized that she was actually glad to see him.

"Thanks." She smiled up at him. "How's the hangover?"

Blake blushed a little. "I'm sorry you had to see me like that. When the visions get too much I have to escape. Tequila is the easiest, more effective way I know to tame the crazy. I hope I didn't say anything ... inappropriate?"

"Of course not." Jamie took a sip of the coffee. "But I'm not sure that pickling yourself in tequila is a long-term life strategy."

"You can talk," he said, grinning. "Riding around town like some kind of vampire Goth when you should be looking after yourself."

He paused, his eyes full of compassion. "I'm so sorry about your daughter."

Jamie turned to the wall, hiding the tears pricking her eyes.

"Thank you ... Well, since you're here, what do you think?"

"It's definitely yellow," Blake said. "A bit bright for me at this point."

Jamie pointed to the collage.

"Check this out. It's on body snatching, and it looks like a full-scale investigation into her parents' past and the history of Neville Pharmaceuticals."

Blake came to stand next to her, close in the small space. He smelled of spicy soap and coffee and Jamie felt a sudden desire to lean into his tall frame. She pushed away the feelings.

"Wow, this is some serious investigative work," he said. "She was a journalist?"

"A lawyer," Jamie said, "but this is personal. That's her mother and that there is her father." She pointed at the aristocratic portrait of Christopher Neville, dressed in his regalia for the House of Lords but with his head turned towards the camera in a smile. The photo was softer, more emotionally resonant, than the one of Esther. Her choice of image painted him as someone Jenna had loved. But had he ultimately betrayed her?

Turning her head, Jamie caught a glimpse of another face she recognized.

"That's Edward Mascuria," she whispered. "He works for the Nevilles."

Jenna's research wall had linked him to various projects at Neville Pharma and there was a picture of him with Esther, an obsequious look on his face as she presented him with some award. Jamie remembered how she had felt in his flat, a crawling across her flesh, the look on his face that she had glimpsed as she rode away.

"What was on the document in the safe?" Blake asked, interrupting her train of thought, his head on one side to examine the material tacked up on the other wall.

"A property deed," Jamie said. "For land in West Wycombe. I'm not sure what it means yet."

They were silent for a moment as they continued to scan the densely packed walls of information.

"I think you should look at this," Blake said.

Jamie turned to look at the montage, the word Lyceum scrawled in the center of the mass in Jenna's looped handwriting. The images circling it were cut from old newspapers and magazines, others printed from the internet. They showed bacchanalian scenes of orgies and feasting, sacrificing to the Devil, sex on altars and then in one, a corpse being cut up and dissected as figures copulated around it, faces distorted by lust. A chill crept over Jamie's skin.

"What is this?" she said, a frown creasing her brow as she bent closer to examine the pictures, trying to work out what they were about.

"Look here," Blake said. "It says that the Hellfire Club had its headquarters in caves under the hills of West Wycombe. This picture shows a map of the cave system and Jenna's research seems to point to this as the meeting place for the Lyceum."

Jamie looked confused. "I'm sure I've heard of the Hellfire Club before."

"It's infamous," Blake said. "It's been in lots of films and books, but it was actually a real club. Back in the eighteenth century, it was established by Sir Francis Dashwood under the motto *'Fais ce que tu voudras'* or *'Do what you want'* and history is rife with rumors of what they did down there in the dark, beyond the reach of the law."

Jamie looked at one image, a man carving his own heart from his chest and offering it to a laughing figure, who bent with jaws open to bite into it.

"If they met in the caves back then, maybe they still do now. So who owns it?"

She turned and bent to the safe again, removing the title deed to look at it more closely. It was registered to the Neville Foundation, one of the many holding companies of the Nevilles.

"I still don't know what's going on," Jamie said, rubbing her eyes. "But clearly Jenna linked the Lyceum to this location and her family. Maybe she challenged them about it. Maybe she threatened to expose them."

"And that may have been what got her killed," Blake said, turning to her. He was so close inside the unit and as he looked down at Jamie, his blue eyes showed deep concern. Jamie felt the weariness of the last twenty-four hours pressing upon her, the emotional exhaustion and the edge of physical collapse. All she wanted to do was lean into his strength and wait for him to put his arms around her. She could sense an attraction between them, even in these desperate times, despite her overwhelming need to find Polly.

Jamie bit her lip, the stab of pain helping her to refocus. "According to Jenna's diary, the Lyceum meets tonight."

There was a beat of silence.

"You want to go, don't you?" Blake said finally. Jamie didn't respond, staring at the images in front of her. "But I think it's time to let your friends in the police deal with this."

She looked at her watch.

"There's no time," she whispered.

Blake took her hands in his gloved ones, spinning her towards him.

"No, it's too dangerous. You can't go. Think of your daughter. She wouldn't want you to put yourself in danger like this."

Jamie snatched her hands away.

"I *am* thinking of Polly," she shouted, tears spilling from her eyes. "I'm only thinking of her."

Blake turned and banged his fist on the wall, the metallic sound echoing through the empty corridors. His face betrayed his frustration and Jamie was surprised at his vehemence, but she also felt a flicker of gratitude that he cared enough to protest.

"I need to call this in," she said. "So the police team can get round here and follow the new leads. But I know they won't be fast enough to get to the Lyceum tonight. There's too much information to process. I have to go myself."

"I'll come with you, then," Blake said, his eyes pleading.

Jamie sighed. "Thank you for your support, seriously. But I need to do this alone."

"You don't have to do everything alone, Jamie." He took a step closer to her. "Taking the world onto your shoulders will only crush you unless you let people help ... people who care."

At another time, Jamie knew that she would have leaned into his embrace, but she felt her resolve would crack if he

192

touched her. The deep grief she was barely holding in check would break over them both and she would never stop crying. She had to keep it together, and being alone was the only way.

She stepped back, her face stony and her voice cold.

"I'm a police officer, Blake. This is my job and I know what I'm doing. You wouldn't be of any use."

He looked at her and she held his gaze, unflinching.

"Fine." Blake's voice was curt, his jaw tight with emotion. Jamie almost begged him to stay, craving his strength and support. Instead, she turned to look at the wall again, studying the images there without seeing. "I'll leave you to it then."

Blake walked out of the lockup and took a few steps down the corridor, then stopped. Jamie thought he was going to turn and say something. Perhaps that's all it would take to break her resolve. But then he walked on, without looking back.

When his footsteps had faded to nothing, Jamie took a deep breath and put her thoughts of Blake aside. She used her smart phone to carefully photograph the evidence that Jenna had collected: the title deed, the photos of key suspects and some of the newspaper cuttings. Jamie was convinced that Cameron or someone at the department was trying to frame Day-Conti, but this evidence would surely get him released and the investigation refocused on the Nevilles.

She called Missinghall, knowing that she couldn't direct this to Cameron in case he really was involved with the Nevilles. The phone rang three times before he picked up.

"Jamie, are you OK? I heard about the theft of your daughter's body. I'm so sorry."

"Thanks Al, I think it's related to the Jenna Neville case, but I need you to keep that quiet for now."

A beat of silence as her words sunk in. "Sure, but shouldn't you be resting or something? This is a difficult time for you,

Jamie."

"I have to work, Al, there's no time for me to wait around, and I've found new evidence you need to get the team onto."

"Are you at the scene? I'll come over right now. Shit. How are we going to handle this?"

"Nothing to handle," Jamie said. "I'll text you the address and you get started."

"Won't you be there when we arrive?"

She was silent.

"Jamie? Where are you going? Seriously, what are you up to?"

Jamie knew her actions were reckless, crazy, but mostly she didn't care anymore. She had nothing more to lose.

"I can't tell you yet Al, but I'll call it in when I can."

"Then at least be careful, and let me know if I can help."

"Later, then," Jamie said and ended the call.

With some cleaning materials she found down the hallway, Jamie wiped any fingerprints from the key so that O and Blake's involvement couldn't be traced. She knew it was tampering with evidence but with her suspicions of Cameron, she couldn't have them under suspicion and her actions were for a greater good. She placed the key on top of the safe and then left the lockup, telling the manager on the way out that her team would be coming along later that day.

CHAPTER 21

As Jamie traveled West along the motorway out of London, she felt a sense of purpose again, as if by moving she could outrun the pain of Polly's loss. She had briefly gone home to shower, change and pack a small rucksack, expecting to be away for the night and in need of a torch and other gear for investigating further. She had also downed another coffee and taken several more ephedrine tablets. Jamie felt the beginnings of shakiness from the sleep deprivation and the pills, but she was also running on a kind of nervous energy that fueled her need to go on. She couldn't rest until this was over.

The M40 motorway was busy, but her bike helped her to navigate the snarls in traffic, and soon Jamie reached the turnoff for High Wycombe. Dominated by industrial warehouses, there was still evidence of the medieval market town amongst the concrete modernity. As Jamie rode through the outskirts, she caught sight of the Neville Pharmaceuticals logo on some of the warehouse buildings: they were one of the biggest employers in the area.

She continued out of the town towards the village of West Wycombe in the Chilterns, and even this close to the motorway the English countryside welcomed her. Jamie rode under a great canopy of beechwood trees, grey-green trunks stretching high, bare branches reaching to the sky forming a guard of honor. A cool winter sun dappled patches on the road and Jamie felt a touch of its rays like a blessing.

As she entered the village of West Wycombe, Jamie realized that the Hellfire Caves were now a popular tourist attraction, and her hopes sank as she realized the Lyceum couldn't possibly meet somewhere so public. Parking the bike, she walked up to the entranceway of the caves. It was designed as a Gothic church, with tall arched windows revealing the wooded forest behind, a cathedral revering nature. Jamie hesitated at the entrance, then decided to take a tour anyway. If there was nothing here, she would have to revisit all of the evidence in the photos but why else would Jenna have the title deeds in the safe? This location had to be important.

As she stood waiting for the tour, cold air seeped into Jamie's bones, sapping her energy further. She shivered. Was this just a wild goose chase? Right now, the only clues she had that could lead to Polly pointed at these caves. There must be something down here that would help her with the next steps.

A guide gathered a group of woolen-wrapped tourists together and Jamie joined them.

"Welcome to the Hellfire Caves," the guide said. "Originally of ancient origin, these caves were extended in the 1740s by Sir Francis Dashwood. They were dug by villagers in need of employment and you can still see the pick axe marks on the walls. Here's your maps." She handed out a page. "You won't get lost, just follow the guide ropes and it's well lit. But watch out for the ghosts." She smiled, trying to inject some enthusiasm into her voice but Jamie caught an edge of boredom there. Another day, another tourist. Our lives are so dominated by minutiae, Jamie reflected, the day to day, never-ending grind. She could understand the attraction of something secret and exclusive, where people felt special and chosen. Membership of such societies was common across all cultures, but more so amongst the rich and powerful with time and money to spare. The Freemasons, and indeed, the Hellfire Club, had counted some of the most senior British aristocrats and statesmen of the time as members.

Jamie looked down at the little map, and waited until the rest of the group had gone in before she entered. She wanted to sense how the place felt without others around and she couldn't cope with the noise of tourists intruding into her thoughts. Part of her was breaking inside, desperate to hold Polly's body in her arms again, but she had to assume the mantle of the detective and focus on being objective.

She stepped inside the entranceway and began to walk down the slight incline, the ground hard under her feet. The temperature was warmer in the caves as they retained the heat and in the winter were more comfortable than the air outside. A straight entrance tunnel led to a small cave, stacked with tools similar to those used by the eighteenth century workers. Jamie looked at the picks and crowbars, wondering whether they might have seen violence beyond digging in the caves.

Walking on into Paul Whitehead's chamber, Jamie read the notes next to the grand urn and bust of the man. A steward of the Hellfire Club, Whitehead had left his heart to Sir Francis Dashwood. A mental image of the dying man suddenly came to Jamie, Whitehead's chest cracked open so his still pulsing heart could be ripped from his body. She shook her head. Where did these thoughts come from? She shivered, realizing that the temperature in the caves had dropped as she descended. Reading on, she noted that Whitehead's ghost was thought to watch over the caves, remaining with the desiccated relic of his heart. The man had protected the club in life, even burning papers containing evidence that might have revealed the Hellfire activities just before he died.

Walking deeper into the caves, Jamie entered Franklin's Cave. The American Founding Father and polymath, Benjamin Franklin, had been a great admirer of Dashwood and his diaries revealed that he had visited the caves, although not as an official member of the Club. Further on was the Banqueting Hall, forty feet in diameter with statues of classical figures in chalk niches. In between the wider caverns, tunnels were shaped into beautiful Gothic arches, giving the impression of an underground castle. There were dark portals off the side of the main corridor, shut off with rope and No Entry signs. Jamie decided to check further into one, but just beyond the light of the lamp, the tunnel had a metal gate, heavily reinforced and locked. Jamie shook the bars, testing their strength, wondering what was in the caves beyond her sight. What went on here after dark when the tourists left?

Navigating the tunnels hacked into the chalk, Jamie finally reached a small waterway that ran through the caves. It was studded with stalactites that hung from the ceiling, twisted shapes dripping stagnant water into a stream. Named the River Styx, it represented the boundary between the living and the dead in ancient Greek mythology, where the wrathful drowned each other for eternity in Dante's Hell. It could only be crossed by paying the ferryman with coins that were laid on the eyes of the dead. At the end of the channel was the Cursing Well, where a strange mist hung over a pool, like the fetid breath of slimy creatures dwelling in the shadows. The lights flickered and Jamie felt her pulse race. She felt as if she was being watched, as if footsteps followed her into the bowels of the cave system. She looked behind her. There was no one, but she was suddenly eager to get out of the eerie cavern.

Crossing the waters quickly, Jamie emerged into the Inner Temple, where the Hellfire Club had allegedly met for celebrations of debauchery and Satanic ritual. She read that the layout of the caves was claimed by some to correspond almost exactly to the sexual organs of a woman being penetrated by a man. Given the reputation of the Hellfire Club, it seemed entirely possible that fertility rituals had been performed or that the design at least reflected the activities that went on down here beneath the earth. But were those depravities still happening today?

From the ceiling hung a great hook, presumably for a chandelier. But as Jamie glanced at it, she imagined a body hanging there, suspended above the table, tortured in front of those seated below, their eyes shining with delight. She looked away and noticed stains on the floor, as if pools of blood were seeping from the ground beneath. She blinked quickly and the vision was gone. Jamie rubbed her forehead. It must be lack of sleep, for why else would her mind play these tricks? Her imagination was clearly affected by the dissections of the Hunterian and her concerns about Polly. There was nothing here to suggest that the caves were used for anything other than tourism. They sometimes had ghost tours in here at night, but other than that the place closed at dusk. But Jenna Neville has been convinced this area was important for the Lyceum, so there must be more to it than just the official sanitized version that the public got to see.

Returning to the entrance, Jamie bought a guidebook to West Wycombe and went to a local pub to read while she ate a quick meal. Inside one of the Appendices she found a copy of a poem that referred to a secret passage running from the church of St Lawrence, intersecting at the River Styx directly below the altar. Eating without tasting, Jamie pulled up the photo of the title deed Jenna had found. The land included Hearnton Wood and the area surrounding the church of St Lawrence, so Jamie decided to head up there next.

As she was reading, her phone buzzed with a text from Missinghall.

Lockup discovery sparked a mad scramble on evidence.

Day-Conti released from custody. Be careful, whatever you're doing. Let me know if you need help.

Jamie felt the ghost of a smile on her lips at his words. Missinghall was a decent man, a good officer and she felt lucky to have someone who cared enough to watch her back. She had pushed people away for so long, protecting her precious time with Polly, but now she realized how alone that left her. She looked at her watch. It was time to finish this and the church was the next logical place to investigate.

The church of St Lawrence was on the summit of West Wycombe Hill, visible from the village below. It was a brisk walk up the steep slope and Jamie found herself breathing heavily, but she pushed upwards, the pain in her legs and lungs a welcome distraction. At the top, she stood to catch her breath, gazing at the odd building behind the Dashwood mausoleum. Originally an Iron Age fort, the medieval church had been built in the fourteenth century, but little of the original structure remained. It had been radically remodeled by Sir Francis Dashwood in 1752, pieces of the new stuck onto the old, with no aesthetic sense of retaining the medieval beauty.

On top of the tall Gothic tower was a shining gold orb that caught the last of the winter sun, a copy of the Golden Ball from the custom house at Venice. Ivy climbed the walls of the mottled stone as if nature was trying to reclaim the land, but Jamie still found the church a little crass, the simplicity of faith perverted into a glorification of the Dashwood name.

The churchyard was dominated by white crosses and the tombs of the aristocrats who had been buried here over the centuries. Jamie paused at the lych-gate and then walked slowly through the graves thinking of Polly. Somehow the lichen-covered tombstones comforted her, for death is our constant companion, walking alongside us through life. It edges closer over the years until it is all that supports us and we long to relax into its final embrace. Polly was beyond pain now, and all Jamie wanted to do was find her and let her ashes rest beneath the carpet of earth, bringing new flowers to life.

Jamie entered the church, her eyes drawn to a central panel, richly frescoed in the style of the Italian Renaissance. The walls were a mustard color with deep red columns topped by Corinthian capitals, supporting a coffered ceiling decorated with a floral pattern. Jamie walked to the altar, looking for some secret passageway or hint of Satanic ritual, but disappointment soon rose within her. Once again, there was nothing here that suggested anything untoward. It was just a slightly odd parish church with little tourist appeal. She left the church and walked back out into the churchyard. What was she missing? Jamie sensed the truth was just out of reach, but she was sure that Jenna had been killed because of the knowledge she had discovered about the Lyceum. There must be something here.

Standing on the hilltop, Jamie could see for miles around. In front of her lay the village and behind her was Hearnton Wood, a densely forested area that ended in a finger surrounding the church. Bare branches stood out against the cool sky, its absence of color epitomizing the English winter. When covered in leaves, the branches would conceal everything but, with the sparse cover of winter, Jamie could make out a shape in the distance, something cornered that broke the natural lines of the forest. She opened the map and searched for the structure but there was nothing shown in that direction. It was supposed to be pure forest. The title deeds showed that this whole area was now owned by the Nevilles, so this forest would be under their care as well. Was there something hidden within the wood?

Feeling a pulse of excitement, and daring to hope that this would lead her to Polly, Jamie took a bearing with the compass from her pack. She followed a path down from the church to the wood in the direction of what she had seen.

When the well-trodden path started to circle back towards the church in a large loop, she set off between the trees, following the compass heading.

It was dusk now, the forest shielding what little light was left of the day. Jamie listened to the rustle of leaves around her, as woodland animals scurried away at her approach. She remembered when Polly had been able to run as a child, how she had loved foraging in the New Forest, finding field mushrooms for their dinner. Jamie smiled at the memory. There had never been much money, it was always a struggle, but there had been a lot of joy until Polly's pain had overtaken her and the little girl hadn't been able to run or explore again.

Jamie pushed on through the trees, letting her eyes adjust to the encroaching darkness, not wanting to use torchlight until it was really necessary. Finally, she saw something looming up ahead, a patch of darker grey between the tree trunks. As she approached, she realized that it was a wall, made of solid metal panels over ten feet tall with a sign indicating it was private land and warning trespassers to stay out. Jamie put her hand flat on the metal, as if somehow she could feel what was behind. It was cold and lifeless on her skin, and she felt her body heat leaching into it. She leaned forwards until her forehead was resting on the metal. Part of her just wanted to sink down to the forest floor and weep, but night was encroaching and she knew there was little time left to find Polly's body before the Lyceum, whatever it was, began.

Jamie listened to the night forest, straining for some indication of which way to follow the wall around. She had to find other some way in, because there was no way that she was getting over this barrier without any special gear. She could hear nothing so she went West, remembering from the map that there was a tiny lane running close to the forest. Keeping the wall on her right, Jamie picked her way through the undergrowth. She kept the torch off, preferring imperfect night sight, walking carefully and trying not to make a sound.

After twenty minutes of walking, the fence was still impervious, but Jamie heard the sound of a van in the distance. The barrier began to curve inwards as she walked, and suddenly she saw the outline of another color ahead, a darker grey indicating a change in material and finally, a gate. She froze against the trunk of a tree, waiting to catch any movement, but all was silent, so she crept forward to look at it more closely. The gate was electronic, clearly activated from the inside. There was an intercom and a camera mounted where a driver would pull up. Jamie made sure to stay out of range, circling behind to inspect the side of the gate. There was no way to climb, so she pulled back into the trees and considered her options. She could wait until much later and try to get back into the caves, or she could call Missinghall and see if the local police would cooperate in investigating this location. But she still had no evidence that anything was going on, and it would take time she didn't have.

Suddenly, she heard the engine of another truck and this time it seemed to be slowing as it drove along the road. Jamie crouched down to avoid being caught in the beam of the headlights as it swung into the short driveway in front of the gate. She quickly circled back through the trees as the truck driver spoke into the intercom. The gate swung open and Jamie ran up behind, hopping onto the back board and clinging to the material there. The truck drove through the gate and, once on the other side, Jamie jumped off again before it could speed up too much. She dropped to the ground and crawled into the trees, now on the other side of the fence. Once she was sure that the truck was out of sight, Jamie started to walk after it, her night vision slowly returning as its lights faded.

Looking at her watch, Jamie felt an urgency building

inside her that crushed the exhaustion she felt. Whatever the dark purposes of the Lyceum, there wasn't much time. I'm coming, Pol, she thought. Jamie started to jog down the road, ready to sprint back into the trees if the truck returned and soon she saw lights on a low warehouse building ahead. There were no markings, nothing to indicate which company the place belonged to. It looked to be only one story, camouflaged by the dense trees that surrounded it. The truck was parked outside and a man was offloading boxes from the back onto a trolley. He wheeled them into an open loading bay area and left them neatly stacked, before reversing the truck and driving away. Jamie hugged the side of the building and slipped into the loading bay, checking the top of the box for the address slip. Neville Pharmaceuticals.

Brilliant light suddenly flooded the loading bay and a ferocious barking filled the air. Jamie was blinded, her heart pounding as fear flooded her system. She turned towards the sound, ready to defend herself, squinting into the light.

"Detective Brooke, what a lovely surprise."

Edward Mascuria stepped forward and Jamie saw the satisfied look on his face. He held a Taser pointed at her and an enormous Rottweiler stood leashed at his side, snarling lips pulled back over sharp teeth.

"You've been doing quite a bit of investigating I hear," Mascuria said. "Shame that will now have to come to an end." He smiled and his eyes were cold. "But what an end it shall be."

CHAPTER 22

JAMIE STOOD HER GROUND, holding her hands out in an unthreatening posture. She felt vulnerable but she also had nothing to lose anymore.

"Do you have Polly's body?" she asked, head held high.

"Such a beautiful specimen," Mascuria said, and Jamie couldn't help herself. She started towards him, violent fury on her face but the Rottweiler leapt forward barking, teeth snapping at her. She had to retreat before it began to rip at her legs. It stood in front of Mascuria, straining at the leash, desperate for the command to attack, salivating at the possibility of blood. She could see that Mascuria was relishing the power he held over her now.

"You bastard," she said, bile rising in her throat. "Why Polly?"

"I needed a female with her kind of spinal deformity for my teratological collection. When you came round to my flat with your - attitude - I found out more about you and your desperate family situation. But don't worry, I'm taking very good care of her body." He indicated a doorway with the Taser. "This way, Detective. You're a little early for tonight's Lyceum, but I think you might enjoy a tour. Don't even think about running. Max here will bring you down and rip your throat out on my command. He's not fed often and he enjoys the taste of human flesh."

Jamie heard the pleasure of reminiscence in his voice and imagined the poor victims that Mascuria had used to train his dog, skin shredded from their bones as screams echoed in the dark forest. She shuddered, but she didn't want to run. She was so close now and once she was with Polly's body, she could consider her options. Dealing with this bastard would have to wait, and she tried to calm her anger, shutting away her feelings and concentrating on her surroundings.

Jamie walked ahead of Mascuria through the open door. Inside was a short corridor and another door at the end with retinal scan entry. Next to the door was a waiting room with glass windows.

"In there, Detective," Mascuria indicated the room. Jamie walked in and turned to face him. "Now strip for me, and I mean everything." His eyes glinted at her hesitation. "Oh, don't worry, I'm not going to touch you - yet. Warm flesh is not really my thing, but I need to check that you're not armed before I take you inside."

Jamie shut her eyes for a moment and gathered herself. He was playing a dominance game but her body was just a body like any other. He would only take pleasure from her resistance and embarrassment.

"Sure," she said, pulling her jacket off and swiftly shedding her clothes. She steeled herself to ignore the dog's growling as her bare skin was revealed. She met Mascuria's eyes as she unhooked her bra and pulled down her panties until she was naked. She stood tall and didn't hug her arms around her body even though the cold made her nipples harden and her skin pucker. She felt a moment of victory when he broke their stare, his eyes dropping to her breasts.

"Turn," he said, and there was a gruffness in his voice. She turned slowly all the way around. "Now face the wall." She did so and he advanced into the room, the dog's growling louder now. Jamie could feel the heat from it just behind her legs. Every inch of her wanted to run and she couldn't help imagining vicious teeth tearing into her intimate, vulnerable flesh. Mascuria could do what he wanted here and she cursed her own independence at proceeding without backup.

Mascuria passed a scanner over her clothes, checking for concealed weapons and bugs. He stood close to her, and she could feel his breath against her back. He pressed the Taser against her buttocks.

"I'd love to press this button," he whispered. "I want to see you writhing in your own piss on the floor, arching in agony for the way you treated me, bitch."

Jamie realized that he was turned on by the thought of her pain and that was terrifying. She wasn't afraid of death, but didn't want to die by his sadistic hand. "But that's not enough for someone like you. You think you're so strong, but I'll break you when you watch me slice up your daughter's body."

Jamie forced herself to remain still as he whispered close to her ear. Every fiber of her being wanted to turn and beat him to a pulp. She would kill him for what he intended to do, but not yet.

"Please," she whispered, feigning submission. "Let me see Polly."

Mascuria walked out of the anteroom and the dog padded after him.

"Put your clothes back on and cuff yourself," he said, brusquely. "There's a lot to do tonight."

Pulling her clothes on, Jamie felt relief at the flimsy barrier between her and the dog, as well as respite from Mascuria's stare. She put on the plastic tie cuffs, pulling them with her teeth so that they were still loose about her hands, tucking the end between her palms. Mascuria put his eye to the retina scan and the door clicked open. He indicated that she should walk in first. Jamie held her head high and made to walk past him, but he stopped her and yanked at the tie cuffs, so they tightened and bit deep into her wrists. Jamie winced at the sudden pain.

"Wouldn't want you trying to get away now, would we," Mascuria said, and up close his breath smelled of rotting flesh. "Max is staying out here, but remember, I still have the Taser."

Jamie pulled away from him and stepped through the door into a large conference room decorated with cream colored easy chairs, potted palms and framed photographs of aspects of biological research. It was business-like and professional, clearly used for visitors to the facility, and Jamie wondered who came to this secret lab and what they were here to buy.

Mascuria made her stand to one side while he used his thumbprint to open the next door. Security was certainly tight, and Jamie was anxious to see what was inside. She kept glancing around for possible weapons, for an alternative exit but, in truth, she didn't want to get away from Mascuria yet.

Through the next door, a long corridor stretched into the distance and on either side were windows, displaying labs within. Jamie could hear noises, animal hoots and moans, and it smelled like a zoo.

"What goes on here?" Jamie asked, staring into one lab that was almost a replica of the one she had seen at the Neville Pharmaceuticals official headquarters. But here the glass-fronted fridges contained specimens that seemed on the edge of abomination, perversions of nature. In some, the creatures' skin was ruptured or scaly and others had limbs like animals on the bodies of human babies. Jamie saw one fetus with only blue eyes in its blank face, open in the clear liquid. With no mouth or nose, it had no way to breathe and her heart thudded with the desperate end it faced as soon as it was torn from its mother's placenta. In the Hunterian, the specimens had been medical history, accidents of birth, but this was deliberate experimentation. What other horrors were here, and was this what Jenna Neville had discovered?

"Neville Pharma has branched out into some of the more interesting aspects of genetic splicing," Mascuria said with pride. "We use stem cells between species. After all, it's easier to create monsters to order than to find them by chance. We've also been exploring the effects of certain drugs in populations where the governments have more relaxed guidelines on testing." He indicated a map on the wall with shaded areas in West Africa, South East Asia and even Eastern Europe. Jamie's mind buzzed with the grotesque possibilities, the lives that even now were being experimented on.

"This research is far bigger than you could imagine," Mascuria said, pushing Jamie onwards. "But what you're really looking for is much deeper inside the facility."

At the end of the corridor, another retinal scan and thumbprint opened a large metal door, this one reinforced like a bank vault with a thick outer wall. Although it was protected like a bunker from the Soviet era, inside it was just a round room, the walls lined with medical and research texts. In between the bookshelves were sculptures Jamie recognized, plastinated corpses of skillful dissection including the little boy with his spine exposed. Jamie felt a surge of pity and a rigid determination that Polly's body would not end up like this.

A wooden lectern stood in pride of place against the very center of the back wall, spotlights shining on a large notebook filled with handwritten notes and intimate drawings in a glass case. Above it was a picture of a clean cut young man in the black and white uniform of the SS, silver skull shining on his smart helmet. Jamie recognized Mengele, vivisector and perverter of science, honored here as an inspirational role model. The spotlight also illuminated a shelf by the notebook that lay empty. Blake had seen the Anatomical

Venus figurine with Mengele's notebook in his vision, so Jenna must have been here and stolen the figurine, using it as evidence to challenge her parents.

With a grunt, Mascuria turned to a panel in the wall and entered a code. A scraping noise filled the room and the large Persian carpet in the middle of the floor slid back by some hidden mechanism. One of the flagstones sunk below and sideways, revealing a staircase down into the earth.

"The real secrets are down there," Mascuria chuckled, with an edge of maniacal glee. Jamie had the impression that Mascuria wanted to show his treasures to someone with a pulse. He pointed at the staircase and Jamie stepped down carefully, trying to keep her balance with her hands still cuffed.

There were muted lights on the stairs so she could see a few steps ahead as they wound downwards. Jamie heard Mascuria step behind her, and then he must have closed the trapdoor because the darkness thickened and the lights at her feet were the only illumination.

"Just keep walking, Detective, it's not too far now, and your curiosity will be satisfied."

Jamie continued carefully down, counting nearly fifty steps until the staircase opened out into another corridor. The ceilings were carved into arches like the Hellfire Caves and down here the air was temperate, warmer than the surface. There was an earthy smell, not unpleasant.

"Welcome to the heart of the complex," Mascuria said. "It's connected to the Hellfire Caves in the opposite direction from the official tourist entrance. There's a mirror image set of caves behind the public area where the Hellfire club really met. The fake caverns were created for delicious scandal and media interest, but Dashwood knew what he was doing."

"And now the Nevilles continue the Hellfire tradition?" asked Jamie, still unsure as to how Jenna's strange family fitted into the mix.

Mascuria laughed. "You'll have to wait and see, but right now, I want to introduce you to my collection."

He pointed at a door of ornate dark wood, carved with alchemical and fertility symbols. In the center was an ouroboros, a snake eating its own tail in a never-ending circle, representing immortality and the continuation of life.

"That is my God, Detective. Nothing we do matters, because it's all just an endless turning. But I will leave my legacy by preserving the extraordinary in nature. I will be remembered, like Hunter, as a man who appreciated the freaks." He paused, then pushed open the door. "Like your little girl."

CHAPTER 23

JAMIE'S HEART THUNDERED IN her chest. She wanted to see Polly's body but she was also terrified. She remembered her daughter as perfection but her flesh would surely be decomposed and rotting by now. Mascuria laughed, sensing her hesitation.

"Don't worry, Detective, I've kept her on ice and she's only showing a hint of decay."

He pushed her forwards and Jamie was surprised to find that the cave was set up like a morgue, with pristine floors and white tiled walls. One side was dominated by a cooling unit and drawer freezers, presumably for bodies. Opposite the dissection gurneys were racks of open shelving containing specimen jars. Jamie stared at them in horrified recognition. They varied in size from large drums on the bottom shelves to tiny jars on the higher levels and each one contained some kind of anatomical preparation.

"I am the true heir of John Hunter," Mascuria said proudly, "and this will be my legacy to the world. While he lived, Hunter was criticized and feared for his scientific methods. In the same way, if what we did here was revealed, I too would be treated as an outcast. But this way, I can perform my great work in peace, and soon I will be as celebrated as Hunter." He waved his arm at the shelves. "I think you'll agree that I have some particularly amazing specimens from the labs upstairs."

"Where's Polly?" Jamie said, uncaring for the rest of the dead. Only her daughter's remains mattered. Mascuria's eyes hardened and he raised the Taser.

"No. Not yet. First appreciate my collection and under-stand the importance of my work, then you may be allowed a glimpse of my next subject."

Jamie wanted to rush him and smash one of the jars into his face, obliterating his perverted brain. She could barely contain her need to see Polly but he still had the advantage. She turned and walked towards the rack of shelving, her stomach churning as she saw what was inside. Like the Hunterian, it was both fascinating and revolting to see the freakish remains, grouped according to type, the first shelf containing fetuses and babies, nightmares that Jamie wished she could un-see.

The fluid around each was yellowish, making it seem as if they rested in a kind of amber. In one, she glimpsed a baby with a normal body but two heads, squashed onto the same neck, with skulls flattened as if the child had been violently murdered as it exited the womb. In another jar, triplet fetuses were suspended, tiny arms wrapped around themselves as if they were cold, each with a tuft of hair on its bald head. But there were only patches of skin where their eyes should be and their faces were featureless. Next, a huge baby's head, its skin wrinkled like an old man, on top of a round body, the limbs only stumps of fingers and toes. Jamie felt an over-whelming compassion for these unborn children, but also a kind of gratitude that they had not had to endure life as monsters. She knew that the physical body didn't define the life inside, but she also understood through her daughter the pain of rejection, the instinctive human response to turn away from those who were less than perfect. But who are we to say what perfection is? And does that make the Creator a eugeneticist, choosing only those good enough to live?

Jamie gazed into other jars, wanting to bear witness to the myriad forms of forsaken humanity that were left alone here, motherless. Here was a true monster, aspects of humanity in the facial structure and arms, but the rest of its body was more like a fish. Its skin was puckered and ruptured in places, as if it had been sewn together. In the next jar was a pitiful specimen, its head perfect but the body just an abdomen with skin split open to reveal the guts within. This was dead flesh, no spark of life, for what is the human body except for us to dwell in briefly, ruin and burn, bury or dissect, returning it to the stardust from which it came.

"Were these children born here?" Jamie asked, her voice echoing round the lab. "Were they created by Neville Pharma?"

"Some were created as a by-product of the teratology research." There was pride in Mascuria's voice. "We investigate the effects of various drugs on pregnant women, to find the stage that affects the fetus the most. After Thalidomide, it became illegal to test on pregnant women but of course, it has to be done, and the money is excellent, so some are willing to be part of the research. Others are unwilling, but … well, let's just say, they end up joining us anyway. They are from the margins of society so none of the women are missed, and they often end up part of the Lyceum, their offspring preserved forever. Who would object to such a fate?"

Jamie's head was reeling with the implications of what went on here but then his words sunk in.

"So this isn't the Lyceum?" she asked.

Mascuria's hollow laugh blurted out, the sound quickly absorbed into the shelves of fluid glass.

"Oh no, they butcher the living, but I use only the dead. Of course, I have to prepare specimens differently, depending on their future use. Removing flesh is only one task. Here's one of their last victims."

Mascuria walked over to a huge copper vat in the corner. It was as pristine as the rest of the lab, but as he lifted the lid, the putrid smell made Jamie wince and her nostrils flared at the familiar stench of death. He beckoned her over and she met his challenge, walking to the vat, the anticipation of what she might see making her heart pound. Jamie peered over the edge, her cuffed hands on her mouth and nose to stop the gag reflex. The liquid inside was a deep brown color, with fat glistening on top. Mascuria grabbed a long handled ladle from the bench and poked it into the soup, fishing for something more solid. There were thicker, heavier parts at the bottom of the vat and he hooked one of them, dragging it up to the surface. It was a human femur, mostly bone now with just a little flesh hanging off. Mascuria smiled at her evident revulsion.

"One option to destroy flesh is to put the body in an enclosed space with flies which eventually clean the bones completely. But an alternative is to hack it into pieces and boil it in a vat until all the flesh and sinew is gone, like this. Of course, anatomy is always a sensory experience, the permanent stench of the dissection room lingers on clothes, the pervading odor of decay. Did you know that Hunter was known for tasting bodily fluids?"

Jamie grimaced as he raised the ladle towards his mouth. Mascuria laughed again.

"Come now, Detective. You know nothing human lingers here. The first time you clutch the cold flesh of a body, when you smell decay and corruption, you know it's not a person anymore. It's only entropy in action, chaos disintegrating the body, returning it to the atomic state. We're only revolted by the dead because the corpse represents the end of life, which we are meant to fear. But I don't fear it, I'm tempted by it. I only know what life truly is because I embrace the death in it." Mascuria replaced the lid on the vat and walked back to the wall units. Pulling one of the freezer doors open, he slid a gurney out, the wheels loud on the tiled floor. "Now, come and see your daughter."

Jamie walked slowly to the open freezer, as Mascuria unzipped the bag in which a body lay. Silent tears ran down her cheeks as Jamie looked down at Polly's face, her skin a lighter shade now, all color gone. Her eyes were shut and she looked more than asleep.

"How dare you?" Jamie whispered, barely controlled anger in her voice. "How dare you disturb her rest. She's suffered enough."

Mascuria reached out a fingertip and stroked the girl's cheek, running it down over her lips, then he poked it into her mouth.

"I dare what I want with the dead," he said, drawing it out again and then thrusting the finger back inside.

Jamie's face contorted with disgust at the offensive action and she whipped her cuffed hands up, striking him across the face double handed as she leaned over the gurney.

"Bastard," she screamed. "Monster."

Mascuria's head snapped back and he stumbled from the blow. Jamie rounded the gurney at speed and slammed into him, sending him to the floor as she fell on top of him, using her legs to try and immobilize him. But she couldn't hold him and he twisted beneath her, pushing her away to make a space between them. She heard the crackle of his Taser and felt pain shoot through her body. Jamie's muscles spasmed into rigidity and she lay prone as the agony pulsed through her, centering in the place where he had thrust the device. Mascuria rose and stood over her as Jamie fought to try and regain control of her body.

"You have no power here, Detective," he said, patting himself down, dislodging any dust and brushing it off onto her. He reached down and grabbed her cuffed hands, dragging her, unable to resist, over to the wall near the door. He pulled down a meathook to lever around the cuffs and then started to winch the thick steel cable up. "This will hold you still while I work. I seldom have company when I process a body, but we have some time before the Lyceum commences tonight. Time for you to witness what I have planned for pretty Polly."

Jamie felt some feeling return to her limbs and she tried to fight the winch, but it just kept rising until she was high on her toes, calf muscles taut. She couldn't unhook herself in this position, she had no leverage. She opened her mouth to beg but only a rasp came out.

"Hmm," Mascuria said, noting her attempt. "I like quiet in my lab, so you'll need a gag." He fiddled around on a nearby lab table, producing a wad of surgical gauze. Jamie tried to move her head, resisting him but he grabbed her jaw in a skeletal grip and forced it into her mouth. He wrapped a bandage around her mouth, tying it behind her head to stop her spitting the gauze out. She tried to scream then, feeling her strength returning but it was too late and Mascuria only laughed at her tears of frustration.

He looked at the clock on the wall.

"Time to get started," he smiled at her with malice, "and just enough time to make you truly pay for the way you treated me."

He picked up a scalpel and approached Polly's body, standing on the far side of the gurney so that Jamie could see his actions. She looked at her daughter's body and in her mind, she screamed for God to help her, a God she didn't even believe in. Part of her was trying to rationalize that this wasn't her daughter anymore, that Polly's spirit was gone, that she wouldn't feel any pain at this man's abuse. But her eyes told her this was still her beloved daughter, the baby born from her blood and pushed from her own body, who had grown into a lovely young woman. Jamie couldn't hide the pain in her eyes, even though she didn't want to give Mascuria the satisfaction of seeing it.

He cupped the budding breast of the corpse with a bare hand, his fingers rubbing at the pale pink nipple. Jamie felt herself gag and had to force the vomit back down. She wanted to look away but knew she had to bear witness to his cruelty.

"Sometimes I keep the body whole," Mascuria said. "Kept frozen like this, they stay perfect for a while longer. I bet little Polly here was a virgin as well, and she will be all tight and cold inside. Perfect."

Jamie struggled furiously against her bonds, rattling the chains. She swore then that she would kill Mascuria, whatever it took. He couldn't be allowed to continue his depraved practices.

"I see the fury in your eyes, Detective, and it inspires me. I shall make Polly a perfect specimen for my collection. She will live on here amongst the monsters, labeled and tagged, her spine a source of fascination in death. And will it hurt you more, I wonder, to watch me take pleasure with her body or to see me cut her into pieces?"

Mascuria looked into Jamie's eyes and she stared straight back at him, daring him to make any move on her daughter. He laughed and reached around the body, flipping Polly over so that she now lay on her front. Her body couldn't lie straight on the table, and the deformity was clearer from the back, the twisting exaggerated. Jamie screamed, moaning into the gag, wrenching on the hook in an attempt to get to her daughter.

"When dissecting a body," Mascuria began, pointing at the corpse as if giving a lecture, "the guts are the first parts to putrefy so usually one would begin by slitting open the abdomen, folding back the flaps of skin and fat and removing the digestive parts, stomach, intestines, spleen, gall bladder and pancreas. Then one would open the chest, sawing apart the ribcage to remove the lungs and expose the heart." His fingers danced down Polly's spine, dipping between her buttocks as he smiled at Jamie's fury. "Of course, the mastery of dissection requires intricate knife skills, but also brute strength to saw through bone and hack off the parts not required for a particular preparation. Removing the limbs so that I have a nice, clean torso to work with is always a good first step, because a big part of the artist's job is deciding what to leave out," Mascuria grinned wildly as he saw the panic in Jamie's eyes. He turned and wheeled over a trolley, on which were laid out scalpels of various sizes and a large bone saw. "I think I'll start with removing her legs." He reached for a scalpel.

CHAPTER 24

THE DOOR SLAMMED OPEN, hitting the wall inches from where Jamie hung behind it. Mascuria froze, one hand holding Polly's leg and the other clutching the scalpel above her thigh. His face fell as he saw who had entered. Jamie tried to twist around but she couldn't see.

"Edward, darling," Esther Neville's crisp British vowels filled the room. "Do you really have time for that?"

Mascuria's eyes flicked to Jamie and the door was pulled back. Esther stood there, no trace of the mousey scientist, the grieving mother or wronged wife remaining. Instead she was the proud ruler of this underground domain, channeling dark spirits below while she created abomination in the labs above. Her clothes were curious, her waist nipped in with a corset and the dress an extravagant eighteenth century costume, out of place in the modern lab. Esther's serpent green eyes drilled into Jamie.

"Detective, why am I not surprised to find you here?" She stepped forward to check that the bonds were secure, nodding her head. "Good job, Edward." Jamie could see that Mascuria reveled under this compliment from his mistress. "But we already have a vivisection subject for the Lyceum tonight." Esther paused and Jamie could see that she was considering the options. "I'd like the Detective to witness her future fate, but we can get more for her at an exclusive event, for those select few who might enjoy intimacy with her kind of flesh." Esther stepped closer, her smile one of triumph. "And what do you think of the wonders we have here, Detective?"

Esther pulled away Jamie's gag, wanting to hear her speak. Jamie's mind flashed over all the insults she wanted to spit out, but she still held onto some hope that she would get out of here. Perhaps Esther could be goaded.

"You're just sick and depraved. There's no real science here."

Esther's eyes flashed with anger.

"Of course, I couldn't expect a mere police detective to understand, but this is truly magnificent work. We're developing weaponized teratology. By introducing pathogens into an environment, we can corrupt a region, making the inhabitants into monsters who will be rejected, murdered and thrown into mass graves. We can target genetically, causing extra limbs to sprout from bodies, horns from heads, perversions of nature. It will justify the killing of those groups in the eyes of those considered normal, but more than that, it becomes a judgment from God, afflictions sent as punishment for sin. Humans are so ready to slaughter those considered Other."

Jamie thought of the gas chambers of Nazi Europe filled with the bodies of the Other - Jews, gypsies, the mentally ill and those considered defective. She thought of Rwanda and the description of 'cockroaches' stacked in mass graves, seen as inhuman by people who were once their neighbors. It was terrifying to think that this lab could hold the key to unleashing atrocity on an even grander scale. But she still didn't have all the answers.

"What has the Lyceum got to do with this?"

"Why, Detective, it's just a little fun, in the medical tradition of course." Esther did a little twirl in her costume, meager breasts pushed up by the tight bodice, full skirts swinging. Against the backdrop of the bottled remains, her delight was all the more macabre. "The Lyceum Medicum Londinense is an old institution, first started in 1785 in the days of the great anatomist John Hunter to replicate his experiments, a crucible to facilitate his scientific legacy. Hunter only trusted his own eyes, so now, in turn, this is what we offer in the resurrected Lyceum. We experiment as Hunter did, exploring the very edges of human experience. Unlike you, most people don't get to see the dark side of reality anymore, it's all so sanitized. They don't get to see death or experience the end of life until they meet it themselves in some pathetic care home. But people want a taste of the extraordinary in their boring lives, they want the freak shows, the crazies. Otherwise this world is just one long dull day after another. These elite seekers are desperate for a glimpse of the other side. They crave this interaction with the dead, for it is like seeing our own future. On the slab, we are all the same."

Esther stepped closer, holding Jamie's gaze. "At the Lyceum, we remove the veneer of civilization and deliver raw truth through vivisection of the body. We want our members to see, to weep and experience deep pleasure. It matters not what they feel, only that they feel something. This becomes an addiction, an expensive one, for sure, and when we find a new member, we try very hard to find them an experience that will change them. Religion offers a way to look into the divine, but the Lyceum offers a way to look into our base physical selves. For what truth is greater than the realization that we are meat, mere chunks of flesh that can be cut away? If we dissect to the last capillary, will we find the essence of the person? No, we cannot, because it has already gone."

Jamie saw the promise of her own death in Esther's eyes, an end through flayed flesh and agony. Where Mascuria delighted in the dead, Esther was addicted to killing. It was a perfect partnership.

"Enough." Esther turned and addressed Mascuria. "Use the ketamine and dress her in something more appropriate, then string her up next to the altar. And Edward, I mean now. You can return to your - specimen - later."

Esther strode from the room, her heels clicking on the stone as she walked away. Mascuria rested the scalpel gently on Polly's back and patted her buttocks.

"I'll return for you later," he whispered, almost lovingly. He looked up at Jamie and the veil in his eyes came down, obscuring any humanity. He picked up a syringe from the surgical table and then filled it from a bottle.

As he walked towards Jamie, she began to struggle, aware that ketamine was a powerful sedative but also that it could produce a dissociative state, hallucinations and visions. She wanted to remember Mascuria's perversions and she wanted to punish him for it.

"It would have been better for you to watch your daughter's preservation than to experience Lady Neville's particular pleasures," Mascuria said. "But now, you have no choice."

He pressed the needle into her arm and within seconds, Jamie felt a heaviness in her limbs and her eyelids drooped. She forced them open again, as the winch lowered her to the floor, but she couldn't fight the drug and she slipped into unconsciousness.

CHAPTER 25

JAMIE BECAME AWARE OF the bonds around her as she woke and it took her a few seconds to figure out what was happening. Her body felt as if she were underwater, heavy and compliant, the sedation of the ketamine still in her system. She was lying on a chill stone floor, hands cuffed in front of her, wearing a mask with tiny slits for her eyes that obscured her facial features. As her senses slowly returned, Jamie realized she was only wearing a sheer black wrap over her own underwear. That bastard Mascuria had stripped her as he had the bodies of the dead. For a fleeting moment, Jamie wished to be next to her daughter on the slab. But then she remembered how much Polly had believed in living until it hurt and making the most out of every minute that we have the grace to be alive. Jamie grasped at a glimmer of hope, that she might make it out of this and revenge the abuses inflicted on Polly and the other innocent victims here.

She moved slowly, trying to take in her surroundings, fighting to clear her head. Still gagged, her throat hurt from the raw material and she was desperately thirsty. She pulled against the chain that bound her cuffs to the wall and managed to lever herself up, resting back against the stone, finally able to see. She was in a twin chamber to the Inner Temple of the Hellfire Caves, but it had been transformed into a dark cave of corrupted medical history.

The walls were hung with twisted poles wrapped with bloody used bandages, a tribute to the red and white staffs of the original barber surgeons. There were skeletons attached between them, posed in positions of torture, their limbs stretched in crucifixion. Candelabra stood around the edge, throwing an incongruous warm light into the dark space and giving off a pungent scent. Tendrils of smoke licked the walls, clouding the cave with a heady atmosphere.

Behind an altar was a long wooden pole, an intricately carved snake curled around it, forked tongue flickering to taste the air. Jamie recognized the rod of Asclepius, the Greek god of healing and medicine, but here it resembled some kind of demonic god. Around an empty central space were rows of tiered seating facing the altar where she sat. Jamie wondered who the members would be, since the original Hellfire Club had been made up of aristocrats, businessmen and politicians. Could it still be so powerful?

Jamie heard footsteps and slumped in her bonds, pretending to be drowsy as Mascuria came to check on her. He lifted her chin, and she groaned softly, playing the part. His fingers dug into her jaw.

"Time to wake up. After all, you'll want to watch the entertainment tonight and reflect on your own future." She opened her eyes slowly to see Mascuria's excited smile. But she realized that his enthusiasm wasn't for her bondage, it was for something that appealed to his darker nature, and Jamie felt a heavy sense of foreboding at what was to come. He forced her to her feet, adjusting the chains so that she was held tighter, standing against the wall, shackled by her wrists and ankles. The sheer wrap barely hid her body and she shivered as the cold seeped into her exposed skin.

"The chill is preferable to being center stage, believe me," he said, pulling out a hip flask. "But this will warm you up." He pulled her gag away and holding her chin firmly, poured some of the liquid into her mouth. The wine was strong and some dribbled down her chin, but Jamie gratefully swallowed it to assuage her thirst. Mascuria tipped another swig into her throat, and Jamie started to feel light-headed. Mascuria saw the question in her eyes.

"A touch of hallucinogen. Altered reality will help you experience the heights of the ritual tonight, since I believe our guest is an acquaintance of yours."

Jamie's thoughts flashed to Blake, Missinghall, the nurses at the home. Who could it be? She dared hope it wasn't someone she cared about, but with the thought of what might come, she pitied the victim, whoever it was.

A drum beat started, a heavy, slow thudding that echoed around the chamber. It seemed to signify the start of proceedings because silhouettes started to enter the room, emerging through the smoky haze.

"Watch carefully, Detective, for this will soon be your fate." Mascuria whispered, slipping away from her into a shadowy tunnel at the side of the room.

Jamie watched as the figures walked slowly in, wearing buttoned long coats covered by hooded capes. Their faces were obscured but Jamie could tell by their stature that both women and men were present. Some glanced in her direction, some for a longer time than others, but she could see none of their features. Each wore the leather apron of the anatomist that Jamie had seen in the paintings of Hunter's time, and they carried small wooden cases. Some had handsome canes with finely wrought handles to complete their eighteenth century costumes. They filed into the tiered seating as the drum began to speed up, a double beat like a heart pounding.

A figure stepped from the shadowed corridor. Esther Neville, resplendent in a swirling black cape over her extravagant dress. Her hood was back and she didn't hide her face, which was now made up with gold and metallic swirls around her eyes, matching the detail on her costume. As she strode to the front of the altar, the drum pounded harder and faster and Jamie felt her heart thumping in time, jumping to the rhythm, making her blood race. She felt heady with the noise and the smoke that made the figures weave in front of her.

As Esther raised her hands into the air with a dramatic gesture, Mascuria wheeled in a metal gurney covered in a white cloth. Strapped on top of it, naked and struggling, was Rowan Day-Conti, his elaborately tattooed body arching in terror. Jamie gasped to see him restrained, and desperate to help him, she twisted in her chains, pulling against their hindrance. Bands round his wrists, ankles, waist and neck held Rowan to the table and, although he writhed in his bonds, Jamie could see that he would not escape them and neither could she reach him.

Mascuria wheeled the gurney into the middle of the space as the drum reached a crescendo and then fell silent. Esther spoke into the silence, calling out in a strange language that Jamie didn't recognize: clearly it was some ritualized welcome as the gathering responded with a chant, sipping from their goblets as they joined the words. Had the Lyceum ritualized their vivisection in this way? Was this a dark perversion of the physician's oath?

Jamie noticed that some of those present drank more heavily, perhaps gaining strength for the ritual to come. As they chanted, Mascuria moved forward and slipped Day-Conti's gag off, forcing him to drink as well. Some of the wine tipped onto the white cloth beneath his neck, staining it a deep red. He couldn't help but drink as Mascuria held his nose and tipped the stuff down his throat. Day-Conti turned his head, coughing and groaning but Jamie knew that the woozy feeling would make his limbs heavy soon enough and she was glad that something would dull the pain to come.

"Tonight we honor our medical heritage, the curiosity

that has driven physicians throughout history," Esther said, her tone imperious. "For with every body we cut into, we slice into our own skin. For every drop of blood we shed, we are draining our own into the earth. For every heart that is silenced, our end is a beat closer. And every bone we break reveals our own inevitable decline."

She raised a goblet to her lips and drained it, then spun to the altar and took up the ritual knife that lay there. Holding it up to the roof of the cave, she spoke words in the strange language again and turned to the crowd. Jamie watched the proud curve of Esther's back, feeling the resonance of her power in the space, a vibration of expectation emanating from the gathering. Day-Conti's eyes were wide open, his head bowed back to try and see what was happening above and behind him, panic evident even through the haze of drugs. Then he saw her and in his eyes, Jamie understood his plea for help. Did he recognize her in the depths of his pain, or did he just see another captive bound for the same fate?

Esther stepped down to the level of the gurney and pulled a black hood over Day-Conti's head, negating his individuality. Jamie had a flashback to the artist's studio, where the body of the decapitated woman lay, waiting for the knife to etch into her dead flesh. Now the sculptor himself would feel her pain. Jamie watched Day-Conti's chest rise and fall faster, his heart pounding as he awaited his fate.

"The vivisection begins," Esther said to the gathering, holding out the ritual knife. A tall figure stepped forward, pulling back his hood to reveal a face Jamie recognized, a prominent politician from one of the more radical right-wing parties. Esther handed the knife to him and he received it reverently with two hands. Jamie felt her own heart thumping hard against her ribs, anticipating the first cut. She twisted against her bonds, desperate to get away even as the man held the knife against Day-Conti's right shoulder and sliced diagonally across his chest, the first stroke of the autopsy, the beginning of the Y incision. But this man wasn't dead yet, and blood welled up under the knife.

A hiss broke from the crowd, a forced exhalation of breath, and as one they moved forward to see better. A muffled scream came from Day-Conti as the man drew the knife across his flesh again and the drum beat began once more, muting the sounds of horror. The thudding animated the crowd and they pushed back their hoods with excitement. Smoke made their features hazy and her head spun with drugged wine and residual ketamine, but Jamie was sure she saw members of government and the upper echelons of business. The crowd parted for a second and she thought she saw Detective Superintendent Dale Cameron, his face transformed by blood lust. Jamie blinked, unable to believe it was really him, and then the robed figures swirled and he was hidden again, if it had even been him at all.

At a sign from Esther, the members pulled out their own scalpels and crowded round the gurney. They began with tentative cuts and a semblance of scientific restraint, but soon all decorum was forgotten. Their robed bodies shielded Day-Conti's mutilation from Jamie's view and she could only watch their arms as they worked. As the drum beat speeded up, the rhythm turned to slashing and thrusting as vivisection turned to dismemberment. Sickened, Jamie swallowed down the bile that filled her throat, but she refused to look away. Here was evil in the bowels of the earth, committed by men and women in power, who held sway over the lives of many. Did they consider themselves as gods, with the ultimate power of life and death?

As Jamie watched, a figure stepped from the crowd, walking towards her with a measured step. It was Christopher Neville, gore staining his robe a darker pitch and a bloody scalpel in his hand. Jamie struggled as he approached her, unnoticed by the group who were engrossed in their orgy of blood-letting. His eyes glittered in the candlelight and she sensed his dangerous arousal, remembering how compliant he liked his women as he stepped onto the altar stage and bent towards her.

CHAPTER 26

CHRISTOPHER NEVILLE LOOSENED THE chains, unhooking Jamie from them so her body sagged, pushing her to the floor out of direct sight of the crowd. As she sank down behind the altar, hands and feet still cuffed, she saw Neville place the scalpel on the edge of it, just out of her reach. Jamie felt the heaviness in her limbs, the drugs making her unresisting, but through the haze in her mind, she remembered how hard Polly had fought the deadening of her own limbs. In that moment, she surged up, trying to fight Neville's dominance, smashing into his legs with her constricted shoulders.

The drum beat hid the sound of his stumbling and the crack of his hand across her face in retaliation, but as he moved to right himself, Neville knocked the scalpel to the floor and it slipped beneath the folds of the material covering the altar. Jamie fell back from the heavy blow to her face but she saw where the blade had fallen, even as she lay dazed, her head ringing.

Neville dropped to his knees and started to paw at her body, groping her breasts. Jamie struggled to get away from him, trying to wriggle across the floor, inching towards where the scalpel lay. If she could somehow roll towards it, she thought in desperation, but Neville dragged her back towards him and she knew her attempts to escape excited him further. Jamie's breath was ragged through her nose as she tried to breathe, the gag making it hard to get enough air. She knew she couldn't stay conscious for much longer and suddenly sagged, letting her limbs go limp. Neville smiled, the wolfish grin of a predator who knows he has won his prize. He turned her body over so she faced the floor, shifting her legs up so that they were bent under her and she lay like an offering for him to take.

He knelt behind her, pulling his robes apart, and it was as if time slowed. Jamie saw him reach for the scalpel, perhaps to cut his way through her clothes, perhaps to hurt her further, but he averted his eyes from her in that second. She moved fast, rolling and twisting so her pinned arms could swing free, catching Neville's hand that now grasped the scalpel, diverting it towards his own body. At the same time, she kicked out with her bent legs, thrusting them back so that they smashed into Neville's thighs, knocking him off balance. He fell forwards, onto her, onto the blade and Jamie saw his eyes widen in shock as it pierced his neck. His eyes widened and his sharp sound of alarm was lost in the drumbeat that drove the frenzy of the room to fever pitch. Jamie could smell the metallic scent of blood mingling with the smoke and it galvanized her into action.

She twisted further, knocking Neville sideways, so he lay gasping on his back, the scalpel sticking out of his neck as he clutched at it with weakening hands, his mouth opening and closing like a beached fish. With two hands still cuffed, Jamie yanked it from him and blood pumped from his wound. Neville started to try and rise, to attract the attention of the others and get help. Jamie rose to her knees and sat astride him, some part of her wanting to use the weapon, but at the last moment she stopped. She couldn't stab the man, even though she wished him dead. Instead, she grabbed Neville's head and slammed it back against the stone floor as hard as she could, then again and again until she saw his eyes roll back in his head and he went limp.

Maneuvering the scalpel, Jamie sawed through the plastic tie cuffs that held her feet bound and then used Neville's body to brace it so she could free her hands. The drum beat still pounded, echoing in the chamber, but Jamie couldn't count on remaining unseen for much longer. Finally free, she crawled to the edge of the altar and peered around, shocked to see that the gathering had now descended into a depraved mass of blood stained bodies, shed of their robes. The smoke was thicker now, partially obscuring the details of what was going on beneath the vapor but Jamie could see that some were engaged in sexual acts and others still crowded around what was left of the bloody mass that had been Day-Conti, hands deep in gore and faces transfigured. No-one was looking in Jamie's direction, engrossed as they were in their own drug-fueled depravity.

Jamie turned back to Neville and stripped him of his robe. He groaned and she knew there wasn't much time before someone discovered he was missing. She pulled the robe around herself and looked at the corridor where Mascuria had emerged with the gurney. That had to be the way back to the morgue area, back to Polly. She rose from behind the altar and moved swiftly to the tunnel, painfully aware of eyes on her back but hoping that somehow she would be able to escape. She had barely made it inside the corridor when she heard a shout behind her and a faltering of the drum beat. Jamie didn't turn, but ran straight up the corridor, following the most well-lit tunnels, praying that they would lead her back to the morgue.

Footsteps echoed in the tunnel behind her, before the drum beat resumed its frenzied beat disguising the sound. Moving faster now, Jamie turned a corner and suddenly saw the wooden door and stairs heading up to the trapdoor. She dashed to the morgue door, running in and slamming the heavy door shut behind her. She pushed the bolt home just as the men behind her reached it, banging and shouting at her with foul language. Jamie imagined them covered in blood, their eyes full of hatred, with a taste for murder. She knew the bolt wouldn't hold them for long.

Turning, Jamie scanned the room. A heavy cabinet with medical instruments stood in the corner and there were oxygen cylinders placed in holding units against the wall, used in morgues when decomposition was advanced enough to require breathing apparatus. Jamie opted for the cabinet, pushing it over as glass shattered inside while she bumped it over the floor to put in front of the door.

That would buy her a few minutes at least. Jamie turned to look at the gurney where Polly's body lay with her own clothes discarded next to it. She tuned out the shouts of those who hunted her and went to her daughter's side, turning her body over and gently kissing the girl's forehead. The corpse was cold and Jamie felt the absence of life keenly as she brushed a lock of hair away from the impassive face. Finally, she could acknowledge that this wasn't Polly anymore, that this shell had been cast aside while her true essence had become part of the stars. But Jamie still wouldn't leave the body to be desecrated by Mascuria.

She looked around the lab again, realizing that there was no way out. If she left the room, she would likely be taken to the slaughter of the Lyceum. The madness of that underground crypt right now meant that they would tear her limb from limb, like the madness of the Dionysians, followers of the god of all things wild. As brave as Polly had believed her to be, Jamie knew that she didn't want to die like that, but in here, she could choose her own way. She could die in here and ensure that Polly's body was at peace. Without her daughter, she was nothing anyway. The banging grew louder at the door and the cabinet moved. In that moment, Jamie saw a way to achieve a final end.

Near the shelves full of monsters was a neat pile of sacking used to wrap specimens for transportation. Jamie picked up Polly's body, cradling her little girl as she had when she was alive. She laid her down gently on the pile, using one sack to cover her nakedness and another under her head as a pillow. It wasn't quite the pyre of the Viking princess that Polly had admired in her history class, but it would be enough to take them both onwards.

Jamie moved swiftly across the room as the door rattled furiously. She opened the valves on the oxygen cylinders, twisting them to full capacity, hearing the hiss as they started to expel gas. Jamie couldn't help but breathe deeply for a second, relishing the purity as it chased away the last of the hallucinogens from her brain. She found two bottles of ethanol and hurled them to the ground, the vapor from the absolute alcohol making her cough. Turning, she grabbed one of the heavy medical textbooks from a shelf and started to smash the glass jars containing the anatomical specimens. Jamie couldn't help her tears as the liquid formalin released its contents and at the sound of breaking glass, Jamie heard the attempts of the men outside redouble in effort. Mascuria would be desperate to rescue his beloved specimens, his life's work.

Twisted body parts plopped onto the floor in a wash of preserving liquid, and dissected fetus corpses joined them in a hideous soup of human remains. Jamie stepped carefully, not wanting to damage them any more. Where Mascuria had seen the deformed beauty of teratology, Jamie saw only the worship of suffering and deliberate cruelty. Nature would not have let these poor innocents live, and now she would release them, along with her daughter.

Jamie's tears obscured her vision, as the formalin evaporated into the highly flammable formaldehyde gas. Now all she needed was a spark. Her eyes fell on her own leather jacket, with cigarettes and lighter in the pocket. She grabbed the jacket and rummaged through the pockets as the men outside broke the lock and the giant cabinet began to move. Jamie threw two of the large specimen jars at the base of the cabinet, then dropped to the floor and crawled under the sacking next to Polly's body. She leaned out and with one arm flicked her lighter open, plunging the lever and creating a spark.

The air flashed around her and as her arm burned Jamie dropped the lighter, igniting the formaldehyde and the body parts soaked in the flammable liquid. The air itself seemed to blaze and a frustrated scream came from outside the door as smoke billowed up and out. Jamie knew it wouldn't take long for the fire to reach their pile of sacking and together they would burn, a pyre of flame, just as Polly had wanted. Her heart hammered at the thought of dying this way but as she gathered Polly's body in her arms and pulled her jacket over herself, she knew it was the only way. The heat surrounded them and she closed her eyes, breathing in the toxic smoke, hoping that she might be overcome before the flames licked her body and the pain began.

A smashing came from the doorway and suddenly the men were in, but the flames had taken hold now and smoke filled the room, even as some of it billowed out into the corridor. The fire spread quickly in the morgue, amplified by the gaseous accelerants. Jamie opened her eyes, watching the vague shapes of three men approaching and she prayed that they wouldn't drag her alive from this place.

Mascuria was shouting desperately, his words barely audible over the crackle of flames, burning body parts dripping melted fat into sticky pools at his feet.

"No! My babies ... Help me."

He was picking up pieces of macerated flesh from the floor, hugging them to his chest and wailing in anguish. Jamie wrapped her arms tighter around Polly's body, pressing her face to the girl's back. As her lips met her daughter's skin to kiss it one last time, she heard Polly's voice in her head, clear as it had been when she had lived. *'Dance for me, Mum'.*

CHAPTER 27

FOR A MOMENT, JAMIE couldn't believe it but then the voice jump-started her resolve, for in that moment, she knew she couldn't just lie here and die. Polly's death didn't have to be her own end, it could be the beginning of a different life. If she died, the Nevilles could continue their sick practices and Mascuria might live to start a new collection. She couldn't let that happen.

Jamie pulled the leather jacket tighter around her, and peered out from beneath its protection. She clutched her burned arm tight to her body, the pain sharpening her senses. As the men moved further into the room, she could see a way out through the open door, as long as she could stay out of sight in the billowing smoke. She crawled away from Polly, then turned and wrapped her in the flammable sacking, pushing the precious body back towards the flames, willing it to be consumed before the fire was controlled. Jamie didn't want to leave her, feeling an emotional tug to what was left of Polly's physicality, but she knew that her pragmatic daughter would have loved being part of bringing this evil to justice.

Still kneeling, Jamie grabbed another of the bottled specimens with a piece of sacking and hurled it toward the opposite end of the room. It exploded in the air from the heat, raining glass shards down and the smoky outlines of the men turned towards the combustion. In that second, she ran, ducking low to the floor and slipping out into the corridor. She coughed, choking in the smoky atmosphere, knowing that she had to get out. Jamie ran for the staircase towards the trapdoor and the labs above and suddenly saw a figure ahead of her in the smoke. It was Esther Neville, her slight figure stepping upwards towards her escape.

Jamie shadowed her up the staircase, remaining far enough behind that the smoke would obscure her form, but as Esther emerged through the trapdoor at the top, Jamie rushed the last few steps, diving for the closing gap and rolled out into the circular room. Esther turned at the noise and flew at Jamie, screaming in anger and frustration, a scalpel still in her bloody hand. The barking of the guard dog outside the room mingled with her sounds of fury, and Jamie could hear its claws scratching at the door, desperate to join the fight.

"You bitch, you've ruined it all." Esther panted, her blade thrusts clumsy with anger. Jamie rolled away and scrambled to her feet.

"Why did you do it, Esther?" Jamie asked, as she circled, keeping her distance from the knife. Esther's face was marked with blood, highlighting her cheekbones like murderer's rouge and her teeth were tarnished burgundy. Her dress was stained with gore and chunks of wet flesh adhered to the sleeves, sticking in the folds. She stank of blood, sweat and sex and Jamie's nose wrinkled at the odor that rose in waves. The pristine scientist was gone, replaced by this base creature marred with death.

"Did Jenna find out about the Lyceum?" Jamie asked. "Is that why you had to kill your own daughter?"

She saw a flash of what might have been regret in Esther's eyes, but it was dampened immediately by her fury as the woman darted across the room, thrusting with the scalpel.

Jamie spun and swatted her arm away, thrusting Esther in the direction she was moving, using the momentum to push her off balance. The knife went wide and Jamie danced away. Esther whirled around, ready to come at her again.

"Jenna was created here," Esther snarled. "A product of my lab, the perfection of my process. She lived while others died as we refined the genetic structures, so she was always mine to destroy."

Jamie thought of the monsters burning in the lab below, pieces of defiled flesh cradled in Mascuria's arms. Those creatures had been Jenna's brothers and sisters: no wonder she had wanted to rescue them in whatever way she could.

"She was going to reveal the lab's secrets," Esther spat. "She had some crazy idea that the specimens we created here had rights. She wanted to expose us, and I couldn't let that happen."

"What about her child?" Jamie tried to keep Esther talking, circling round, waiting for an opportunity to strike.

"An unexpected miracle," Esther laughed. "Somehow her genes together with Day-Conti's created something astonishing, for she should have been barren. Her death was too early, though. I wanted to bring her here for experimentation but she resisted me. I pushed her as we argued and she fell, but then I couldn't leave her fetus. It has sparked a new line of research, so you see how nature rewards my work? How can it be wrong?"

Esther started across the room again, this time holding the scalpel with a firm grip, adjusting her stance for a lower thrust. The Rottweiler was going crazy outside the room, howling and barking.

"I will slash you until your blood runs freely and then let the dog hunt you in the forest." Esther laughed again, and Jamie heard anticipated pleasure in her voice. "You aren't worthy of the Lyceum anyway, and now they're scattered, escaping the fire you have brought on us." She crouched, light on her feet. "But the Lyceum will meet again, Detective, for there is an insatiable need for its extreme pleasures in this civilized world."

Jamie watched the way Esther moved, feinting left and seeing how she adjusted her stance.

"And only you can bring them that?" she asked, keeping her eyes on Esther, watching the knife weave in the air.

"Only I am willing to, and they're happy to pay hand-somely for the privilege."

Jamie let Esther advance further as she backed towards one of the plastinated corpse sculptures on the wall. Smoke was now curling up from the trapdoor and Jamie imagined Polly's body consumed by the fire, finding freedom in the flames.

"What part did Christopher play?" Jamie asked, feeling the memory of his hands groping her own flesh.

Esther's face wrinkled in disgust at the mention of her husband.

"His only use is to find appropriate people for the Lyceum within the networks of the upper class, those weary of the usual pleasures, those looking for something more - visceral." Esther's eyes glittered green, and Jamie saw that her addiction had taken her to the very edge of sanity. She felt drawn to that threshold too, feeling the battle of her police training against the vicious desire to end this woman's life. Jamie wanted to grab the knife, slash it across Esther's throat and let her stinking blood join that of the murdered Day-Conti, to hack at her body, each cut for one of the mutilated victims she had created in the labs.

Esther suddenly thrust the blade, aiming at Jamie's exposed throat. With her back against the torso of the twisted sculpture of flesh, Jamie ducked away and the scalpel embedded deep into the sculpture, leaving Esther's ribs exposed. Jamie moved, grabbing Esther's body and pulling her forward, driving her knee hard into her solar plexus, winding the woman as she let go of the weapon. Jamie pulled it out of the sculpture as Esther sank to the floor. For a moment, she wanted to yank back Esther's head and slash her throat, finishing the woman's miserable life. But something stayed her hand, some sense of what she could allow of herself. Instead, Jamie thrust the blade downwards into Esther's thigh and then twisted it as the woman howled in pain. Blood spurted from the wound, adding to the stains on her clothes. The dog barked ferociously, clawing to get in.

"That's for Jenna," Jamie said, and ran for the door, picking up the edge of the thick rug as she reached it. She pulled the rug about her body, using it as a shield for her soft flesh in case the dog tried to attack her. Esther looked up and in her green eyes, Jamie saw that she knew what was about to happen.

"No!" Esther screamed, and Jamie pulled open the door, letting the Rottweiler in, snarling and barking, teeth bared in vicious savagery. The scent of blood and gore on Esther was too much and the dog bounded across the room. She tried to get away from it but its teeth ripped into her leg by the open wound. The powerful dog began to shake her and Esther fell to the floor, the blood on her torso and face driving the dog wild. As it bit and wrenched at her exposed body, Esther's cries grew weaker.

Jamie was momentarily transfixed by the brutal savaging and the sound of the dog feeding on Esther while she still lived. The animal was deep in the blood lust of the recent kill, but Jamie knew it wouldn't be long before it turned on her. She dropped the rug and darted out through the door, slamming it closed behind her as the dog swung its head from the dying woman, baring its teeth in a bloody grimace, defending its prey.

Jamie stood shaking in the lab corridor, the pristine environment a strange juxtaposition to the unholy chaos she had witnessed down in the caves. But what had been created up here was a part of that dark underworld. Science walked a knife edge, and in the wrong hands it became a tool for evil: the legacy of Mengele still lived on in these labs. Jamie rested her forehead on the door, listening to the sickening sounds of the dog worrying at Esther's body, an agonizing groan indicating that the woman was still alive. For a moment, Jamie felt revulsion at the fate she had left Esther to. Part of her wanted to find a weapon and go in to face the dog. She had sworn to protect people, to help them, to be on the side of good. Where did her actions leave her now?

Smoke started to seep under the door and she heard the dog start to bark and whine in fear. The noise of a massive explosion came from below, followed by a rumble deep under the earth. It was too late to save Esther now, and Jamie backed away from the door, stumbling away down the lab corridor. She heard the faint sound of sirens outside, alerted perhaps by the fire that must be billowing out of the building, the flames visible from the nearby village. Jamie felt her strength break within her. The long hours of the night, what she had seen in the depths of the caves, Polly's final end, it all welled up within her and tears began to run down her face as her mind struggled to focus on escape.

She pulled open the final door, and sank to the floor in the loading bay as the flashing lights of the police and fire service vehicles filled the clearing in front of the lab. She closed her eyes against the glare of spinning red, hearing shouts as officers moved swiftly into position. She knew what she must look like, a victim of some kind of attack dressed in only a diaphanous wrap, bare legs and feet marked by ankle cuffs, her face cut and bloodied, her limbs burned and smoky black. She didn't even have enough strength to say that she was a police officer. She just let one of the uniforms enfold her in a blanket and help her to a waiting ambulance as firemen streamed into the building.

CHAPTER 28

JAMIE DREAMED OF DEFORMED bodies emerging from specimen jars, the eyes of the abandoned fetuses open and accusing as their limbs charred and crackled in the flames. They dragged their stumpy bodies across the floor toward where she crouched in the billowing smoke, moans emanating from their tiny misshapen mouths. She felt the first touch, clammy like a frog on her bare leg as one began to pull itself up her body, wanting to fill her mouth with corrupted flesh.

"Jamie, Jamie, wake up. It's OK, you're safe now." The voice pulled her from the nightmare and Jamie opened her eyes, clutching at the bedclothes with shaking fingers. Her first lucid thought was of Polly. Was her daughter safe?

Then Jamie remembered what had happened and her world dimmed and nausea washed over her. The best part of her had died and yet, after everything, she was still alive. She wanted to sink back into drugged sleep and forget, anything to dull the raw pain inside. But she remembered the voice in the flames and Polly's desire that she dance again, and she forced herself to concentrate. Dragging herself mentally to consciousness, Jamie realized that she was in a small hospital room, wearing a surgical gown. Her head ached and her lungs felt squeezed in her chest, her breath ragged.

Blake sat by the bed, watching her, his gloved hand close to hers and Jamie felt comforted by his presence, for he understood the inherent darkness within people. She had pushed him away, but he was here now and she was grateful.

"Glad you made it out," he said, smiling. "Sounds like you almost didn't."

His vivid blue eyes were intense and filled with concern. Jamie lifted a hand to touch his face, his jawline now smoothly clean shaven so he looked much younger. His eyes darkened and he leaned into her palm. She felt a connection with him, he had experienced horror and known loss and she didn't have to explain herself with him. Blake had seen her vulnerability and it was a relief to know that he saw the truth.

"Jamie, I …" Blake started to speak but Jamie heard an edge of emotion she couldn't face right now. His kindness would break her into pieces.

"What have you heard about the fire?" She interrupted him, wheezing a little.

"Only what's on the news," Blake said, and she saw understanding of the evasion in his expression. "Fire in a chemical lab spreads to the Hellfire Caves, sparking all kinds of rumors about what was actually going on that night. But the police say further investigations are needed before they reveal any more." He raised an interested eyebrow. "So tell me the gory details, because they've taken all your personal effects so I can't read them."

Before Jamie could reply, the door opened and Missinghall entered, his face a picture of concern.

Blake stood up. "I'll leave you two to talk," he said. "You know where to find me when you're ready, Jamie."

He turned and walked to the door, nodding in acknowledgment at Missinghall, whose look of guarded interest made Jamie wonder what the two of them had talked about in the waiting area.

Missinghall sat down by the bed.

"I know you're a senior officer and everything, but seriously, Jamie, what in hell were you thinking? Going in there alone was idiotic. You could have been killed."

Jamie couldn't help but smile at his concern, and the effort made her face ache. Her body felt so beaten up, and exhaustion sapped her strength.

"They had Polly's body, Al, and I knew that the team wouldn't get the evidence processed in time for the Lyceum's meeting." She thought of Esther Neville's savaged body in the lab and Polly's remains in the morgue below. "So what happened? Did you find anything left down there?"

"It's all a big mess, and the Commissioner is trying to keep a lid on everything." Missinghall shook his head. "But we found Esther Neville's body ripped to pieces, and the remains of Edward Mascuria and several other men in the morgue downstairs. There were other body parts too, none recognizable, as well as a teenager's skeleton, mostly burned to ashes."

Tears welled in Jamie's eyes and she took a deep breath.

"That's Polly," she whispered. "That's my daughter."

Missinghall closed his eyes for a second and then let out a long exhalation. "Oh Jamie, I'm so sorry. Her remains are being looked after, and once the investigation is over, I'm sure they'll be released to you for burial."

Jamie felt a kind of relief that Polly's physical body had been committed to the flames, her Viking princess sent onward through the fire.

"What about the caves?" she asked, her voice cracking with the memory. "They murdered Rowan Day-Conti down there, Al."

Missinghall nodded. "There were several bodies in the caves, badly burned, but we were able to ID Christopher Neville and parts of Day-Conti. That's what we're trying to keep a lid on, because he had only just been released from police custody when he disappeared again, presumably abducted by the Lyceum. There are also some pretty senior people in hospital with smoke inhalation, picked up by officers in the village as they emerged from the caves. Did you see any of the others involved?"

Jamie thought back to the swirling smoke and hallucinogenic nightmare of blades and blood. Had she really seen Detective Superintendent Dale Cameron amongst the Lyceum members, or was that some mirage fabricated by her own mind?

"I might be able to identify some of them," she said, frowning. "But I was under the influence of drugs and, given the involvement of Polly's body, I was emotionally distraught. I'm not exactly a reliable witness."

Missinghall's shoulders sagged with disappointment. "Oh well, Cameron's assigned two officers to keep you safe until we wind up the investigation, just in case. They're outside the door right now." Jamie felt a prickle of concern. If Cameron had really been down in the caves, he would want to make sure that she didn't identify him. Was she safe even now, she wondered, or were her suspicions just a result of the trauma? Missinghall continued. "And of course, the investigation into the Nevilles has been blown right open."

"But they're all dead," Jamie said softly. "The Lyceum has no purpose now that it has claimed the lives of the whole family."

"But the pharmaceutical company can go on without them, so that's been kicked up into a bigger investigation. For the murder case, it's just tying up the loose ends now, and of course, the dreaded paperwork." Missinghall snorted with laughter. "Guess you'll skip that this time."

"And what are they saying about me, Al?"

Missinghall sighed, his eyes darting away as he spoke with reticence. "Of course, your actions are being debated and some are calling for your dismissal. You committed offenses Jamie: breaking and entering, concealing evidence which amounts to obstruction." He shook his head. "Although, of course, it was understandable given the circumstances and Polly's disappearance. You also managed to find the evidence that led to the Lyceum, even though it sounds as if you used some dubious methods." Missinghall's eyes flicked back to the door where Blake had left. "Despite everything, Cameron is campaigning for your return. But with everything that's happened, do you even want to come back?"

Jamie wondered at Cameron's actions to protect her from dismissal. Was he keeping her in debt to him because of what she had seen? Part of her wanted to just turn away and never go back, but what did she have in her life now? She thought of the sleeping pills in her bathroom cabinet, the emptiness of her flat and the hole in her heart. Life without Polly was unthinkable, but without her job, there would be no meaning at all.

"I want to come back," she said. "I need to be busy, Al."

Missinghall nodded. "But for now, you need some rest. I'll visit again tomorrow, keep you up to speed on the gossip."

He rose and walked to the door, then with a smile and a wave he was gone. Jamie turned her head to look out at the grey London sky, her thoughts only of Polly. As the wind whipped dry leaves past the window, she imagined her little girl out there, her soul soaring, finally free from the constraints of her physical pain. Jamie would always be a mother, but there would never be another Polly. The child born of her flesh and blood was no more and grief was like a solid bowling ball in Jamie's gut. But her every breath was a decision to live and perhaps she would dance again, in Polly's memory.

ENJOYED DESECRATION?

Thanks for joining Jamie and Blake in *Desecration*. Their adventures continue in *Delirium* and *Deviance*. If you enjoyed the book, a review would be much appreciated as it helps other readers discover the story.

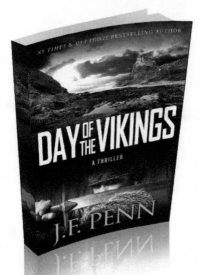

Get a free copy of the bestselling thriller, *Day of the Vikings*, an ARKANE thriller featuring Blake Daniel, when you sign up to join my Reader's Group. You'll also be notified of giveaways, new releases and receive personal updates from behind the scenes of my books.

Click here to get started:

www.JFPenn.com/free

AUTHOR'S NOTE

This book is rooted in my own fascination with how the physical body defines us in life as well as after death. Here are some of the factual details behind the story, but of course, it is fictionalized and any mistakes are my own. You can find pictures of my research at:

www.pinterest.com/jfpenn/desecration/

Hunterian Museum, Dissection and Teratology

You can find the Hunterian Museum at the Royal College of Surgeons in the heart of London and I based most of my initial research around the facts of John Hunter and 18th century medical dissections. When I first visited the Hunterian, I was physically overcome with weakness and nausea at some of the specimens I saw. This visceral reaction to human body parts fascinated me and that feeling is part of what I have tried to capture in the book. Despite my initial horror, I have been back to the Museum many times and consider it a privilege to examine the specimens that have given so much to science. If you'd like to read more, I recommend The Knife Man by Wendy Moore.

For this story, I embellished the collection at the Hunterian with artifacts from other teratological collections in museums around the world. My other sources included the Mutter Museum in Philadelphia, the Wellcome Collection in Euston, the fantastic Morbid Anatomy blog and a brilliant exhibition at the Museum of London on Doctors, Dissection and Resurrection Men.

Teratology is the study of abnormalities in physiological development and it is truly a disturbing field to investigate.

Corpse art, body modification and Torture Garden

The use of corpses for art was inspired by my visit to the Von Hagens Bodies exhibition in New York, where plastinated sculptures are displayed in the exploded way described. In all my research, I couldn't find a definitive answer on the legality of using donated bodies for art. The offense of stealing or abuse of a corpse differs by jurisdiction but if there is no 'ownership' of the corpse then the lines seem blurred. So I have taken fictional liberties with Rowan Day-Conti's artwork.

Body modification by choice is an extreme form of self-expression that has a vibrant sub-culture. Torture Garden is a real fetish club in London where modification, as well as other forms of expression, are embraced. The inspiration for O's character was a painting of a man with a large octopus tattoo at the National Gallery and I'll be writing her complete story in another book as she keeps returning to my thoughts.

Psychic reading of objects/ psychometry

My obsession with the supernatural continues to be a theme in my writing. When I visited the Hunterian, one of the first things I saw was a wooden table with one of the earliest dissections of blood vessels. I imagined the person who had lain there, the rest of their flesh dissected away and that's when I wondered what it would be like to read objects as Blake does.

Police procedure

Although I have used books and expert readers to help me with the police procedural aspect of the book, I have taken creative liberties with Jamie's role. The story is less about police procedure and more about Jamie's journey and the exploration of deeper themes, so all mistakes are purely my own. The use of psychics by the Police is fictionalized.

Tango

I have always wanted to dance tango and the scene of Jamie dancing was inspired by the book Twelve Minutes of Love. A Tango Story by Kapka Kassabova. I dare you to read it and not want to head straight for a milonga.

Mengele and vivisection

Josef Mengele used human vivisection in the Nazi camps and was particularly interested in twins and genetic abnormalities. There are reports that he indeed conjoined a pair of Roma twins. The notebook and anatomical Venus are fictionalized, although there are many specimens of the latter in collections around the world.

Hell Fire Caves, West Wycombe

The Hell Fire Caves are real and you can visit to read the rumors of what went on down there in the dark nights, which I have taken the liberty of expanding into something more dramatic for modern times.

MORE BOOKS BY J.F.PENN

Thanks for joining Jamie and Blake in *Desecration*.

Sign up at www.JFPenn.com/free to be
notified of the next book in the series and
receive my monthly updates and giveaways.

* * *

Brooke and Daniel Psychological Thrillers

Desecration #1
Delirium #2
Deviance #3

* * *

Mapwalker Dark Fantasy Thrillers

Map of Shadows #1
Map of Plagues #2
Map of the Impossible #3

If you enjoy **Action Adventure Thrillers**, check out the
ARKANE series as Morgan Sierra and Jake Timber solve
supernatural mysteries around the world.

Stone of Fire #1
Crypt of Bone #2
Ark of Blood #3
One Day In Budapest #4

Day of the Vikings #5
Gates of Hell #6
One Day in New York #7
Destroyer of Worlds #8
End of Days #9
Valley of Dry Bones #10
Tree of Life #11

* * *

For more **dark fantasy,** check out:

Risen Gods
The Dark Queen
A Thousand Fiendish Angels:
Short stories based on Dante's Inferno

More books coming soon.

You can sign up to be notified of new releases, giveaways
and pre-release specials - plus, get a free book!

www.JFPenn.com/free

If you loved the book and have a moment to spare, I would
really appreciate a short review on the page where you
bought the book. Your help in spreading the word is gratefully appreciated and reviews make a huge difference to
helping new readers find the series.

Thank you!

ABOUT J.F.PENN

J.F.Penn is the Award-nominated, New York Times and USA Today bestselling author of the ARKANE action adventure thrillers, Brooke & Daniel Psychological Thrillers, and the Mapwalker fantasy adventure series, as well as other stand-alone stories.

Her books weave together ancient artifacts, relics of power, international locations and adventure with an edge of the supernatural. Joanna lives in Bath, England and enjoys a nice G&T.

You can follow Joanna's travels on Instagram
@jfpennauthor and also on her podcast at
BooksAndTravel.page.

* * *

Sign up for your free thriller,
Day of the Vikings, and updates from behind
the scenes, research, and giveaways at:

www.jfpenn.com/free

* * *

Connect with Joanna:
www.JFPenn.com
joanna@JFPenn.com
www.Facebook.com/JFPennAuthor
www.Instagram.com/JFPennAuthor

* * *

For writers:

Joanna's site, www.TheCreativePenn.com, helps people write, publish and market their books through articles, audio, video and online courses.

She writes non-fiction for authors under Joanna Penn and has an award-nominated podcast for writers, The Creative Penn Podcast.

ACKNOWLEDGMENTS

First and always, thanks to Jonathan, for understanding my fascination with death and the macabre and not being freaked out by my consistently dark obsessions. And to my readers, who I write for.

I also have a great team who have helped me to shape the book. A huge thanks to: My Mum, Jacqueline Penn, for her line editing and consistent encouragement; My Dad, Arthur Penn, for his honest appraisal as a crime reader which helped reshape the procedural aspects of the book; Doctor Denzil Gill and Doctor Kim Gill, dear friends who helped me with the medical aspects of the book including Polly's illness and death; Garry Rodgers, author and ex-coroner for answering my morbid questions about methods of murder and anatomical specimens; Clare Mackintosh, writer and ex-police officer, for her expertise and suggestions on procedural aspects; New York Times bestselling authors David Morrell and CJ Lyons, for their feedback, encouragement and mentorship. And to Rachel Ekstrom, my agent for a time, for her hard work on my behalf and suggestions that improved the plot.

Thanks also to my production team: Liz Broomfield, at LibroEditing.com for the proof-reading; Derek Murphy at Creativindie for the cover design; Jane Dixon Smith at JDSmith-Design.com for the interior print design; Suzanne Norris of www.sakurasnow.com for the brilliant interior cabinet of curiosities artwork.

Made in the USA
Middletown, DE
09 April 2021